Praise for Erica James

'Erica James' sensitive story . . . is as sparklingly fresh as dew on the village's surrounding meadows . . . thoroughly enjoyable and fully deserving of a place in the crowded market of women's fiction' *Sunday Express*

'This book draws you into the lives of these characters, and often makes you want to scream at them to try and make them see reason. Funny, sad and frustrating, but an excellent, compulsive read' *Woman's Realm*

'There is humour and warmth in this engaging story of love's triumphs and disappointments, with two well-realised and intriguing subplots' *Woman & Home*

'Joanna Trollope fans, dismayed by the high gloom factor and complete absence of Agas in her latest books, will turn with relief to James' . . . delightful novel about English village life . . . a blend of emotion and wry social observation'
Daily Mail

'Scandal, fury, accusations and revenge are all included in Erica James' compelling novel . . . this story of village life in Cheshire is told with wit and humour' *Stirling Observer*

'An entertaining read with some wickedly well-painted cameo characters. It's a perfect read if you're in the mood for romance' *Prima*

'An engaging and friendly novel . . . very readable'
Woman's Own

'A bubbling, delightful comedy which is laced with a bittersweet tang . . . a good story, always well observed, and full of wit' *Publishing News*

Erica James grew up in Hampshire and has since lived in Oxford, Yorkshire and Belgium. She now lives in Cheshire. She is the author of twelve novels, including *Gardens of Delight*, which won the 2006 Romantic Novel of the Year Award.

By Erica James

A Breath of Fresh Air
Time for a Change
Airs & Graces
A Sense of Belonging
Act of Faith
The Holiday
Precious Time
Hidden Talents
Paradise House
Love and Devotion
Gardens of Delight
Tell it to the Skies

A Breath of Fresh Air

Erica James

An Orion paperback

First published in Great Britain in 1996
by Orion
This paperback edition published in 1998
by Orion Books Ltd,
Orion House, 5 Upper St Martin's Lane,
London WC2H 9EA

An Hachette UK company

Reissued 2008

25 27 29 30 28 26 24

A CIP catalogue record for this book is available
from the British Library.

ISBN 978-0-7528-8345-8

Typeset by Deltatype Limited, Birkenhead, Merseyside

Printed and bound in Great Britain by Clays Ltd, St Ives plc

The Orion Publishing Group's policy is to use papers that
are natural, renewable and recyclable products and
made from wood grown in sustainable forests. The logging
and manufacturing processes are expected to conform to
the environmental regulations of the country of origin.

www.orionbooks.co.uk

*To Edward and Samuel who handled their
mother's tantrums with such patience.
Thanks to Big G and all my friends who helped
and bullied me through the darkness,
especially Helena, Maureen and Rosemary*

Man cannot discover new oceans until he has courage to lose sight of the shore.

Unknown

Chapter One

Charlotte had never seen a man cry before, so she wasn't sure how to react to her husband's unexpected display of emotion. Not once had she ever imagined Peter capable of crying; it went against all she had ever known about him.

At a quarter to eight in the morning and while tapping open her boiled egg in their Brussels apartment, Charlotte Lawrence had finally plucked up the courage to ask her husband for a divorce and to put an end, once and for all, to his assumption that because he was fulfilled, so was she. She had told him that life under the corporate umbrella was not sufficient to satisfy both their needs. And then he had cried.

Charlotte passed him the box of tissues and tried to assimilate her own feelings. To her surprise, she felt indifference towards Peter, tinged with a hint of embarrassment. True, a man of the 1990s was allowed to cry – men were now allowed the full gamut of emotions, it was no holds barred, cards on the kitchen table; like women, men had emotions, too. But when it was in their kitchen and over their table, it felt all wrong.

'I'm sorry,' she said, knowing how hollow and inadequate her words sounded. She watched Peter scour his eyes with a tissue, then blow his nose. She looked away, down on to the street below, and wished, as she did every morning she looked out of the window, that she was back in England.

She knew it was pathetic, but she couldn't help it. She was homesick. Oh yes, she'd been given lots of helpful advice, mostly from Peter's father. 'I was a prisoner of war for two and half years and managed to enjoy myself, don't see why you can't just knuckle down to it, girl.' Then of course there was his old favourite: 'Stop feeling so sorry for yourself.'

And in simple justification of their nomadic lifestyle, that in eight years of marriage had taken them from London to Singapore, back to London and then on to Brussels, Peter would say, 'Other wives are happy here.'

'But I'm not other wives!' she would say in desperate retaliation, knowing that Peter had no comprehension of her basic need for the simple things in life: stability, security and a suburban high street of familiar chain stores, not the sophisticated expatriate regime of uncertainty, cocktail parties, language classes and flower arranging.

In a moment of cynicism and real rock-bottom boredom, she too had joined the ranks of the flower arrangers, and then Peter had tried getting her pregnant, believing this to be the answer. But this was one area in Peter's life where he had to admit failure. A genius in the mergers and acquisitions department he was, but with a low sperm count there was little he could do in the baby-making department.

Looking out of the window, Charlotte watched the softly falling snow. She felt as though they were characters acting out their parts in a well-rehearsed performance; a scene which she had produced and directed in her own mind for nearly a year now – except Peter was ad-libbing; he wasn't supposed to cry.

'Why?' he said, bringing her back to the script.

She turned round. 'Because I don't like what you're doing to me.'

He sniffed loudly and she could see he was willing his body to act according to the rules of his straitjacketed upbringing – boys didn't blub at boarding school. 'This is absurd,' he said, at last, and in a firm loud voice that had the effect of disciplining those dark, unexplored territories of his inner self. He picked up his briefcase, once more in control. 'I'll be back late. I'm in Luxembourg all day.'

'But the snow, it's far too dangerous, you can't possibly go all that way . . . and anyway, we need to talk.'

'There's nothing to discuss. The answer is no.'

Lying back in the bath, Charlotte waited for the warmth of the water to ease away the strain of not just the past hour, but the past eight years. It took only a few moments before she realised that she wasn't in need of a soothing balm. She was all right. After nearly a year of waiting for this point in her life, she was actually all right. The truth of her feelings hit her quite forcibly and she let out a sudden laugh. It echoed horribly in the bathroom with its high tiled ceiling. She chewed her lip guiltily.

But what next?

And now the second act in her well-rehearsed performance ran through her mind. This was when she stopped dancing attendance to someone else's tune, this was when she whistled the melody of her own life.

She would go back to England, to Hulme Welford, and move in with her parents until she got herself sorted; it would be hell living with her mother again, but Dad would be sweet.

And work. What about work?

Before she had been moulded into a corporate wife she had run her own business: an upmarket sweater shop. But then Peter had come home one evening with that silly grin on his face and told her his boss had asked him 'to consider Singapore'. Within three months the shop had gone, along with her identity, and she had found herself living a twelve-hour flight away from all that was comforting and familiar.

She knew it would be hard starting over again; finding work was never easy. Wherever they had lived she had tried to find her own niche – even if it had always been taken away from her. After seven months of trying to find work in Singapore, she had eventually managed to get a job within the personnel department of an international chemical company; then when Peter's contract had come to an end they had moved back to London. She had just found herself work there, when Peter announced they were going to Brussels. For the first six months she struggled to learn some basic French and was then offered a temporary part-time job working as a volunteer for a helpline service for the English-speaking community. When this had come to an end though, there had been no more work available, not until she had met Christina.

At half past eleven, Charlotte decided to call round to see her neighbour, Christina. She wanted to share this moment with someone – wanted somebody to tell her how brave she was, that leaving her husband was the right thing to do.

Christina Castelli had moved into the apartment next door and had become Charlotte's only real friend.

'A high-class tart!' Peter had announced, calling in for his clean shirts en route for the airport, just as the last of Christina's expensive-looking furniture had been brought up to the sixth floor. 'Perfectly obvious what she is,' he had gone on to say. 'The lift stinks of erotic perfume.'

Charlotte had questioned him on this point; how did he know what erotic perfume smelt like? He had fumbled for an answer and then reaching for his suit-carrier had simply said, 'Be back day after tomorrow, any duty-free you want?'

'Yes,' she had told him, 'some erotic perfume would be nice.'

He hadn't laughed, but then he'd forgotten how. His life had become too serious; too full of live-or-die mergers and acquisitions. He was constantly living on his ability to judge whether a thing was a profit or a loss; it was either black or it was white to Peter. The only grey area in his life was her.

Within a few days of Christina moving in, Charlotte had been forced to admit that Peter may have been right. The *femme fatale* fragrance in the downstairs hall, lift and sixth floor landing seemed now to be accompanied by a steady stream of German eau-de-Cologne. Charlotte never actually saw her neighbour's callers, apart from one man, who by accident got the wrong apartment, and when Charlotte tried to point him in the right direction he shot back into the lift, his face hidden behind a copy of *Le Soir*.

One morning Christina knocked on Charlotte's door and invited her in for a drink.

'You must call me Christina,' she told Charlotte in perfect English, beckoning her towards a cream leather sofa that had more than a hint of Milan to it. 'We have no need to be formal, for I do not think we shall be conducting any business between ourselves. And I may call you . . . ?'

'Charlotte, very plain I'm afraid,' Charlotte said, feeling incredibly plain as she sat next to this catwalk beauty.

Christina laughed, a light tinkling laugh, that Charlotte knew would have the ability to whip the boxer shorts off any man in seconds. 'In that case I shall call you Carlotta – that is your name in Rome, where I come from.'

Charlotte never told Peter about her visits next door, not even when Christina came up with a job for her.

'Carlotta, you and I are alike in many ways,' Christina said one day. 'We both need to be kept busy and I know that behind that beautiful smile of yours you are perfectly miserable, so I have found you work, just two mornings a week for a friend of mine.'

Charlotte looked doubtfully at her. 'What kind of work?'

Christina laughed. 'Do not worry, Carlotta, I am not about to turn you into a . . . now what was the expression I heard Mr Carlotta use, the day I moved in . . . ah yes, a high-class tart. No, I would not suggest such a thing.'

Charlotte's cheeks flushed. 'How did you hear that?'

Christina shrugged her silk-clad shoulders. 'It was a warm day, every window in Brussels was open. Mr Carlotta's voice carried well that afternoon.'

In Christina's company, Peter was never referred to as Peter, instead he had simply become the anonymous Mr Carlotta. Christina had told Charlotte on their first meeting that she never wanted to meet or even know the name of Charlotte's husband. 'After all,' she had said, her full lips turned gently upwards in the most seductive of smiles, 'it might be awkward for us both if it turned out that I already knew your husband.'

'No, Carlotta, you are not to work as a high-class tart, but as a receptionist. There now, I think that would suit you so much more, don't you?'

'But I can't speak French very well, never mind Flemish,' Charlotte said hopelessly, and then added, 'I have tried, I just don't seem to be very good at it.'

'Then I will teach you, I am a good teacher.'

Charlotte suddenly smiled.

'Such a beautiful smile you have, Carlotta, but I am wondering why you are smiling. What is it you think I am good at teaching?'

Looking at the reflection of herself in the hall mirror, Charlotte smiled at the memory of that conversation. She would miss her friendship with Christina when she moved back to England; it would be the only thing from Brussels that she would miss. Just as she was about to pick up her keys and go and see Christina, the door bell rang.

She pulled the door open and saw two Belgian policemen standing in front of her. They started speaking in French and even with her limited knowledge of the language, she was able to understand what they were saying.

Monsieur Peter Lawrence was dead.

Chapter Two

Shrilling with all the urgency of a telephone, a child's voice invaded the quiet, Edwardian sitting-room of The Gables in Hulme Welford.

'MUMMY!'

Charlotte's younger sister Hilary, who was quite used to her daughter's demanding cry, carried on pouring out cups of tea. Similarly, the Reverend Malcolm Jackson, a robust forty-five-year-old Meatloaf fan and father of three, barely flinched, but not so Iris Braithwaite, a woman who claimed to live on nothing but the remains of her shredded nerves; she jolted vigorously, as though in response to a proffered red-hot poker.

A six-year-old girl, dressed in an assortment of jumble sale goods, appeared at the sitting-room door. With cheap yellow beads bouncing on her chest and over-sized red slingbacks slapping at her heels, she trotted towards her mother.

'Becky,' Hilary said, 'I did tell you not to play with the clothes from the boxes in the hall. Go and take them off, especially those ridiculous shoes, you'll have an accident.'

'Do I have to?'

'Yes you do. Now say hello to Mrs Braithwaite and Malcolm.'

Six-year-old shyness appearing from nowhere rendered the little girl speechless. She played with the biggest of the yellow beads, turning one of her feet inwards. She then remembered what she had wanted her mother for. 'What does bonking mean, Mummy?'

Flanked by an uneasy rattle of china from one side of her and a stifled laugh from the other, Hilary grappled to save the teapot in her hands and to think of a suitable answer. All she could think of was the terrible unfairness of it all.

She had worked so hard today, had tried to make everything just right. It had all fallen apart though, the moment she had opened the fridge door that morning and realised she hadn't got any eggs. The shop in the village had run out of her usual free-range variety and she had been forced to make do with those battery-farmed eggs instead. The sponge, of course, had turned out a disaster and was it any wonder? She had then had to make a back-up batch of scones for her monthly meeting with Malcolm Jackson and Iris Braithwaite – Chairlady of the St John's Replacement Stained Glass Window Committee. Then, just as she'd got the kitchen cleared up, school had telephoned to say there had been a gas leak and all children were being sent home. And on top of all this her sister Charlotte was arriving in a few hours' time, which meant there had been Ivy Cottage to get ready for her, along with the welcome-home dinner to prepare for that evening. No, life just wasn't being fair with her today.

Then with shame she thought of Charlotte. Life hadn't exactly been fair to her recently.

It was now two and a half months since Peter had died; the funny thing was, it felt longer.

It had been a sad little funeral, on a cold wet day in Aldershot, with their own family far out-numbering Peter's. She had been so sure that Peter's funeral would have been a rather grand affair, had even bought a hat, which thankfully, just at the last minute, she had left behind in the car. In fact there had been few friends present, hardly anyone to mourn comfortingly alongside Charlotte, just a few duty-bound work colleagues; not even Peter's own brother had turned up. She had felt sorry for Peter's parents; sorry, too, that nobody cried, not even Charlotte.

Afterwards they had all tried to talk Charlotte out of returning to Brussels, had tried to get her to leave everything to the company. 'I must go back,' she had said. 'There are things I need to sort out.' She had been adamant. Just as she had been adamant about buying a house in the village. 'I want to be where I grew up,' she had told them on the telephone. 'Hulme Welford is the only place I know as home. It's got to be there.'

Secretly Hilary was looking forward to having her sister to look after, living, as she would be, quite literally on the doorstep. She smiled to herself at the thought of one day taking the credit for getting Charlotte back on her feet. She could almost feel that rosy glow of praise and gratitude, which she knew would be hers within a few months. Yes, she had great plans for her elder sister.

Looking up from the teapot Hilary realised that both Iris Braithwaite and Malcolm Jackson were staring at her, Becky too. Uncharacteristically she chose to ignore her daughter. 'More tea?' she said.

Taking his cue, Malcolm Jackson held out his cup. 'Just a top-up, please.'

Becky was not to be put off. 'But Mummy . . .'

'Have a chocolate biscuit, dear.'

Wide-eyed with delight, Becky took one, thought better, and took another, but then doggedly continued with her line of questioning. 'Philip says he won't give me back my Barbie doll until Ken's finished bonking her. How long do you think that will take, Mummy?'

At the commotion which followed, Becky left her jumble-sale heels behind her and took to her own, whilst Hilary did her best to deal with Iris Braithwaite's tea-soaked tweed skirt and the slice of lemon that had ended up sitting perkily, like a Frenchman's beret, on one of her sensible brown lace-up shoes.

Another cup and saucer was fetched from the kitchen and quickly filled, but conversation, like the tea, was strained, until Iris Braithwaite warmed to her subject: that of the rising sense of apathy in the village. 'It seems to me that people today have lost their sense of generosity,' she said, taking a sip of tea and wincing as she scalded her thin lips. 'Why, I remember a time when we thought nothing of a jumble sale every two months.'

'I think that people are less inclined to throw things away these days,' suggested Malcolm Jackson. 'After all, everyone, in some way, has been affected by . . .'

'It's greed, pure greed,' interrupted Iris. 'People are hoarding things. Greed is such a terrible sin and one to be avoided at all costs.' She punctuated this by reaching for another scone. 'And as the good book says, "Let the wicked fall into their own nets, whilst I pass in safety." '

Malcolm Jackson couldn't resist it and touchéd with 'Ah, but let's not forget "If any one of you is without sin, let him be the first to throw a stone." ' His tone was cynical rather than pious and he received a withering look for his trouble.

'We really could do with one more pair of hands for the jumble sale next Saturday,' Hilary said in an effort to steer the conversation back to where it had been before Becky had interrupted. 'We had seven last time, and to be honest we were a bit stretched.'

'What about Charlotte, your sister?' Iris Braithwaite said. 'She could help, she won't have any commitments so soon, will she? Do her good, get her fully integrated into the village again.'

'Oh, I don't think that would be a good idea. Do you?' Hilary asked, turning to the vicar.

'Nonsense,' Iris Braithwaite carried on, ignoring Malcolm's opened mouth. 'She'll need to be busy. When my Sydney died fifteen years ago, the first thing I did was to spring-clean the house and organise the summer fête.' She paused as though reflecting on those halcyon days, then said, 'I don't suppose Charlotte will be bringing any of her deceased husband's clothing back with her, will she? We could make good use of that at the jumble sale.' And casting a meaningful glance over Malcolm Jackson's faded sweatshirt and jeans, she said, 'Perhaps there might even be something suitable for the vicar.'

'I really couldn't say,' Hilary said helplessly, conscious of the sudden sirocco-style exhalation of breath at her side.

It was always the same. Every month, whenever they had to meet to discuss various fund-raising events for St John's, Iris Braithwaite rendered poor Malcolm speechless. Trouble was, Malcolm, being a clergyman, was like the Queen – not allowed to answer back – and she herself, like so many in the village, was just plain terrified of Iris Braithwaite.

'Well,' said Iris, putting her cup down on the tray and then dabbing the corners of her mouth with her napkin, 'I think we've covered everything quite adequately. So, come along, Vicar, it's time we were going. I'm sure Mrs Parker doesn't want us cluttering up her sitting-room a moment longer.'

Dutifully getting his bulky frame to his feet, Malcolm Jackson smiled at Hilary and thanked her for the tea. 'Will you be in church on Sunday?' he added as they moved towards the hall.

'Yes, it's my turn on Sunday School rota – which reminds me, we really could do with a new trainer seat for the toilet. Poor Joel had an accident with the last one.'

'Really, Mrs Parker!' spluttered Iris Braithwaite. 'I'm sure the vicar doesn't want to hear about such trifling matters.'

Oh dear, thought Hilary, another faux pas.

'I doubt whether it seemed a trifling matter to young Joel at the time,' Malcolm said, a smile on his lips. 'No serious damage, I hope?'

'He hurt his bum!' came a loud voice. It was Becky bumping her way down the stairs on her bottom. She was now wearing a pink leotard with grass-stained ballet tights and carrying her treasured Barbie doll in her hands. 'He hurt his willy wobbler as well,' she added for good measure, when she finally bumped to a stop at the foot of the stairs. 'He was such a cry-baby, he cried all during the story of David and Goliath.'

'Thank you, Becky, that's enough,' said Hilary in a tired voice. She pulled open the front door, anxious for the afternoon to come to an end. But Iris was not finished.

'We're a pair of hands short on the church flower rota. Ask Charlotte, it'll give her something to do. Lovely tea by the way, shame about that sponge, though.'

'Have they gone?' It was Philip, a dark-haired ten-year-old boy, calling from the top of the stairs. Satisfied that the coast was clear, he raced downstairs and shot into the sitting-room to gain possession of the remote control of the television before his sister got it.

'What about your homework, Philip?' Hilary asked, fulfilling her son's expectations of her, as she began clearing the wreckage of tea.

'I've done it,' he replied glibly, thereby fulfilling his mother's expectations of him, at the same time waving the remote control device high in the air, just out of his sister's reach.

Out in the kitchen, Hilary fed the dishwasher, cake crumbs and all, mentally going over that evening's meal, and her plan – supper with a few of the neighbours, just to get her sister acclimatised, and, of course, to introduce her to Alex.

If there was one thing Hilary could never be accused of, it was suffering from an over-indulgence of sentimentality, and whilst it was all very sad and tragic that her sister's husband had died so suddenly, she knew that one simply had to carry on. Charlotte would now have to build up her life again, with a little help. She would need company, and preferably the company of a man, and Hilary had just the man in mind.

Alex Hamilton had been in the village for just two weeks now, renting the granny annexe of Charlotte's new house, Ivy Cottage. He was, in Hilary's opinion, quite the most attractive man to have hit Hulme Welford since a few years ago, when a rather notorious snooker player moved into the village, only to move out again rather rapidly when he lost his potting technique, along with his fortune.

There was no doubt in her mind that Alex Hamilton was the tonic Charlotte needed in order to get herself back on her feet again.

Hilary looked up at the clock above the Aga. Charlotte's plane would be arriving within the hour and Hilary knew the traffic would slow her down.

'I can always get a taxi,' her sister had said.

'Nonsense!' had been Hilary's reply.

Now there was a part of her that was regretting this

rash offer; she had more than enough to do without getting caught up in Friday night's rush-hour traffic.

Living 'conveniently placed for Manchester airport', as her husband David so liked to describe the village in his estate agency brochures, was the only tangible disadvantage to living in Hulme Welford, as far as Hilary could see. They were situated directly beneath the main flight path and David had to work hard at playing down the noise to prospective purchasers who came into his attractive black and white half-timbered estate agency office in the centre of the village.

In recent years house sales in the area had sky-rocketed, as Hulme Welford, with all its chocolate-box charm, had steadily increased in popularity with the more adventurous members of the Manchester commuter-belt set. When the older and quite dilapidated cottages in the village had been snapped up, small exclusive developments, such as Orchard Way and Pippin Rise, had sprung up like weeds on the perimeter of the village. They provided trouble-free houses for the upwardly mobile; fully centrally heated, double garaged and two bathroomed, gold taps and all. The houses had increased the population of the village, and brought to it an excess of BMWs tearing about the lanes, as well as a universally agreed improvement to the shops. The local infant and junior school had responded with equal expansion and now, with its increased numbers and pulsating PTA, could boast not only good academic results, but a swimming pool as well.

Most of these changes Hilary approved of, especially the pulsating PTA, of which she was currently Secretary. Next year she hoped to be Chairwoman. Just recently though, the idea of joining the Board of Governors for the school had taken root, and the more Hilary thought about it, the more the idea appealed to her. She could even buy one of those smart executive-looking suits to wear for the meetings.

Taking a tray of wine glasses through to the dining-room, Hilary's thoughts about whether to buy a navy-blue or grey suit were interrupted by a pump-action ring at the doorbell. 'Get that, will you, Philip? It'll be Tiffany.'

'Oh Mum, *Grange Hill*'s on.'

'Oh, all right, I'll go.' She put the glasses down on the oak table in the hall. 'And Becky, you come out of there, you're too young for *Grange Hill*.'

A shrill wail started up from Becky, followed by a full scale riot, as Philip began thumping his sister to make her be quiet. Unperturbed, Hilary opened the front door.

'Muffin 'ell, what's going on?'

Hearing their babysitter's familiar voice, Becky leapt off her brother and ran out into the hall. Tiffany fascinated her. When she grew up, she wanted to be just like her – black leggings, huge boots, black-rimmed eyes just like a panda and long, long black hair.

'Can I count your rings, Tiffany?'

'Say please.'

'*Please*.'

''Course you can. Let's see how good your maths is today.'

With tongue-poking-out-of-the-mouth concentration, Becky started to count. First on Tiffany's left hand then on her right. 'Four and three, that makes . . . seven,' she announced after careful consideration.

'Who's a clever little madam then. And what *was* you doing to your brother when I came in?'

'*Were*,' corrected Becky.

Hilary smiled. Tiffany's subversive teaching methods with Becky never failed. She and David could shout until they were blue in the face about the correct use of speech and Becky would just throw it back at them.

'Okay if I dash off straight away, Tiffany?' Hilary said. 'I'd like to try and get there early.'

'Yeah sure, no problem.'

'I'll be a couple of hours at most. David might even be back before me, though I doubt it.' She reached for her keys hanging up on the hook by the telephone. 'Oh Lord!' she suddenly cried out. 'I've forgotten to give the children any tea, I've been so busy thinking about tonight and what with Mrs Braithwaite and Reverend Jackson, I've . . .'

'Got any fish fingers in the freezer?'

'Yes, and there's some cake left over from this afternoon. Oh Tiffany, you are wonderful. What would I do without you?'

Tiffany smiled. If only her mother thought the same.

Pushing her trolley of luggage, Charlotte's eyes searched the crowded arrivals hall for her sister's welcoming face, but all she could see were rows of bored-looking men holding drooping placards bearing the names of their charges. There was no sign of Hilary.

Charlotte felt anxious. She wanted to get this bit of the day over with. Knowing her sister's intense desire to do and say all the right things, Charlotte viewed the drive home with a mixture of uneasiness and hostility.

She paused for a moment with her trolley, letting her fellow passengers push ahead of her. She suddenly felt overwhelmed by the juxtaposition of this large, bustling, uncaring crowd around her and the thought of Hilary lavishing well-intended sisterly love on her. Frightened she was about to cry, she reached into her jacket pocket for a tissue. Instead of a tissue, she found the envelope

Christina had given to her at the airport in Brussels. She had kept it in her pocket until she was soaring over the Belgian coast with a glass of champagne in her hand. Then she had opened it and read the card with Christina's beautiful words.

'Leave your sadness behind, Carlotta; leave it in Brussels where it can no longer harm you. Take only your beautiful smile with you and offer it to everyone you meet; it will bring you and them such happiness.'

It was the loveliest thing anyone had ever said to her.

And then as if by magic there was Hilary rushing towards her. To Charlotte's surprise, relief flooded through her.

Chapter Three

'I'm doing a little supper party for you tonight,' Hilary said, stretching her hand out of the car window to insert the parking ticket in the required slit.

'Oh Hilary, not tonight, I can't.'

'Nonsense, you'll be fine,' Hilary said firmly. She hoped to goodness her sister wasn't going to play the grieving widow round the dinner table that night. Moussaka, mirth and a little matchmaking were what she had in mind, not moussaka and misery. 'You know,' she said, choosing her words carefully, 'you know how desperately sad we all are about Peter, but at some stage you have to pick up the pieces of your life again, so it might as well be tonight.' Especially after all the trouble I've gone to, she thought. 'And anyway,' she added with forced brightness, 'it will be a nice way for you to meet Alex.'

The initial flood of relief Charlotte had experienced on seeing her sister's capable face in the crowd had completely flowed out of her. The familiar twinges of irritation that went hand in hand with the sisters' affection for one another were now beginning to surface.

And Charlotte also knew what Hilary was up to. Ever since the contract for Ivy Cottage had been signed and David had found a tenant to live in the granny annexe, Hilary had never stopped mentioning this Alex Hamilton on the telephone: 'Such a nice man . . . very pleasant . . . he'll be no bother to you . . . quite handy really, you know, should you run out of coffee, or anything like that.'

Well, tonight she would meet him, would make up her own mind. In her opinion, Hilary had been watching too many Gold Blend adverts.

She decided to move on to firmer ground. 'How are the children?'

'As wonderful as ever.'

Charlotte grimaced. Wonderful was not the description that instantly sprang to her mind when she thought of her nephew and niece – seismic savages more like it.

'They're really looking forward to seeing you. You'll be a real aunt to them now, living so close.'

'I hadn't thought of it quite like that,' Charlotte said, horrified at the thought. Living opposite her sister had been the only fly in the ointment of her plan to move back to Hulme Welford.

'Philip's just been awarded his thousand-metre swimming badge and Becky has cracked breaststroke. She's a real natural, Mrs Pulman says.'

Charlotte knew it was always best to let her sister ramble on with motherly pride, and over the years she had mastered the art of half listening and oohing and aahing in the appropriate pauses. 'So, who's coming tonight?' she asked, when at last Hilary had run out of glowing reports of her offspring. 'Will it be smart? I haven't brought everything, the rest is following on in the removal van.'

'No, of course it's not posh,' Hilary said, thinking of all the luggage they had just loaded into the back of David's Volvo. 'It's only family and a few neighbours. There'll be you, me, David, Mum and Dad, and Derek and Cindy. Remember I told you about them moving into Rose Cottage just before Peter . . .'

Hilary's unfinished sentence hung stiffly in the air and an awkward silence filled the car.

'Go on,' Charlotte said at last. 'Say it, Hilary, don't be afraid of using the word. *Died*. Peter died. Okay? His car skidded on ice and hit a barrier at a hundred and twenty kilometres an hour. He was killed instantly. Peter's dead. There, I've said it, you try it.'

Hilary found herself unable to respond to what, in her mind, was an appalling outburst of bad taste. Surely even in grief one had to employ a certain amount of dignity? Looking after Charlotte was going to be more difficult than she had supposed. Her eyes firmly fixed on the road ahead, she decided to return to the subject of supper that evening. 'And the only other guest who'll be there is Alex, of course.'

'Of course,' repeated Charlotte, looking out of the window, not trusting herself to look at her sister.

Adopting a cheery voice, Hilary said, 'Have you thought any more about my offer for you to stop the night with us? I just can't bear the idea of you being all alone. You'll be so lonely.'

It was difficult for Charlotte not to laugh out loud. She had spent the last few years of her marriage feeling alone and isolated.

'Stay with us, Charlotte. Come on, why don't you? Just your first night.'

Charlotte considered The Gables for a moment: the noise, the constant bickering, the fighting – and that was just Hilary and David. She smiled to herself, thinking of the calmness and tranquillity she hoped to have at Ivy Cottage. 'It's kind of you to offer,' she said, 'but I'd rather like to get settled in straight away, there's so much to do. I'm quite looking forward to it really.'

'Yes of course, I understand.' She didn't understand at

all. How could Charlotte be looking forward to moving into that house all alone?

They entered the village, and as they passed the prettily painted sign that had helped Hulme Welford win the North-West's 'Best Kept Village' title last year, Charlotte began to feel uneasy. Supposing she had made a mistake in coming back? It was a fact of life, one of those clichéd phrases, trotted out with diligent reverence to the worldly wisdom of those unfortunate enough to have tried it for themselves – *you can't go back*.

Only her mother had actually had the courage to say this to her. 'Charlotte, are you sure you're doing the right thing? After all, everyone knows, only a fool tries to turn back the clock.'

'Thank you, Mother,' she had said. 'I can always rely on you for support, can't I?'

'No point in me lying to you, Charlotte, never lied to you before, why should I start now?'

'Because my husband's just died?' Charlotte had replied, knowing how pathetic she was sounding, whining like a small child. 'And it might be nice to be . . .'

'What?' Louise had said, frowning. 'Mollycoddled? You want me to mollycoddle you? You of all people must know I'm not that kind of a mother.'

It was true. Louise Archer had never been the kind of mother to rush to a bleeding knee-cap with a box of plasters, nor soothe an exhausted child with a bedtime story. She had always been busy at some auction or other, or working in her antique shop, buffing up and restoring her 'finds'. From an early age, both Charlotte and Hilary had learnt where the Germoline and aspirins were kept.

They drove along the main street with its plentiful supply of shops; their mother's antique shop, the baker's, butcher's, grocer's, paper shop and Post Office next door, and then the more upmarket chic clothes shop and the kitchen and bathroom shop. It was just after six-thirty and, apart from the paper shop, everything was shut. She spotted David's office. Charlotte could see a light still on. She thought for one awful moment her sister might want to stop the car and take her in to see David. But to her relief Hilary turned left at the church, drove down Daisy Bank and then turned again into Acacia Lane, a leafy cul-de-sac made up of a handful of small terraced cottages and four large houses set well back from the road.

On the right-hand side was The White Cottage. The house was exactly what its name suggested, a neat cottage with a perfect covering of unadorned white rendering. The garden was equally neat with well-dug, weedless flower beds. Daffodils, now well past their best, had been neatly folded with rubber-bands, thwarting any untidiness. This was where Iris Braithwaite lived.

Beyond The White Cottage was Rose Cottage. This came as a complete surprise to Charlotte. Not so long ago Rose Cottage had been a pretty, pale-coloured house. Now it was painted shocking pink, and at the end of the drive was a large sign informing Charlotte it was called 'In The Pink'.

'Derek and Cindy,' Hilary said to Charlotte's look of horror. 'They have a chain of hair salons right across Cheshire and they've turned the house into a sort of health and beauty centre, in record time too. They seem to be doing very well out of it.'

'But it's ghastly. However did they get away with painting it that disgusting colour?'

'Don't ask me. And please, don't ask them. Derek thinks it's quite the thing. By the way, watch out for Derek.'

'Why?'

'Don't be naïve, Charlotte.'

Dropping down into second gear, Hilary turned off the road and carefully drove between two peeling white gates and up a narrow driveway to Ivy Cottage.

Since she'd grown up in Hulme Welford and had made regular visits home throughout her marriage, Charlotte was familiar with every house in the village, except those on the new developments, Orchard Way and Pippin Rise. Ivy Cottage had always been one of her favourites. As a child, she had been fascinated by the house and its occupant, a woman who had been something of a celebrity as a writer of romantic fiction. Blanche Blair had drifted about the village with the glamour one might have expected of a woman of her profession, and she had managed to create an air of mystery around her large Edwardian cottage and beautiful garden. The last years of Blanche Blair's life were spent in a nursing home and the cottage had stood empty. On her death, Ivy Cottage had been snapped up by the Cliffords from Doncaster, who, bringing an elderly mother with them, had the house redesigned to provide an independent granny flat at one end of the house. But the elderly occupant of the granny flat rather ungratefully died and the Cliffords had felt the pull of Doncaster. The house still looked to be one from the outside, but there were two driveways, an original of gravel and one of tarmac.

An abundance of ivy and peeling paint gave the impression that the house and garden were badly in need of work. Yet Charlotte thought it was wonderful. A little sad and drab perhaps, but compared to the elegant, sterile apartment she had left behind in Brussels, with its marble and fake neoclassical gilt work, it was real, and it was hers.

Between them, they took the luggage out of the Volvo and into the house.

'There now,' said Hilary, 'everything's in. Shall I show you round?'

'Haven't you got a meal to prepare?' Charlotte wanted more than anything to be left alone.

Hilary looked at her watch. 'Oh Lord, you're right, I must fly, but are you sure you've got everything you need?'

'I'm fine, really. I'll unpack a few things, have a bath, then be right over.'

'Good idea. I put the immersion heater on for you earlier.'

Charlotte knew she should be grateful to Hilary for thinking of having hot water ready for her, but she felt childishly possessive; it was her house, her immersion heater.

She watched her sister reverse down the drive and turn into her own drive to The Gables. Closing the door behind her, for the second time that day Charlotte felt an overwhelming sense of relief; she had made it this far.

Then for no good reason she could think of, she started to cry.

Chapter Four

Pound coins chinking in her jacket pocket – the financial rewards of babysitting – Tiffany Rogers sauntered across the road towards In The Pink. She was in no hurry to get home, had even offered to stay on a bit longer to help Mrs Parker set the dining-room table. She was nice, Mrs Parker, though she could do with slowing down a bit; she'd been like a headless chicken just now in the kitchen.

As she walked up the drive, her heavy Doc Martens clomping on the tarmac, Tiffany paused to look at the damage her parents had done to what had once been an ordinary-looking house.

When they had bought Rose Cottage, her parents had taken it in hand, treating it like a client. Only this time they worked in reverse, stretching it to twice its original size by adding two enormous extensions, providing room for a complex of saunas, jacuzzis, gymnasiums, massage rooms and a hair salon. Now Rose Cottage was beyond recognition, smelling permanently of a combination of hospitals, public swimming baths and hairspray.

The walls, which had once been a delicate pastel shade of pink, were now the colour of a vivid Mediterranean geranium. Tiffany knew they stuck out in the village as flagrantly as she herself did.

Coming to Hulme Welford had not been as bad as it might have been; at least she and her brother could stay at the same school, so had kept all their old friends who were now a short bus ride away. Since she was eight years old they had lived in Wilmslow, but then last year Dad had got this idea that the big money lay in buying a large old house and converting it into a health and beauty centre. Tiffany viewed it more as a temple of indulgence for the privileged few and said as much to her parents at every possible opportunity.

Alone in the salon, Cindy Rogers turned off the lights and, carrying her expensive Italian shoes in her hands, made her way along the corridor that separated the work area from the living area of the house. On her feet all day, Cindy knew she should wear flatter shoes, but she also knew that her slim, tanned legs looked even better in a pair of high heels.

She was tired and not looking forward to going out for dinner to the Parkers'. She would have much preferred a good long soak in a lavender-oil-scented bath. Instead she would have to face the ordeal of coping with the excessive amount of food which Hilary would present her with. Eating out always filled Cindy with dread.

She found Tiffany in the kitchen, frying some bacon and making a cup of tea, and at once Cindy felt the familiar surge of disappointment as she looked at her daughter.

She had so badly wanted a daughter. The birth of her first child, Barry, had been a bad enough blow, but nothing had prepared her for Tiffany. The black patent shoes and smocked dresses she had longed to dress her daughter in had been denied her by this wayward, head-strong child. The shopping trips she had envisaged, the shared girl-talk and mutual understanding of all things feminine had been snatched away, right from the moment

Tiffany, at the age of four, had stood in the middle of her bedroom and pulled off the beautiful little dress Cindy had just bought for her in Manchester. 'Don't like it,' Tiffany had shouted defiantly, stamping all over the expensive fabric, 'won't wear it, want to be like Barry.' And she had followed this to the letter, fastidiously copying the way her older brother dressed, until she had started menstruating. At that point, she decided to grow her hair. And then, a year ago, on her fourteenth birthday, she had emerged from the bathroom with her long sandy hair completely jet black. From then on, it seemed to Cindy, Tiffany grew each day more and more like Morticia from the Addams family.

Cindy frowned, then immediately relaxed her facial muscles, knowing how damaging it was for the skin. But the strains of her morning argument with Tiffany were still there, hanging in the air of her bleached ash kitchen. Nothing was going to change her mind; Tiffany and her friends were too young to go off for a weekend in the Lake District on their own. Surely her stubborn fifteen-year-old daughter could see that?

It was Tiffany who spoke first. 'Want some tea?'

'No, thanks. Where have you been?' It came out all wrong and she felt her daughter bristle.

'Muffin 'ell, I've been over at Mrs Parker's babysitting. I told you this morning I'd be going there straight after school. You obviously weren't listening.'

They were off again, their mood to one another cold, combative.

'Where's Barry?' Cindy asked, trying to sound conciliatory.

'Up in his room studying.'

'What, already?'

'You should be proud of him. After all, if he does

become a surgeon he'll be able to give you the facelift you'll need after all that rubbish you pile on your face.'

Cindy gave up. 'I'm going to have a bath, seeing as you've nothing civil to say to me.'

Tiffany watched her mother go. She hadn't meant to be rude, but her mother's complete misunderstanding of Barry really got to her. Didn't she know how important it was to Barry to get not just good grades in his A levels, but brilliant grades? Their mother and their father just had no idea of the strain Barry was under.

Derek Rogers was having a sauna. He liked a good sweat before going out. At forty-five, when most of his contemporaries were beginning to look their age and were quite prepared to forget about their bodies, Derek Rogers was obsessed with his.

Physically he was in great shape, but mentally he was not. He was bored, bored to death.

The five salons he and Cindy owned throughout Cheshire practically ran themselves and now that In The Pink was up and running and gaining more clients every day, he felt the need for something more challenging. He was bored with the women of Hulme Welford too. They were no challenge to him. They were all so bored themselves that they leapt at the chance of an added drop of excitement in their lives.

Since the age of sixteen when Derek had discovered he was irresistible to women of any age, and discovered at the same time that he was driven by a compulsive need for a variety of women in his life, he had embarked upon countless affairs, leading up to and during his twenty-two-year-old marriage to Cindy. Affairs to him had never been an added bonus; he needed them like a gambler needs the next roll of the dice. He viewed Cindy as his morning cup of coffee: strong and bitter and always there. He never considered whether he loved her or not, that was irrelevant. She was just there, a part of his life.

Out of the sauna, he rubbed himself down with a towel, pulled on a pair of Paisley boxer shorts then walked through to the gym. A quick ten-minute work-out on the exercise bike and then he would shower and get ready. He was looking forward to this evening. It held the promise of something new. He knew Hilary and David of course, living so close, and he and Cindy had been introduced to Louise and Neville Archer some weeks ago. The two guests he didn't know at all were Alex Hamilton and Charlotte Lawrence. He had noticed that chap Hamilton moving into the granny flat of Ivy Cottage two weeks ago and had seen a lot of books and computer stuff coming out of the back of the removal van, which meant they would have nothing at all in common.

But Charlotte Lawrence, Hilary's sister – now she was a different matter, she intrigued him. He had seen a photograph of her when they had been invited over to the Parkers' for drinks one Sunday lunchtime. Defiant eyes had stared back at him from the framed photograph on the mantelpiece. He had noticed that there was a strong similarity between the two sisters; noticed, too, that while Hilary was a pleasant enough-looking woman, Charlotte was the more attractive, more complete some-how – as though the two women had been painted by an artist who had started work enthusiastically on the elder sister, only to run out of paint and motivation by the time he reached the younger woman. Poor Hilary looked like a watered-down version of her sister, Derek thought.

All Derek actually knew about this sister of Hilary's was that her husband had recently died and she was coming to live in Ivy Cottage. He slowed the pedals down on the bike, began to think seriously of the evening ahead and the potential it offered. Should he wear casual – navy chinos and cream polo shirt – or one of his new Italian suits? He favoured casual; the cream shirt would set off his tan better. Looking at his paper-thin wristwatch, he considered a quick five-minute session on the sunbed.

Chapter Five

Thank heavens for Tiffany, Hilary said to herself for the umpteenth time, as she stepped out of the bath and started rubbing her legs with a towel. During the time in which she had collected Charlotte from the airport, Tiffany had not only cooked the children's tea, cleared up afterwards and then coaxed them up to bed, but she had also found time to read a few chapters of *George's Marvellous Medicine* for them. Tiffany really did have the most fantastic effect on both Becky and Philip.

Hilary bent down and tugged at the bath plug, allowing herself a small smile. There'd be no shower for David when he eventually made it home – she had used up all the hot water and there would be no more until half past six tomorrow morning, which was all down to David's excessive desire to economise. It was one of his most infuriating habits, that and being a lousy host. No doubt he would excel himself tonight, drink too much and forget all about their guests. Well, blast David's economising. As soon as she was dressed she would go downstairs and light a fire in the sitting-room. It was the coldest room in the house with its north-facing position, and even at this time of year it could feel miserably damp.

She went over to the chest of drawers by her side of the bed. Hunting at the back of the drawer, she pulled out a brand new pair of ivory-coloured silk pants and a matching bra. One of her few luxuries in life was buying and hoarding new underwear and saving it for just the right occasion.

Just as she was cutting off the price tags in the bathroom, Hilary heard the familiar noise of her own car coming up the drive. Hurriedly she hid the evidence of her indulgence at the bottom of the bin, pulled on the pants and wriggled into the bra. She was disappointed, though, not to be able to savour the moment alone.

Downstairs the front door banged. This was followed by the sound of David's exploratory footsteps pacing through the hall to the kitchen, the sitting-room, the dining-room, until eventually they could be heard coming up the stairs.

'There you are,' David said, coming into the bedroom, pulling off his silk tie and tossing it on to the bed. 'Mm . . . you look nice.' He eyed her more closely. 'Been shopping?'

She laughed and parried his question. 'You look pleased with yourself.'

'I've every right to be pleased. I've sold three houses today, including that architect-designed monstrosity I thought I'd be stuck with for ever. Could be a sign the recession really is letting up at last.'

'That's wonderful, darling,' Hilary said, opening the wardrobe door and trying to sound more pleased than she was. Ordinarily she would have been delighted for David, but not today, not tonight. For David would be feeling in need of some reward, which would involve an effort on her part – and to be honest she just didn't have the energy this evening after the day she'd had. He would also feel the need to celebrate by drinking too much over dinner, which would mean he'd be as good as useless at helping her with the meal.

'I'll just have a quick shower before the mob turns up,' David said.

'There's no hot water left, sorry.'

'Well in that case,' he came towards her, 'I'll have to do something else to fill in the time. Are you sure these knickers aren't new?'

Irritation flickered through Hilary as David stroked her silky bottom. She felt cheated; the pleasure was supposed to have been all hers, not David's.

Half an hour later, opening the front door to the first arrivals, David found himself poleaxed by a mouthful of Miss Dior and an equal measure of Paco Rabanne. He stood back for air as he let Cindy and Derek in, taking from them a bottle of wine and a box of chocolates.

'Go through,' he said, grimacing behind their backs. 'You know the way.'

In the sitting-room the curtains were already pulled across and a fire was blazing furiously. Minutes earlier, in an effort to save wood, David had flung most of the contents of the kitchen bin on to the gently smouldering logs, and now there was a distinct aroma of burning plastic accompanied by an occasional high-pitched whistling noise. Hilary would give him hell later.

'Do sit down.' David gestured to the chintz-covered sofas. Cindy did as she was told, perching birdlike on the edge of the sofa. Derek made himself at home, taking up pole position by the fire, feet a statutory twelve inches apart, hands pushed down into trouser pockets. After a couple of seconds he started to sniff and looked behind him.

'Think your chimney needs sweeping, David. Bit of a whiff coming from it, isn't there?'

That's rich coming from you, thought David, turning to Cindy. 'So Cindy, what can I get you to drink? No, don't tell me, let me see if I can remember. Gin and tonic?' She shook her head. 'Of course not, glass of white wine, that's got to be it.'

Derek laughed, taking his hands out of his pockets, gold bracelet chinking. 'Must be your other girlfriend. Cindy's practically a teetotal merchant, always has been, always will be, isn't that right, love?'

Cindy laughed politely, but her perfectly made-up lips remained tightly shut.

David laughed too, it was easier that way. He never knew quite what to say to Derek. After all, what sort of man was a hairdresser? But what really went against the grain with him was that Derek had legitimate access to every woman in the village and surrounding area – he was like a doctor, but without the background or ethical code of practice.

'What's that smell?' It was Hilary, her Royal Horticultural Society apron still on, a *hydrangea petiolaris* working its way up her front. Her eyes were trained on the fireplace.

'That's a fine way to greet our guests, darling.' David knew he was on thin ice, so why not go down with the *Titanic*?

'Hello Cindy and Derek,' she said pleasantly. She gave David one of her slightly stern looks, and said, 'Haven't you got the drinks going yet?'

'All in hand, dear, all in hand. Cindy, what would you like?'

'Perrier please.'

'Mine's a gin and tonic,' said Derek.

It would be, David thought, bustling off to the drinks cabinet.

'Hilary, I hope you haven't gone to a lot of trouble,' Cindy said, hoping against all the odds that it might be

35

just a light supper. 'After all, it's only friends and neighbours, like you said.'

'And family,' called out David, trying to decide whether Cindy and Derek came under friends or neighbours, at the same time trying to conceal the bottle of gin which was Sainsbury's and not Gordon's.

'So Hilary,' Derek said, picking up the framed photograph of Charlotte from the mantelpiece, 'tell us what your sister is like.'

Cindy, her perfectly manicured nails digging into the palms of her hands, closed her eyes. Surely he wouldn't? Not with a woman whose husband had so recently died.

Chapter Six

Charlotte was late. She had spent longer than she intended in the bath, with a large gin and tonic, and when the bath water had gone cold for the second time, she had wrapped her bathrobe around her, topped up her glass and wandered aimlessly about her echoing, unfurnished new home. The removal van from Brussels wasn't due to arrive until Monday morning, so until then all she had was a put-you-up-bed and a couple of chairs which Hilary had loaned her.

Despite this, and despite the dusty wooden floorboards, the naked walls with their ghostly marks where once there had been pictures, Charlotte was delighted with each room she went into; especially the shambling, wooden-constructed conservatory at the back of the house. It was not a neat modern conservatory sold by an aggressive young man on the doorstep, but one built many years ago that recently had fallen into disrepair. Certainly it looked as though the Cliffords had not made it as far as this part of the house in terms of adding their personal touch.

Opening the stiff door, which creaked and groaned for a good rubbing down and some oil and led out on to the garden, Charlotte let in the cool evening air. The air inside was warm and as thick as syrup with flies buzzing wearily against the smeared glass. In this hothouse warmth, Charlotte began to feel lightheaded. Suddenly she had a very real image in her mind of Blanche Blair sitting at her typewriter in the almost tropical atmosphere, conjuring up one of her torrid romances, hearts beating and aflame with desire.

Laughing, she went back into the house. Buoyed up by three large gins, she felt convinced that she had made the right decision in moving back to Hulme Welford. Ivy Cottage, she decided, was going to be the best thing to have happened to her in a long while.

Peter's idea of a home had been an impersonal base that was neat and tidy, without any added complications such as flower beds, leaking gutters and windowsills that needed painting. Each time they had moved, Charlotte had requested they live in a house, but each time Peter had over-ridden her wishes and insisted they rent an apartment. Admittedly, the apartments they had lived in had not been mean and cramped, far from it. The one in Singapore had been ridiculously palatial, even bigger than Brussels, but it had still felt like a prison cell to Charlotte. 'A prison cell!' Peter had shouted indignantly, when Charlotte complained about their latest home. 'Are you mad, Charlotte? Look about you and see how some of the locals live, ask them whether they think we're living in a cell.'

Perhaps, though, it had not been the physical walls of their various homes that had made her feel a captive. It was the mental confines of a marriage going disastrously wrong that had caused her to feel such a prisoner.

Upstairs, in what was to be her bedroom, Charlotte opened a suitcase and pulled out the first dress that came to hand. She tried to gear herself up for the evening ahead. Trouble was, she had no idea how to play her part. Was she to be doleful, demure or stiff upper lippish, displaying shoulders back and best foot forward? It should, of course, all come naturally, but it didn't, because she herself did not know exactly how she felt. With each day that passed she was conscious only of a deepening sense of guilt which most people around her mistook for grief. She had convinced herself that because of her Peter had tried to drive to Luxembourg when he was no longer in control of his emotions and had died as a result. She had told no one of this, not even Christina, and nobody knew what she had told Peter over breakfast. So there was no one to suggest that perhaps her husband – his mind already on his business meeting – had quite simply hit a patch of ice? And why had she told no one? Because then no one would be able to blame her for Peter's death.

Other than this growing, self-imposed culpability, Charlotte had not experienced any great trauma. After all, she had already experienced every level of emotion during the months leading up to that point of no return when she knew that she could not go on pretending. She had cried gulping great tears alone, night after night, lying in a half empty bed. She had cried in the bath, streams of tearful loneliness. She had even wept in the local supermarket, angry tears of frustration over the *pain de blé* when she had finally come to realise that she would never be the wife Peter needed; the kind of wife who didn't mind her husband having an all-consuming mistress – his work.

She shut the front door behind her, and locking it with the unfamiliar key Hilary had given her earlier, Charlotte started to walk down the driveway. But with each step she took away from her new home, her recently gin-induced confidence began to ebb away, until by the time she had reached the gate, she wasn't at all sure she had made the right decision in coming back to live in Hulme Welford, searching, as she was, for the familiar security of what she'd known P.P. – pre-Peter.

She stood on the pavement and looked across to The Gables. She felt like a small child who has just been given its comfort blanket, only to find the silky edging has come away.

Her mother, Louise Archer, opened the door to her. 'Charlotte!' she cried out, as though her elder daughter was the last person on earth she had been expecting to see that evening.

'Mother,' Charlotte replied, finding it difficult to respond in any other way. They almost made contact as they leaned towards each other for a perfunctory kiss.

'Hilary's on the telephone, she won't be long. You look tired.'

'You always say that.'

'Well, isn't that the kind of thing mothers are supposed to say?'

They walked through to the sitting-room, Charlotte following behind her mother.

'Look, everybody, look who's here,' Louise said, in a loud voice. It came out like an over-rehearsed line from a play.

'Charlotte!' Neville Archer said with obvious delight. He levered himself out of a florid armchair and came towards her, spilling a few drops of whisky as he did so. 'How about a hug for your old dad, then? Sorry we weren't there to meet you at the airport – your mother had an auction over at Chester and needed the car.'

Charlotte hugged him warmly. She was always pleased to see her father, with his familiar Toby jug appearance – stout and highly coloured.

'Don't worry,' she said. 'Hilary was there in full control.' Stepping back from him, she said in a voice deliberately aimed at her mother, 'You're looking great, Dad. The new diet's going well, then?'

He smiled at her and at the same time, with great effort, he pulled in his stomach, causing his buttoned cardigan to collapse like a balloon. Lowering his voice so as to exclude everyone else from their conversation, he asked, 'You okay?'

She nodded, grateful for his quiet concern, and said, 'How are the gooseberries?'

He looked worried. 'Not sure, they don't seem as good as last year's.'

Like a number of men and women in the village, Neville Archer spent months preparing for the annual gooseberry-growing contest, but as yet her father's gooseberries had never got anywhere near the weights required to be in the running for a prize. But each year Charlotte hoped that he might be lucky.

She rested a hand on his arm. 'They'll be fine. You'll win something this year, I'm sure of it.'

'Don't, Charlotte, for goodness' sake, just don't start him off about those wretched gooseberries,' Louise said vehemently, shaking her head. 'You know how unbearable he gets on the subject.'

'Talk to you later,' Charlotte whispered to him. Noticing that there were others in the room whom she did not know, Charlotte looked for her sister or David to make the necessary introductions. There was no sign of either. Staring straight at her was an overly tanned, slim woman with a perfect bob of blonde hair, looking for all the world like a candidate for *Come Dancing*. Cindy, Charlotte decided. And over by the hi-fi, it had to be Derek, a dead ringer for Phil Collins if ever there was one.

'Charlotte, you're here at last.' It was Hilary, coming in with a tray of nibbles, and her choice of words did not go unnoticed by Charlotte. 'Have you been properly introduced? I can't think where David's got to, I only asked him to fetch some logs. That was Alex on the telephone, by the way. Poor man, he just called to say he had been stuck in traffic in Manchester, but would be with us as soon as he'd changed. Cindy, let me introduce my sister.'

Cindy stood up, met Charlotte eye to eye, and was convinced she could smell gin.

There were very few women in the village whom Cindy liked; most of them she considered a threat, with the exception of Hilary. Cindy had decided her neighbour was far too busy coping with her own marriage to stray beyond it and so wouldn't recognise a come-on from Derek, even if he handed her a condom with her name on it. On the other hand, she knew instinctively that this woman, standing in front of her, *was* a threat. Those huge, dusky violet eyes and all that luscious raven-coloured hair would be like a gift from heaven to Derek. And she was free and vulnerable. It certainly didn't take too much effort on Cindy's part to see how Derek could make up his mind to take this woman out of herself; to get her over the death of her husband.

Charlotte sensed Cindy's reluctant hand slip in and out of her own and the brittle smile that went with it. She was aware, too, how simply but effectively Cindy was dressed, unlike herself she now realised. The expensive linen suit she had slung on only minutes earlier should have been ironed, but she had been in too much of a hurry and too lazy to bother.

'You must come and pamper yourself some time,' Cindy was saying. 'Grief can have such a devastating effect on the skin.'

'Yes,' Charlotte said awkwardly, wanting suddenly to step away from Cindy, who with her perfect complexion was probably already sizing up Charlotte's skin as pumice-stone texture.

Almost as though Cindy had been pushed to one side, there was the Phil Collins lookalike standing before Charlotte, cool as you like, a strategically unbuttoned cream polo shirt revealing a sprinkling of fair hairs on a tanned chest. 'Don't be naïve,' Hilary had said earlier in the car. Charlotte smiled to herself, thinking how she might have fun being exactly that.

'Now you do remember, don't you?' said Hilary. 'I told you about Cindy and Derek and In The Pink.'

Charlotte felt the hackles rising. Of course she remembered – she had lost her husband, not her mind. 'No,' she lied for the sheer hell of it, 'no, I don't recall you mentioning a Cindy or a Derek.' She heard her sister's sharp intake of breath.

'Continentals don't go in for much handshaking, do they?' Derek said, moving closer to Charlotte. 'They kiss a lot instead.' Which he promptly did, kissing Charlotte on both cheeks.

'How wonderfully flamboyant,' Louise said, raising her eyebrows.

'Well,' gasped Hilary, slightly flustered, 'that's one way of breaking the ice. Now come on, everyone, sit down, make yourselves at home. Anyone for chicken tikka-flavoured nuts?'

'Somebody mention food? I'm starving.' It was David with a large basket of logs, which he dropped with a crash beside the fireplace. 'Charlotte, you've arrived. Good to see you. Everything all right over the road?'

'Yes thanks, David, just as Hilary said it would be.'

Shaking his hands clean of log dust, he came over and kissed her. 'This isn't on,' he said. 'You're the only one without a drink. Let me get you something.'

'Only a quick one,' chipped in Hilary, who, like Cindy, was sure Charlotte smelled of gin. In answer to the query written on her husband's face, she said, 'We'll be eating soon.'

The doorbell rang.

'I'll get that.' Hilary almost barged past David in her hurry to get to the front door. 'It'll be Alex.'

The rest of the guests sat in awkward silence, listening to the front door being pulled open and the sound of Hilary's voice carrying from the hall. 'Oh Alex, how kind, but you shouldn't have. Really, I don't deserve them.'

You're right, thought Charlotte, you don't deserve them, whatever they are, you scheming little monkey.

The sound of Hilary's voice grew louder until she stood in the doorway, a sparkling smile on her face, a bouquet of gypsophila and pink carnations in one hand and a bottle of wine in the other.

'Sorry I'm late, everybody,' said a voice from behind Hilary. Alex Hamilton made his appearance. 'I hope I haven't kept you all waiting.'

Smooth, thought Charlotte.

'No, no, of course you haven't,' fawned Hilary. 'Think nothing of it. We're just delighted you're here.'

Oh, for goodness' sake, Hilary, stop larding it on, cringed Charlotte, you'll be bobbing and curtsying next. It was quite obvious to Charlotte that this party had very little to do with welcoming her home; this was all about Hilary's honoured guest, Alex Hamilton, and making the right impression on him. While her sister carried on making a fool of herself, Charlotte weighed up the recipient of all this red carpet treatment: about six foot, she reckoned, with fair hair that was showing signs of greying. He was casually dressed in an understated kind of way: striped shirt beneath a pale blue cashmere sweater, jeans and a pair of well-worn Reeboks. He was probably about her age, she decided, mid-thirties.

'Now let me introduce you to everyone.' Hilary was off again and beginning to steer Alex round the room, as though he were a prize bull at an auction. 'And this is my sister, Charlotte,' she said at last.

'Hello,' he said, taking her hand. 'Welcome home to England. What time did you arrive?'

'Er . . .' Charlotte was nonplussed. She wasn't expecting such an ordinary question. For the past two and a half months nearly everyone who talked to her spoke in clichés – *oh it must be so hard, oh poor you, we're thinking of you.* People spent all their time telling her how she must be feeling, or how they felt; nobody actually asked her anything. It seemed as if nothing was expected of her, as though her role as a widow was to be passive. 'Oh, a couple of hours ago,' she answered vaguely, at the same time withdrawing her hand.

'I hope I prove to be a good tenant,' he responded, then, smiling, he placed a hand on his heart and said, 'I promise not to hold any all-night parties or to hang out washing on a Sunday.'

'What a shame,' she said, offering him a small smile. 'I like a good party and it's surprising what you can learn about a person from looking at their washing.'

'Especially their underwear,' cracked Derek.

'Well, yes, I suppose so,' said Hilary, thinking of all hers upstairs. 'Now if you could all go through I'll just put these lovely flowers in water and then follow on in a moment.'

They made their way slowly into the dining-room which, after the warmth of the fire in the sitting-room, felt a little cool. They found themselves confronted with a table laid with rigid military precision: glasses standing to

45

attention, cutlery lined up in ranks, napkins with knife-edge creases and flowery name plates pushed to the front of each place setting . . . and just as Charlotte suspected, she had been positioned next to Alex.

'What an interesting painting, David,' she said. 'Is it new?' And while everyone predictably turned to admire a rather nondescript watercolour above the sideboard, Charlotte switched Alex's name for Derek's.

At the head of the table, Hilary was doing her level best to steer the conversation on a straight course, but somehow it kept slipping away from her. And who, she wanted to know, had ruined her seating plan? Secretly she suspected Derek, all that kissing at the start of the evening. And what did Charlotte think she was doing, whispering and tittering like a schoolgirl, down there with Derek at the other end of the table. Lord knows what Cindy must think. A sideways look told Hilary that Cindy was obviously bored and, by the way she was poking at her chocolate mousse, she was not going to finish it. Hilary felt slighted. Cindy had barely opened her mouth all evening, had only said anything when she was spoken to. Alex, bless him, had tried several times to talk to her, but Mother was making that exceptionally difficult, mono-polising the poor man with all her talk of antiques. And Dad, of course, was just being Dad, and for all his scintillating talk, he might have stayed at home. David was predictably drunk now and telling another of his Rotary Club jokes.

'What's the difference between a Skoda and Prince Charles?'

'Not now, David,' she said warningly, knowing the punchline only too well. She got to her feet and started to gather up the dishes. 'Bring these out for me, will you?'

'Right you are, my little sweetie-pie,' he said jumping smartly to his feet and managing to pull part of the tablecloth with him. Glasses crashed against plates and red wine bled on to the white damask cloth.

'Don't worry, everyone,' shrieked Hilary, who seemed to be the only one who was worried, 'a bit of salt rubbed in and a cold soak overnight will do the trick.'

'And that's just for David,' giggled Charlotte.

Everyone laughed and started to clear up the mess, dabbing the table with their napkins, while Hilary disappeared to the kitchen.

'Bit of a boob that, old mate,' said Derek, the only one not bothering to help. 'Though personally, I'm not a boob man.'

Again everyone laughed, except Cindy.

Derek looked up round the table. 'Nothing wrong in that, is there?'

David shook his head and poured himself another glass of wine. Taking the bottle from him, Derek filled his own glass and then Charlotte's. 'Anyone else?' he said holding up the bottle. 'What about you, Alex?'

'No thanks.'

Derek laughed. 'No, not the wine. Are you a boob man?'

'Stop it, Derek,' hissed Cindy.

'No, let the man speak.'

'I prefer the whole body.'

Smooth all right, thought Charlotte.

'Cheese and biscuits,' said Hilary, reappearing with a large plate. 'Cindy, dip in first before it all disappears.'

'No, really I couldn't, that was all quite delicious.'

Liar, thought Hilary, looking disappointed.

'Mother, how about you?'

'Sorry, that moussaka really finished me off.'

David roared with laughter. 'Has that effect on most people.'

'Is that a piece of Cheshire Blue?'

Hilary smiled gratefully at Alex and passed him the plate.

'*Very* smooth,' muttered Charlotte.

'What did you say, Charlotte?' asked her mother.

'I was just saying how smooth this red wine is.'

Hilary looked warily at her sister. She had the most awful feeling that this moment was the lull before the storm. Something terrible was about to happen. 'David,' she said, in an effort to keep the evening on track, 'what about some port?'

Getting slowly and very cautiously to his feet, David reached for a near-empty bottle of port on the sideboard, along with a tray of glasses, and for those who wanted port, he poured it out as sparingly as Communion wine.

Separate conversations began springing up around the table. Charlotte eavesdropped on what was being said.

'. . . you know, Cindy, Tiffany is such a godsend to me,' Hilary was saying. 'I don't know how I ever managed without her. She's wonderful with the children, nothing's too much trouble for her.'

'Really, I find that difficult to believe. At home she's quite difficult.'

'. . . So Alex, you're in computers, are you? I would think that would be extremely tedious. Can you prove to me it isn't?'

'I'm not sure I can, Louise, not right here and now, but I can see why you might think that.'

Alex turned away from Louise and looked down the length of the table and stared Charlotte straight in the eye. 'What plans have you got, Charlotte, now that you're back in England?'

'Plans?' she repeated. He smiled, a smile, she realised to her horror, that was duplicated, as was the cheese in front of her. Hell, she was drunk!

'I just wondered what you might want to do next?' he said, his elbows resting on the table and leaning towards her.

He wasn't going to give up, was he? 'Get a job of course,' she answered brightly.

Her mother laughed derisively. 'It won't be easy, Charlotte,' she said. 'Haven't you heard, there's a recession on and you're not exactly overly qualified, are you, apart from now having a little French under your belt, of course?'

'Thanks,' Charlotte said, picking up her wine glass and tossing back the last mouthful.

'I'm only being realistic,' Louise persisted. 'Firms have been closing down at a terrifying rate all over the country.'

'But not the antiques trade, that right, Mother?'

An uncomfortable hush fell round the table. It was Derek who broke it.

'I'm sure someone like Charlotte won't find any difficulty in getting a job,' he said, leaning into her and refilling her glass. 'Bet you sound dead sexy speaking French.'

Charlotte giggled and Hilary looked up sharply. 'David!' she snapped. 'Coffee!'

Hauling himself out of his chair once more, David looked pie-eyed round the table. 'Coffee for how many?'

'For eight of course,' came Hilary's swift reply, and then, remembering her manners, she looked round the table. 'Unless there are any takers for tea.'

'Better make it for seven,' Louise said tartly. 'Your father's fallen asleep again.'

And looking at her father, Hilary stifled a low groan. What must Alex think of them all?

'So, what kind of job?'

Charlotte silently screamed to herself. Why couldn't that smoothie just shut up and leave her alone? How on earth did she know what sort of work she could get? 'Oh, I don't know, something will turn up,' she murmured, 'and anyway, there's no need for me to get a job immediately. Peter has left me very . . .' Her voice faltered and trailed away.

'A job would keep you busy though, wouldn't it?' said Hilary. 'Keep your mind off things.'

'Why don't you come and work for us?' Derek said, winking at her. 'Classy French-speaking masseuse, that would open up the business, eh Cindy?'

'Shut up, Derek,' Cindy said quietly.

Underneath the tablecloth, Derek placed his hand firmly on Charlotte's left thigh.

Charlotte slowly pushed back her chair and rose unsteadily to her feet. She picked up her glass of wine and brandished it in the air, and in a wavering voice said, 'To Hilary, that was a wonderful lasagne . . . I mean moussaka . . . I'd just like to thank you all for a lovely evening, I haven't had so much fun since . . . well not since I told Peter I didn't . . . Oh I'm sorry, I think I'd better go home.' She banged her glass down on the table and, spilling some of its contents, she slumped slowly down into her chair and started to cry.

A stunned silence followed, then a crescendo of activity with Derek offering to take Charlotte home and Cindy hissing like a swan, saying he'd do nothing of the kind. Hilary told David to get Charlotte out of the dining-room and upstairs before she was sick all over their antique Chinese rug. But Louise surprised them all by saying, 'No, don't be silly, Alex can take her home. He lives nearest, after all.'

'Mother!' cried Hilary, a look of horror on her face. 'Alex can't possibly . . . she must stay here with us.'

'No,' wailed Charlotte. 'Not here. I want to go home.'

'No problem,' Alex said. 'I'll take her back to Ivy Cottage. Could someone find her bag for me, please?' And before Hilary could protest any more, Alex led the snivelling Charlotte towards the hall. 'Goodnight, everyone,' he said. 'Don't worry, she'll feel better after a breath of fresh air.'

Chapter Seven

A cup of coffee in his hand, Alex pushed open the door of his office, or what had once been Mrs Clifford Senior's small dining-room. He could feel the warmth of the early morning sun streaming through the window, even though it was only a quarter past eight. He reached up above his desk and opened one of the windows, looking out at the garden as he did so.

High up in the silver birch tree at the far end he could see two magpies building a new nest. Only yesterday morning these same magpies had been forced to defend their old nest from the onslaught of a large black crow. The noise had been incredible, quite unlike anything Alex had ever heard before, as the birds attempted to protect their home, screeching and squawking, their wings beating furiously, while the crow relentlessly swooped and dived, its wings flapping as menacingly as a vampire's cape. Looking at the two determined birds this morning, Alex wished them well, admiring them for their resilience. He watched them for a while and then sat down at his desk. He took a sip of his coffee, leant back in his chair and wondered how Charlotte was feeling.

After they had crossed the road to Ivy Cottage last night he had walked Charlotte round and round the moonlit garden. At one stage she had even recited the words 'round and round the garden like a teddy bear'. With each circuit completed Charlotte began to lean on him less, until finally she reached the stage when she was completely upright. At that point, coming to a halt in the front garden, Alex took her key from her bag and let them both into the house.

They stumbled around in the dark for a while, because neither of them knew where any of the light switches were. As they crashed about, Charlotte started telling Alex to be quiet. 'Ssh,' she whispered, a finger against her lips. 'You'll wake Peter and he won't like that and then he'll be cross.'

'I'll try to be quiet,' he said in a hushed voice, attempting to placate her.

They found the kitchen and the light switch. But Charlotte immediately turned the light off. 'Look!' she said, smiling and pointing up at the sky through the kitchen window, her eyes wide like those of a small delighted child. 'Isn't it lovely? The moon's shining on us, we don't need a light at all.'

On the draining board stood a kettle, along with a glass, a half empty bottle of gin and two empty tonic bottles. He filled the kettle, plugged it in and then turned round to ask Charlotte where the coffee was. But she was gone.

He went out into the hall and found her coming down the stairs. Her smile, which in the kitchen just now he had decided was quite beautiful, had vanished. 'He's not there,' she said in a small, angry voice.

'Who's not there, Charlotte?'

'Peter.'

This confused discovery on Charlotte's part had the effect of instantly sobering her up. She went into the kitchen, flicked on the light switch and rummaged through the cupboards until she found a small jar of Nescafé. He had left her twenty minutes later.

Alex switched on his computer and prepared himself for a few hours' work, even though it was Saturday. Just this week he had been taken on by a small manufacturing company over in Congleton to install and set up a system encompassing accounting, planning, production and stock control. It was going to be a big job, at least five months' work.

Computers had been Alex's 'thing' since leaving university and it had been generally acknowledged, within his field of expertise, that he was brilliant. Henderson & Wyatt PLC, the huge insurance organisation with a head office in London, had known this only too well, which was why the board of directors were so shocked when Alex, their most experienced IT Project Manager, handed in his notice. Large amounts of money, followed by even larger amounts were offered to keep him. But Alex was adamant. He gave the company six months' notice, and when that was up, he relinquished his company car, sold his flat and put his furniture into store. He then acquired the necessary visas, filled a large backpack and headed east – to Poland, Latvia and Estonia, and for no other reason than that he fancied going there.

Friends and especially family were horrified, and after much exchanging of anxious telephone calls, they decided quite simply that Alex was at 'that age' – Alex Hamilton, they came to the conclusion, was having his mid-life crisis early and was best left alone to get on with it.

His return to Britain coincided exactly with his thirty-sixth birthday. Arriving at Heathrow airport a stone lighter, he had a very firm idea as to just what he was going to do next. He wanted to start up his own consultancy, to be his own boss, to do with his life as he chose. What he wasn't so sure about was just where to do it. He had no desire to live in London again, did not want to pick up his life where he had ceremoniously dumped it eight months previously. From now on he wanted his life to be full of spontaneity, decisions to be made by the hazardous toss of a coin. While still in the confines of the airport, he bought a map of the British Isles, laid it out – Scotland balanced on his backpack and the Home Counties covering the bottom of a sleeping girl – and asked another traveller to point out on the map where he had spent his last British holiday. The man said he had spent a very agreeable few days in Cheshire in the New Year. With a pencil poised over the county of Cheshire, Alex closed his eyes. He brought the pencil down on the village of Hulme Welford – this was to be his new home.

A week later, staying in a smart little bed and breakfast on the outskirts of the village, Alex made his first recce of Hulme Welford. His initial impression, on seeing the black and white half-timbered cottages – some even with thatch – was that he liked what he saw. Strolling into the estate agency in the centre of the village, he was soon on his way to take a look at 1a Ivy Cottage, with a view to renting it.

'As you can see, all the alterations are of a high standard, so you'll have no trouble with the property,' David Parker told him, as they stood in the small empty bedroom looking out over the garden and the open field beyond. A tractor was slowly ploughing ridges with a storm cloud of crows following behind. 'Not a bad view either,' David Parker said, smiling, piling it on a bit more, obviously hoping to clinch the deal there and then in the bedroom.

But Alex didn't need any convincing, his mind was made up. Before stepping foot in the estate agent's office he had already tossed a coin – heads, and he would take the first rented property he saw. It had turned up heads.

They went down the stairs and out through the kitchen door into the garden. Alex stood on the lawn and looked up at the house. 'I'd like to take it, please,' he said. 'But, just as a matter of interest, who will be my landlord?'

'Your landlady actually. My sister-in-law.' Locking up the property and walking back into the village, David Parker explained, briefly, Mrs Lawrence's reasons for moving back to Hulme Welford. 'She needs her family round her,' he added.

Alex hoped that this was indeed the case. Sometimes families were the last thing one needed.

Back in David's office, Alex filled out the necessary forms, giving names and addresses of people whom he hoped would supply him with 'a good character reference'.

'And your line of work, Mr Hamilton?'

'Management Consultant, specialising in Information Technology,' Alex answered, deliberately making himself sound like a contestant on *Mastermind*.

'Right. That sounds . . .'

'Respectable enough?'

The two men smiled, understanding each other perfectly.

'I'll have to check these references – that will take about a week – then I'll have to ask for two months' rent in advance and a deposit of four hundred pounds. Is that all right?'

'No problem. When do you think I can move in?'

David Parker looked at the calender on his desk. 'Shall we say in two weeks' time, would that suit?'

It had suited very well. For the past fortnight Alex had begun to establish himself in the village. He was made to feel adequately welcome, in a gentle, probing kind of way.

He set out the spreadsheets that he had been working

on yesterday morning, flicked a few keys on the PC keyboard and set to. His concentration didn't last long. He looked up and wondered at the sound he'd just heard, a little like a muffled cry, or was it the magpies being assaulted again? He peered out of the window. All was well high up in the silver birch tree. Then followed a sound that was more audible and clearly more recognisable. His landlady was awake and obviously suffering. He got up from his desk and went quickly upstairs to the bathroom, before going next door to see if he could help.

Moussaka second time around was disgusting, especially when it got stuck in the nose. If she lived, Charlotte thought she would never forgive her sister. Clutching her head and stomach both at the same time, she looked down at the kitchen floor. It was not a pretty sight. She had only crawled downstairs to get herself a drink and now she had this awful mess to clear up.

The unfamiliar sound of the doorbell made her jump and was enough to set off a second bout of vomiting. This time she made it to the toilet.

When she staggered back into the kitchen, she thought she must be hallucinating. Alex Hamilton was standing at the kitchen sink, filling a washing-up bowl from the hot tap. She stood open-mouthed, not knowing what to do. She was still dressed in the clothes she had worn last night, and she felt like a pair of old tights just pulled out of the washing machine.

'Ah, there you are,' he said, turning off the hot tap and lifting the bowl out of the sink. 'I thought you might need some help. I did ring the bell but there was no answer, so I came round the back and found your door open. You must be feeling pretty wretched.'

Charlotte's mouth opened even further. Sympathy was

the last thing she had expected: mocking contempt, yes; concern, no. She tried to speak but couldn't and instead rushed to the toilet again.

When she reappeared Alex was down on his hands and knees wearing a pair of pink Marigold gloves. She somehow found the energy to laugh.

He looked up. 'What's so funny?'

'I'm sorry, it's just that you look ridiculous in those gloves. I suppose Hilary bought them, she's tried so hard to organise everything for me . . . she means well . . . and I was a perfect cow last night.'

He got to his feet. 'I'm sure she'll forgive you.'

'You know, it would be a lot easier if you could be a complete jerk.'

'Maybe I am,' he said. 'Have you got any disinfectant?'

She felt too weak and too stunned by what was happening to be of any real use. 'Have a look under the sink,' she said, 'Hilary's bound to have put some there.' Thinking about what Alex had said earlier, that he had found the back door open, she wondered how that could have been. Then she remembered. Last night, before going out, she had opened up the conservatory . . . and had forgotten to relock it. But that wasn't all she had forgotten, was it?

'I've never had to admit this before,' Charlotte said nervously, watching Alex turning out the cupboard under the sink, 'but I have no idea how I got back here last night. I suppose Hilary saw me home.'

Alex twisted off the safety top of a plastic bottle of disinfectant and poured some of the liquid on to the kitchen floor. He turned to face her. 'Don't you remember anything about last night?'

Recoiling from the smell, she said, raising her voice, 'Well, of course I do!' She regretted this, as her head began to pound with the resonance of a kettle drum. 'I just don't remember coming home, that's all.'

'Actually, it wasn't Hilary, it was me.'

'You!'

'For some reason, known only to your mother I think, she suggested I did, not that I minded.'

Charlotte was speechless. What the hell was her mother playing at?

Alex peeled off the rubber gloves and pointed to a glass of murky brown liquid on the table. 'You'd better drink that.'

'What is it?'

'A patented morning-after-the-night-before cure, never fails. I was given it in Poland where they have more than their fair share of hangovers.'

Charlotte picked up the glass reluctantly and sniffed it. 'Smells disgusting,' she said, pulling a face.

'Tastes disgusting as well. But trust me, it works.'

Too weak to argue, Charlotte put the glass to her lips, deciding that if it made her sick, she would at least have the pleasure of making Alex clean up the mess. The thick liquid slipped down her throat, reminding her of the only time she had ever eaten oysters. She shuddered violently and felt ready to pass out.

'I suggest you have a bath now, then go back to bed.'

Charlotte, strangely obedient, did as she was told, until she reached the landing and found herself watching a comparatively unknown man go into the bathroom and start running her a bath. At the sight of Alex bending over the taps and rummaging through her newly placed toiletries, she felt an overpowering sense of intrusion. Peevishly she said, 'I can manage on my own, thank you. You're my tenant, not my husband.'

He looked neither hurt nor offended. Turning off the

taps and wiping his hands on his trousers in the absence of a towel, he said, 'Okay, but I'll be next door if you need me.'

Chapter Eight

Iris Braithwaite, armed with a pooper-scooper in one hand and a dog lead in the other, was standing at the end of Charlotte's driveway when she saw Alex Hamilton coming out of the front door of Ivy Cottage.

Hidden by an unruly forsythia bush, and being a founder member of Hulme Welford's Neighbourhood Watch scheme, she had no difficulty in watching Alex unnoticed, as he made his way from one side of the house to the other. She also had little difficulty in piecing together her version of the events of the previous night.

Sin, and sin with a capital S, put all thought of what was on the other end of the dog lead completely out of her mind, until she took a step backwards and found herself slipping on what her eleven-year-old King Charles spaniel Henry had just evacuated. Grasping at a branch of forsythia, Iris Braithwaite managed to remain vertical, thereby keeping intact her highly prized dignity, though not her silk scarf. It floated slowly to the ground and, like part of a magician's act, covered perfectly Henry's squelched offering.

Saturday was Derek and Cindy's busiest day of the week at In The Pink. From the moment they had opened at eight forty-five the salon and gym had been packed. In the back salon, above the sound of the local radio station, Derek could hear Dawn, their beautician, telling a horizontal Mrs Carlton the best way to close up her pores each night before going to bed. Earlier it had been a lesson on the perils of dehydrating the Stratum Corneum by using a defatting something or other. It all sounded pretty convincing stuff, and even if he didn't believe a word of it, the punters did, and that was what counted.

Trying to ignore Dawn's constant stream of prattle, he carried on winding clingfilm around the head of Mrs Jeffs, an attractive bottle blonde from the Orchard Way executive development. She was married to *the* Darren Jeffs, the highly paid key goal scorer for Manchester United – though it was rumoured that Darren was scoring more than goals these days. Until yesterday evening Derek had reckoned Mrs Jeffs was worthy of extra special attention, had thought her to be the most desirable woman in the village.

Now, as Derek looked in the mirror at the sleek face bent over the latest bestseller from Jackie Collins, he viewed her as second rate – he noticed too that she had been reading the same racy page for the past ten minutes. Overnight he had relegated Mrs Jeffs to the second division, for every bit of him wanted Charlotte Lawrence.

He would have to go carefully with Charlotte, he knew: a grieving widow was a harder prospect than a bored housewife. Last night in bed, after making love to Cindy, he had lain awake thinking of Charlotte: of running his hands through her lovely hair with its natural dark colour; of taking her to that secret place, down in the woods near the mere – where he had intended taking Mrs Jeffs.

'*Derek!*' It was Cindy standing next to him, a hot brush in one hand and an aerosol of styling mousse in the other. 'I don't know what you're thinking of, but that's quite enough clingfilm for Mrs Jeffs.'

He looked down at the now unwanted Mrs Jeffs, almost hidden beneath a sombrero of transparent plastic. Frankly though, he didn't give a damn. He decided that from now on, if he was going to get anywhere with Charlotte, he would have to be subtle.

Charlotte woke up just after two in the afternoon. She was amazed how well she felt, so well in fact that she wondered whether the hangover, and what had caused it, had all been a terrible dream. But looking at her pile of discarded clothes at the end of the put-you-up, and recognising them by their creases, it hit Charlotte that she had a certain amount of music to face. Earlier, she'd had only a patchy memory of the events of the previous night; now she could remember *everything*. Oh, what a fool she had made of herself, especially all that wandering around the garden with Alex.

Drunk. She closed her eyes and shuddered. She had never been drunk before. Tiddly yes, but not so drunk that she had been sick afterwards.

The most memorable occasion when she'd had too much to drink was when Peter had taken her to meet his parents for the first time. 'I think you should meet my parents,' he had said one night on the phone.

'Why? Am I in for a shock?' she had replied.

Ann and Godfrey were a shock with their puritanical mores. Grace had been barked out at the start of dinner, just as Charlotte had reached for her knife and fork. The first social gaffe of the evening committed she gulped at her wine, saying 'This is lovely.'

'We never touch it ourselves,' Godfrey stated, as upright as a guardsman in his chair.

She tried appealing to Ann. 'Hasn't Peter done well at work this year?'

'We never wanted him to be an accountant.'

Charlotte looked to Peter for his reaction. His face was expressionless, which made him seem so vulnerable. It was then that Charlotte first thought she loved Peter.

At the end of the meal, and having drunk more wine than was good for her, Charlotte committed the final faux pas. She reached out for her cup of coffee over the top of a flickering candle and let out a sudden undignified yelp. She dropped the cup, spilling coffee everywhere and saw with horror a flame at the end of her finger – her false nail had caught light. 'I'm so terribly sorry,' she squealed, dousing her finger in the remains of her wine. The hiss was short-lived but not the memory of that evening.

In the car driving back to London, she apologised to Peter. 'I'm sorry. I spoiled everything.'

'Rubbish,' he said, smiling for the first time all night. 'You gave them a good shaking up.'

'I don't think they approved of me.'

'Good. Will you marry me?'

That was the impulsive Peter she had loved, and married three months later.

Charlotte pushed back the duvet and got up. She pulled some clothes out of a suitcase, got dressed and went downstairs to get something to eat. She was starving.

There was a strong smell of disinfectant in the kitchen. She opened every window and door and set about making herself a sandwich and tidying away last night's bottles of gin and tonic. As she leaned against the worktop and bit into the bread and cheese, she began to realise just how much her sister had done for her. The refrigerator and cupboards all seemed to be full of basic food and household requirements. She hadn't noticed any of these things yesterday. How ungrateful she must have seemed.

From now on, she decided, there would be no more

wallowing in self-pity, no more blaming herself and then being bloody to everyone else who helped. It was time to move on. What had happened had happened. She hadn't killed Peter, the weather had – all that snow and ice. 'I am not responsible for Peter's death,' she said out loud.

It was time to be strong, to be positive and decisive, but most of all, to be nice. Cynicism had played too great a part in her life recently, so much so that it was possible that she had forgotten what being nice was all about. It certainly wasn't humiliating one's sister at her dinner party; nice wasn't throwing up all over the kitchen floor as a result and then being rude to someone who was trying to help. Even so, that drink had smelt awful. She wouldn't apologise for saying that.

After this self-imposed lecture, Charlotte made herself a cup of tea, stood at one end of the empty kitchen and stared hard at the room. Oblong in shape and bordered with good quality pine cupboards with innocuous cream and blue wall tiles, it offered no obvious horrors. Her pine table and chairs, arriving from Brussels on Monday, would finish it off well, together with a fresh lick of paint and some pretty curtain fabric. Then it would feel like her kitchen. This was what she had wanted for so long – to live in a house that was hers, not an apartment that was rented and had no sense of 'home' or permanence.

She began to feel more cheerful and, rushing upstairs to her bedroom, she unearthed a notepad and pen. She returned to the kitchen, where she started to write out a list. At the top of the list and underlined were the words, 'Apologise to everyone'; next was 'Buy paint', followed by 'Check out curtain fabric', and then, after a moment's pause, she wrote 'Buy a dog'. For years she had wanted a dog, but Peter had always said, 'No, how can we?' Given the circumstances, he was right, of course.

She was just wondering how she would go about buying a dog when the door bell rang.

Opening the front door, she was surprised to see a large bouquet of red roses proffered by a tanned arm. She couldn't smell the roses but she could smell aftershave and so had a pretty good idea who it was hiding behind one of the brick posts of the porch with his arm extended.

'They're lovely,' she said. 'A shame they're not for me.'

'Oh, but they are,' Derek Rogers said, stepping out from his hiding place. 'They most certainly are for you.' And with one hand placed firmly on her shoulder, he took her inside the house, shutting the door behind them. 'You know, Charlotte, I made myself a promise this morning.'

'That's funny,' Charlotte said, 'so did I.'

'I made a promise to be kind to widows and orphans.'

Charlotte laughed, feeling that perhaps she shouldn't. 'And I've just promised myself to be strong, positive, decisive and nice,' she said.

He smiled. 'Sounds interesting. I hope you're going to be nice to me. You'll need to put those in water.' He handed her the roses. 'This way to the kitchen, is it?'

Why, thought Charlotte, does everyone else seem to think they have a perfect right to gate-crash their way into *my* house? She followed behind, and placing the bouquet in the sink, she put the plug in and turned on the cold tap.

'I think I ought to apologise for last night,' she said above the noise of gushing water. 'I don't normally get drunk.'

'No need to apologise,' he said, stepping towards her. 'I like a woman who can let herself go.'

Turning the tap off, Charlotte took a step back. 'It's just that I wouldn't want you to get the wrong idea about me.'

'And what idea would that be?'

'Well, you know, that I always behave badly.'

He laughed, and moved slightly closer. 'I'd say you behaved beautifully.'

'That's all right then,' she said brightly, remembering last night how she had thought it could be fun to flirt with Derek. She wasn't so sure now. She walked over to the other side of the kitchen.

'So beautifully, in fact, that I spent the entire evening wanting to make love to you, there and then.'

She tried to laugh, to sound blasé, as though she was completely *au fait* with this kind of conversation. 'What, in front of everyone?'

Again, he was moving towards her. 'I think we'd both prefer to do it in private, wouldn't we?'

He's joking, she told herself. He's just trying me out, trying to see whether I'll fall about shocked. She tried another laugh. He came and stood next to her.

At first she was totally passive when he kissed her, too surprised to know how to react. Then, because she was really rather enjoying it, she responded. It only lasted a split second but it was enough to convince Derek that he was a welcome guest to the rest of her body. 'No,' she said firmly, when his hands strayed from her shoulders and towards her neck.

'No such word,' he whispered.

'How about this?' Charlotte said, coming to her senses. 'Cindy!'

'Cindy doesn't mind.'

'Bloody hell!' Charlotte shouted, pushing him away from her. 'So you think you can add my name to your long list of ego boosts, do you?' She moved back to the sink and, picking up the roses, she thrust their dripping stems at his chest. 'I want to keep my promise, Derek,' she said calmly, 'so will you get out of my house now . . . please?'

Iris Braithwaite was doing the rounds distributing the parish magazine. She was just on her way up Charlotte's drive when she heard the sound of the front door being opened and saw Derek Rogers coming out. Iris paused for a moment and turned on her heels, marching off down Acacia Lane to the safety of The White Cottage. 'She's past shame, that Charlotte Lawrence! Her husband's barely cold.' She muttered all the way home in a frenzy of outrage. '*Two* men in one day! I must warn Reverend Jackson, no man is safe. Why the poor man himself might even be in danger.'

Chapter Nine

'Well, you do surprise me,' Louise told Hilary on the telephone. 'I thought you would have raced over the road at the crack of dawn to see how your sister was.'

'Not after her appalling behaviour,' Hilary said emphatically, unaware of her mother's pithy sarcasm.

'Oh don't be such an old woman, Hilary. Charlotte only got drunk. You sound as though she committed mass homicide round the table last night, though to be honest, I can think of one person I would gladly let her murder.'

Finding herself in agreement with her mother for once, Hilary said, 'You're absolutely right, of course – that Derek Rogers is entirely to blame. I did warn Charlotte about him, but you know what she's like, thinks she knows . . .'

'Rubbish! Derek's a dear,' responded Louise, who secretly thought that if Derek hadn't been there last night, they would have all died of boredom. 'I was referring to your father. Dear God, ever since he retired, there's been no keeping him awake. He did the same thing when we were over at the Macmillans' for Easter Sunday.'

Annoyed, Hilary sensed her telephone call being hijacked as she listened to her mother setting off down the familiar track of Dr Neville Archer retired.

For thirty-six years their father had been a GP in Hulme Welford, until last year when he could no longer put off his retirement. Ever since then Louise had complained constantly that their father was at a loose end, permanently moping about and getting under her feet. Hilary could sympathise. She had often thought the same thing about David while on holiday.

Well, that was one thing her sister would be spared. At least Charlotte wouldn't have to put up with Peter getting in the way. Thinking of Charlotte made Hilary remember what she had called her mother for.

'Mother,' she interrupted, 'never mind Dad for the moment. Don't you think you should go and check on Charlotte?'

'Why ever should I?'

'Because, well, she might have thrown up and—'

'What, and choked to death? Goodness, Hilary, you do have a vivid imagination, don't you? Look, it's Saturday afternoon and I've got a shop full of customers. If you're so worried about Charlotte lying in a pool of her own vomit, go and do something about it.'

Hilary put down the receiver with a look of shock on her face. She had forgotten her mother had moved the telephone from her little back office to her desk in the main part of the shop. She cringed at the thought of those customers listening to her mother's one-sided conversation. What must they have thought?

As for going over to see Charlotte, that was quite out of the question. She had no intention of calling on Charlotte, not until her sister had apologised for ruining her dinner party.

In the end, it was Neville – his gooseberries tended to and with time on his hands – who called on Charlotte.

He couldn't be bothered walking to Ivy Cottage even though it was only ten minutes away. He supposed that was what retirement did to you, and he got the car out instead. Turning into Acacia Lane, he hoped that Hilary wouldn't catch sight of him. She would be bound to tell Louise and then he'd never hear the last of it and be restricted to even fewer calories. 'If you're going to lead a completely sedentary life, you must expect to eat less,' Louise had told him the last time he had got the car out for what she called an unnecessary journey. She, of course, cycled energetically everywhere and was the same weight now – as she so liked to tell him – as when she fell pregnant with Charlotte.

'Hello Dad,' Charlotte said, opening the door. 'Come in.'

He stepped inside. 'You look better than I thought you might,' he said.

'Let the side down a bit last night, didn't I?'

He smiled. 'Me too. What a pair we are.'

In the kitchen, Neville couldn't help but notice the opened copy of *Yellow Pages* on the worktop. 'Anything I can help you with?' he said warily. These days he was so used to being told there was nothing for him to do, he hardly dared ask the question.

'There is, as a matter of fact,' she said. 'Have you got a spare hour or so?'

'Yes,' he said, brightening. 'I've got a spare twenty-four, if that's any good to you.'

'Right then,' she said, picking up her bag, 'drive me over to Lower Peover and help me choose a dog.'

Neville followed his daughter out of the house.

He suddenly felt happy. He was going to enjoy having Charlotte around again.

Chapter Ten

Charlotte looked at her watch. It was half past six on Sunday morning. She groaned and tried to ignore the noise coming from downstairs. Surely dogs slept for longer than this? She lay there, listening to the persistent whining for a few moments more, before she gave in, got out of bed and padded downstairs to the kitchen.

Opening the kitchen door, she was all set to be firm, but seeing the small face looking up at her – head slightly tilted – all her strong resolve vanished, and she bent down and scooped the little dog up in her arms.

The dog had looked at her like that yesterday afternoon at the kennels. Mrs Ingram-Walker, whom Charlotte had spoken to on the telephone earlier, had greeted Charlotte and her father at the gate, shouting loudly above the noise of the yapping West Highland White terrier puppies. 'Found us all right, then? Bit off the beaten track really. Still, you managed it, that's the main thing.'

They walked round the kennels, Mrs Ingram-Walker determined to give them an official guided tour, and enthusing every step of the way. The place was certainly impressive, spotlessly clean and festooned with certificates and rosettes for Best Dog and Best Bitch.

'You know what this is all about, don't you, Charlotte?' her father said as they were shown yet another certificate, this time for hygiene. 'This is the sales pitch to justify the huge price she's going to quote you any minute now.'

'That's just the kind of thing Peter would have said,' Charlotte replied tersely.

As they were coming to the end of the tour of puppy pens, Charlotte saw a slightly older-looking Westie on its own. 'Why's that one all alone?' she asked.

'Kept her back from an earlier litter, thought perhaps she might be good enough to run on for breeding. Turned out she's not. Always a problem, that. You get stuck with them then – people want puppies, not a dog at seven months. Still, there we are, she's not a bad bitch though.'

'May I see her?' Charlotte asked, bending down to have a closer look at the shy face, tilted to one side and staring up at her from the back of the pen. Charlotte's mind was already made up. It was this dog or nothing.

Holding the little dog to her, Charlotte looked down at the sheets of newspaper she had laid out on the kitchen floor the night before. Mrs Ingram-Walker had said there would be no need, that the dog was completely toilet-trained, but Charlotte hadn't wanted to take any chances. 'So you really are a good girl then', she said, seeing that all was dry.

She put the dog on the floor and began tidying up the newspapers. As she did so, *Deaths and Funerals* caught her eye. All the recently deceased were women and in their seventies or eighties: Mrs Mary Robinson, Mrs Edith Byron, Miss Alice Hayes, Mrs Annie Tompkins and lastly Miss Mabel Unwin. Charlotte looked up from this last entry and turned to the white dog beside her, who responded with another tilt of its head. 'Yes,' Charlotte smiled. 'I think I've found the perfect name for you – Mabel.'

Breakfast was interrupted by the sound of the doorbell. Mabel, her head down inside a small china bowl of Weetabix, didn't even look up.

'Fine guard dog you're going to be,' Charlotte said, putting her own bowl of cereal down on the worktop. 'You'll be back to Mrs Ingram-Walker if you don't pull your weight round here,' she called over her shoulder as she went out into the hall.

Charlotte opened the door. 'Talking to yourself now,' Louise said, then gave her daughter a hard stare and added, 'or have you got someone here?'

'What, at half past seven in the morning, Mother?'

'Anything's possible.' Louise tucked a thick wad of newspaper under her arm and looked up the stairs to the landing above.

Charlotte stared at her mother, shut the door and then wandered back to the kitchen, shaking her head. 'Is there anything you wanted in particular? I mean, it's lovely to see you, but it is fairly early to be paying social calls, especially for you.'

'Don't worry, I shan't stop for long. Any tea in the pot? Oh, what's that?' She stared down at Mabel.

'She's a breeder's reject,' Charlotte said. 'Can't you tell?'

'It's too early in the morning to play games with me, Charlotte. Who does it belong to?'

'*She*,' Charlotte said with emphasis, 'is mine. I bought her yesterday from a Mrs Ingram-Walker.'

'Are you out of your mind? How are you going to look after it, I mean her, while you're out working?'

'Oh, so suddenly I'm capable of getting a job, am I?'

'Well, that remains to be seen, of course.'

'Don't spoil it for me, Mother,' Charlotte said, handing her a mug of tea. 'I've always wanted a dog, and besides, I need the company.'

Louise put the *Sunday Times* on the worktop behind her and cradled the mug in her hand. 'But you've got

Hilary right opposite you, and there's us, no more than a ten-minute walk away.'

'Yes, and you've all got your own lives to lead.' Charlotte thought that right now she'd rather have Mabel than any member of her family, except her father. 'Look,' she said, 'I can't expect you all to revolve around me suddenly. It wouldn't be fair.'

'Well, I suppose you're right.'

'And while we're on the subject of things being right and fair, what on earth were you doing suggesting Alex see me home on Friday night?'

Louise laughed. 'Just a bit of fun, playing Hilary at her own game. You should have seen the look on her face.'

'I can imagine it,' Charlotte said, almost enjoying the thought. 'So what did you come round here for, apart from a cup of tea?'

'Oh yes. To tell you that you must come to church this morning.'

'Why, is there something special on today?'

'No, but I just think you ought to show your face.'

'You've never forced anyone to church before. Why now, and more importantly, why me?'

'Well, Charlotte,' Louise said, putting down her empty mug, 'thing is, you've been found out. I was in the paper shop a few moments ago,' she nodded towards her copy of the *Sunday Times*, by way of supportive evidence, 'and I overheard Iris Braithwaite talking to Mrs Haslip. Apparently it's common knowledge.'

'What is?'

Louise smiled. 'I have to take my hat off to you, Charlotte, you don't do things by halves, do you?'

'Now who's playing games?'

'You are, by the sounds of things. But I'm not sure

Hulme Welford is the right place to be playing them. Too small, too parochial – especially for a woman.'

'For heaven's sake, Mother, what are you talking about?'

'Not just me, what everyone's talking about, that not only have you lured your tenant into bed within twenty-four hours of moving into Ivy Cottage, but Derek Rogers as well.'

Chapter Eleven

At first Charlotte laughed out loud at her mother's revelation, hot from the lips of Iris Braithwaite. 'But *surely* no one is taking these absurd claims seriously?'

'I think you'll find that most people will be only too keen to believe it, Charlotte.'

'But why?'

'Because it's exciting, it's forbidden, and a woman, at that, is doing it here in Hulme Welford, right under their noses. They want to be shocked.'

'So Derek Rogers could go around seducing everyone and everything, left, right and centre, and that wouldn't be newsworthy, you mean?' Charlotte's voice was beginning to rise.

'Not in the same way. Everyone expects a man like Derek to behave badly, that's entirely within the rules of the game. But you're a widow and expected to behave as such and because you're a woman, you can only play the role of victim. Play it any other way and you're wide open to tabloid sensationalism.'

Charlotte was finding the situation less amusing now. 'But that's ridiculous.'

'I'm sorry, Charlotte,' her mother went on, 'but you've broken the rules and you've been found out.'

'You mean, you actually believe all this nonsense?'

Louise shrugged her shoulders. 'It really doesn't matter what I think, does it?'

'Of course it does.'

'Goodness, I don't understand why you're getting so worked up, you've never been bothered by what anyone thought of you before. Conforming has never been your forte, has it?' She laughed. 'I know you'll hate me for saying this, but there's more of me in you than you'd like to believe.'

Charlotte tried to ignore this last unnerving comment from her mother. 'So, just why are you asking me to go to church this morning?'

'What you get up to in your own home has nothing to do with Iris. She shouldn't be allowed to get away with invading your privacy, or anyone else's for that matter. You've got to fight her.'

Charlotte sighed. Fighting was the last thing she felt like doing at the moment. 'But there's nothing to fight about, none of it's true,' she said in an exasperated voice.

'None of it?' Louise asked, eyeing her daughter speculatively.

'None of it,' Charlotte repeated, looking out of the kitchen window and evading her mother's gaze. Well, there was no need to mention Derek kissing her, was there? And she hadn't kept the roses, she'd given those straight back.

Her mother picked up her *Sunday Times*. 'I must be off. But like I say, just go to church, brazen this out and make sure that as many people as possible, especially Iris, see you there, preferably on your knees. If there's one thing the righteous really like, it's a sinner praying for forgiveness.'

Crashing the breakfast dishes into the sink, Charlotte turned on the hot tap. Water gushed directly on to a cereal spoon, sending up a fountain of water in her face. She wiped herself dry and considered the no-win alternatives: do nothing and everyone would assume her guilty; fight back and everyone would think that the lady doth protest too much.

In front of the altar, a smartly dressed Mrs Haslip was reading out the week's notices. The rest of the congregation was so absorbed in working out how best to avoid being roped in for the jumble sale and the fork supper that nobody noticed Charlotte slipping quietly in at the back and settling herself in an unoccupied pew. So far so good, she told herself, wishing that the real purpose of her visit to St John's was to remain discreet to the point of invisibility, instead of being there to clear her name.

She had made up her mind not to come and to hell with everyone thinking she was man crazy. But then she had thought about Cindy and her children, and the terrible unfairness of the situation had hit her and propelled her out of Ivy Cottage and down Acacia Lane to St John's. She would sort this out, not for her own reputation, or Derek's for that matter, but for that of his family. And of course, there was Alex to think of.

The service was under way now. Charlotte stared at the needlepoint design on the hassock in front of her, and thought of the last time she had been in church. Peter's funeral.

Throughout the funeral service Peter's mother and father had sat motionless, their grief kept well in check until the church service was behind them and the funeral party had moved on to the nearby crematorium, where Ann finally allowed herself a restrained display of emotion, the comfort of her husband's angular shoulder supporting her own. It was as though she was responding to the heat of the flames about to consume her son, letting it thaw her customary coldness to give way, perhaps, to a sense of regret.

When Charlotte looked up she found she was no longer alone in the pew. Malcolm Jackson was well into his stride on the theme of spiritual gifts and he was holding up a small pink wallpaper-covered bin as a visual aid.

Sitting on her right was an earnest-looking tall young man of about eighteen, with a strong athletic build. He was wearing a pair of fashionable tortoiseshell-framed glasses, half obscured by an asymmetrical fringe dangling down on one side of his forehead. Covering the rest of him was a well-worn jogging suit. Charlotte guessed, from his slightly flushed and glistening face, that he had recently been wearing the jogging suit for its originally designed purpose. There was an aroma about him too that corroborated this. She could feel his body heat radiating towards her and she also thought she sensed some hostility. But no. She was just being paranoid. He turned and looked at her. She smiled, but he jerked his head away and gave his attention back to the sermon.

'Gifts come in varying shapes and sizes,' announced Malcolm Jackson. 'This was once a discarded tin of coffee, thrown away from somebody's kitchen cupboard, but with the gift of creativity we now have a wastepaper bin. I want to challenge each and everyone of you. Go home . . .' a slight pause, a smile . . . 'No, not now, but later, and search through your spiritual cupboards and see what God has given you. What has God given you, that you have been ignoring all these years?'

Not daring to think what might lie in her spiritual cupboards, Charlotte surveyed the congregation and the choir. Iris Braithwaite was wearing a wide-brimmed, brown felt hat which managed to ensure that she was the focal point of the choir. Taller than the other ladies, now all on their feet ready to sing, Iris stood at least five inches higher than anyone else. As Mr Phelps from the Post Office pulled out all the stops on the organ and the congregation rose to its feet, Iris, with both her hands crossed in front of her as though guarding her virginity, closed her eyes, opened her mouth and prepared to give everyone the benefit of her deep contralto voice. Within a few words of the opening line of 'Give Me Joy' – far too modern a hymn for Iris's taste, as everyone knew – her eyes shot open at the sound of the happy clappers three rows from the front. She stared hard at the offending couple, but they carried on courageously right to the end of the hymn.

The singing came to an end and the service continued with 'the Peace'. Anarchy seemed to be breaking out in the pews, with people greeting each other as though they were long-lost friends. No one greeted Iris. Charlotte, balking at the idea of being confronted by anyone she knew, turned to her lone companion, hoping to engage him in dull, safe conversation. She was in for a shock.

'You look like you've just been jogging,' she said. How ridiculous she sounded.

Looking down at his clothes, the young man said a little sullenly, 'Do you mind?'

'Of course not, but you'll probably find there'll be those who do mind, and they won't be happy until they see you in a boring grey suit.'

He almost smiled, almost looked her in the eye. 'It's just the only way I can come,' he said, nudging his glasses on to the bridge of his nose.

Charlotte was wondering what he meant by this, when he asked her, 'You're Charlotte Lawrence, aren't you?'

'Yes.'

'Do you know who I am?'

'No.'

And looking her in the eye, he said, 'Have you really been to bed with Derek Rogers?'

'No!' she answered, in a shocked voice. She hadn't been at all prepared for this kind of blatant interrogation, especially from one so young.

Vaguely aware that order had once again been restored, Charlotte turned away from this inquisitive lad and tried to pick up the threads of the service.

'. . . *I believe in one God, the Father Almighty . . .*'

'Believe me, I haven't,' Charlotte said to the young man, wanting suddenly to defend herself. She slipped down on to her hassock.

'. . . *Maker of heaven and earth . . .*'

'Do you intend to?'

'. . . *And of all things visible and invisible . . .*'

'No, certainly not.'

'. . . *And in one Lord Jesus Christ . . .*'

'Good,' said her companion.

A few minutes after the service had come to an end a sizeable crush had developed in the porch. Charlotte decided to remain in her seat until the worst was over. She was alone again, her strange companion having left. He had made his exit just as silently as he had arrived, leaving seconds before the end of the service. Whilst she hadn't particularly liked his line of questioning, there had been something about him she had liked – his straightforwardness.

She caught sight of her sister hovering by the font, holding what looked like a miniature toilet seat. Charlotte smiled at her, remembering she had yet to apologise. Was it her imagination, or had her sister just ignored her? Confused, she got to her feet and joined the queue for the escape route out, thankful that those around her were completely taken up in their own conversations and didn't seem to be at all worried by what she may or may not have been up to.

From behind her came a voice. 'Charlotte, there you are.' It was her mother, making one of her absurd statements, with her father bringing up the rear. To Charlotte's surprise her mother kissed her. She knew why and was, for once in her life, grateful to her.

The three of them were now level with Malcolm Jackson in the porch and Charlotte began to feel nervous. Had Malcolm heard the gossip? Heavens, he might have been thinking she had been propositioning the young man who sat next to her.

'So good to see you, Charlotte. How are you?' she heard Malcolm say. She nodded mutely, but instead of looking him full in the face, she found her eyes rooted to a small red wine stain on the left cuff of his otherwise immaculate white robe. She wondered if Iris Braithwaite had spotted this during the service and was even now planning a campaign to clean up the vicar of Hulme Welford.

'She's fine,' her mother answered for her. 'We're all rallying round, aren't we, dear, easing your suffering?'

Charlotte looked on bewildered. She had never heard her mother speak like this before. Suddenly, drawn like a magnet to the word suffering, everything seemed wrong. Yesterday she had been happy. This morning, before her mother called in, she had been happy. But it was wrong, very wrong. She had no right to feel anything other than the burden of Peter's death. All that had just passed inside the church, all those words she had listened to and repeated about love and deliverance from evil – she had no right to be there. Not after what she had done to Peter.

Panic began to well up inside her. She fought it back, tried to control the monster of guilt within and edged towards the open door and the sunshine waiting outside.

'I shan't pester you, Charlotte,' pursued Malcolm, 'because I'm sure you'll have plenty of offers of help and advice, but if there really is anything I can do for you, you know where I am, though Mrs Braithwaite says I'm the most elusive person she knows. Apparently she was looking for me all yesterday afternoon, had something important to tell me.'

Charlotte forced a smile, wanting more than anything for the conversation to reach its conclusion. At the mention of Iris Braithwaite's name, she changed her mind. 'There is something you can help me with.'

'Yes?' Malcolm looked eagerly sympathetic.

'I just wanted to ask who that young man was, the one sitting next to me at the back of the church?'

'That was Barry. Nice lad, seems to carry the weight of the world on his young shoulders though. He's Derek Rogers' eldest.'

Outside in the sunshine and reeling from the shock of what she had just been told, Charlotte leaned against a large ornate tomb, about the size of a Mini, and tried to take in the fact that she had just been confronted by Barry Rogers. *Have you really been to bed with Derek Rogers?*

'Well,' said her mother, 'that wasn't so bad, was it? We would offer you Sunday lunch, but we're off to a car boot sale which starts in an hour, and I need to get there for the pick of the best pieces before the crowds turn up.'

'Don't worry about me,' Charlotte said in a distracted voice, watching her mother walk away. 'I've got plenty to do.'

'Are you okay, Charlotte?' her father said, walking alongside her. 'Only you look a bit strange.'

'I'm fine,' she lied.

'No, you're not,' he said. 'I can tell, I was a doctor once, you know.'

'Oh Dad, don't be nice to me, not now, you'll make me feel sorry for myself and that would never do. Peter's father always used to say I was full of self-pity.'

'Never mind Peter's father, do you want me to speak to Iris? She's no right spreading lies about the village.'

Charlotte looked up into her father's face and smiled. 'No,' she said, shaking her head, 'but thanks anyway.'

He looked puzzled. 'What for?'

'For believing in me and not what Iris Braithwaite's been saying.'

'Neville, do hurry up,' Louise called out. She was already down at the bottom of the gravel path and pulling open the lych-gate.

For a moment Neville Archer hesitated between his wife and daughter.

'Go on, Dad,' Charlotte said. 'I'm fine, really.'

Alone for no more than a few seconds, Charlotte felt herself the focus of someone's gaze. She looked up and met the icy glare of Iris Braithwaite, who, together with her cronies Mrs Haslip and Mrs Bradley, was encircling Malcolm Jackson in a well-practised pincer movement. A combination of fear and confused guilt told Charlotte to run, but something greater, her anger and her sense of justice, told her that this was the moment to shoot from the hip.

'Hello, Mrs Braithwaite,' she called out, as she made her way back towards the church porch.

In response, the older woman clutched her handbag tightly to her.

'You're just the woman I needed to see,' Charlotte said brightly, now standing directly in front of Iris. Post-service hangers-on, pricking up their ears, turned to watch. They sensed that something cataclysmically more interesting than discussing the vicar's handling of the service was about to happen. Charlotte pushed on. 'I think you have something to say to me, haven't you, Mrs Braithwaite?'

'I certainly have not.'

'Oh, but you have, and not only to me.'

The pearls on Iris's silk-clad chest began to wobble. 'Mrs Lawrence, I assure you, I have absolutely nothing whatsoever to say to you.'

This haughty righteousness was too much for Charlotte. 'Do you really think,' she said in a dangerously menacing voice, 'that I am capable of taking two men, whom I hardly know, into my bed one after the other?'

'I know what I saw,' Iris Braithwaite said, holding her ground and looking for back-up from the two women either side of her, who were beginning ever so slightly to distance themselves from Iris.

'You saw two men leave my house, nothing more, nothing less,' Charlotte asserted. 'I suggest you go and undo all the harm you've done with your vile gossip, and you can start by apologising to Mr and Mrs Rogers and their children.'

Leaving Iris Braithwaite looking like a paralysed rabbit caught in the beam of a car headlight, Charlotte turned and walked away, unaware of the silent applause from those around her who had just witnessed the first ever public dressing-down of Iris Braithwaite.

Chapter Twelve

Charlotte felt wretched. Scoring a public victory over Iris Braithwaite should have had her skipping home, happy as a lamb. Instead she was shocked and saddened by what had just happened.

All her life, like so many others in the village, she had viewed Iris Braithwaite as some kind of personal *bête noire*. Iris had ruled the roost of Hulme Welford for as long as Charlotte could remember, her authority never once having been publicly questioned until today. Yet all Charlotte could remember from the short exchange was the terrible look on the older woman's face.

She had noticed that very same look on Peter's face the last time she saw him. She could recall now that look of hurt he was trying so hard to hide from her. So vivid was the picture in her mind that she was back there, in their Brussels apartment, in the kitchen, the smell of coffee, toast, boiled eggs . . . and then her words, words that had stabbed at Peter across the breakfast table: *I want a divorce, Peter*. She thought at first that he had not heard her. Then slowly he put his knife down on the plate in front of him – a blob of butter, half melted, clinging to the serrated edge – and he looked up at her, his lips clamped tightly shut, his eyes never leaving her own. He sat like that for what seemed an age, petrified by his emotionally starved upbringing. Nothing had prepared him for this devastating moment in his life.

Oh God, thought Charlotte, crossing the road, what was happening to her that she could go round hurting people so badly?

Not wanting, just yet, to go back to Ivy Cottage, not with the possibility of being confronted by Hilary, or even Iris Braithwaite, Charlotte turned left and walked down to the main street of the village until she came to Ted Cooper's paper shop.

Behind his back Ted Cooper had always been known as Sleazy Ted. But three years ago, after a lifetime of battling to keep what little greasy hair he had, he'd given up on it and covered the remaining strands with a well-uphol-stered wig. Then he had become Ted the Toup. Now, after three years of accumulated grime and nicotine, his famous false hair gave the appearance of being fused together into one solid piece.

Charlotte pushed open the door. She saw Ted sitting behind his till. He was leaning back in his chair reading a copy of the *People*. The face of a recently disgraced cricketer stared back at Charlotte. His eyes, beneath his cricket cap, watched her as she approached the counter.

'Hello, love,' Ted said, raising his own eyes over the top of the paper. 'Settling in okay, are you? Making new friends?'

'Not too badly,' Charlotte said, registering the ambiguity of Ted's last question.

''Course, nothing's really changed, has it, from when you left?'

'No, nothing's changed,' she agreed, noticing that Ted's tobacco-stained hands with their effeminately long nails were still the same, as were his cracked and blackened teeth.

She scanned the selection of Sundays on offer. The tabloids seemed to have either a 'distressed' or an 'outraged' Royal on the front page, with the exception of the *People*, who had gone it alone, informing its readership of the lurid sex life of a Northamptonshire top-spinner. The heavy brigade all carried more or less the same photograph of a tired-looking John Major. Having no particular loyalty to any one newspaper, Charlotte picked out the *Independent*, which was the nearest one to her. As she handed over her money she reflected that it seemed a very fitting choice.

Leaving Ted to get back to his reading, she opened the shop door to find herself confronted by a blue anorak and a pink hand-knitted cardigan. Although Charlotte didn't know the couple, she had seen them earlier in church and knew that they had witnessed the exchange between Iris Braithwaite and herself. They smiled at her – a full-blown, obsequious, Cheshire-cat grin. Politely she smiled back, hoping to slide past them and out of the shop. But they were having none of it.

'We'd just like to congratulate you,' the anorak said.

'We certainly would,' the pink cardigan echoed.

'It's about time somebody stood up to her,' the anorak said.

'It certainly is,' the cardigan agreed.

There was a rustle from behind the counter as Ted once again lowered his paper, his attention aroused by something other than bums and boobs. He looked over at them and slithered his way into the conversation with consummate ease. 'Afternoon, Reg, Joan. Congratulations in order, did I hear you say?'

'Didn't she tell you all about it, Ted?' said the anorak, who had now been identified as Reg. Charlotte folded the *Independent* in her hands and looked at the floor.

Reg and Joan closed the door behind them and surged

past the displays of greetings cards and racks of magazines in their haste to impart their news to Ted.

'She was very brave,' said Reg.

'Oh, she was, you know,' agreed Joan.

'I really must be going.' Charlotte backed away towards the door. She felt bad enough as it was, without having this misplaced hero-worship to further fuel her considerable guilt.

'She certainly put Iris Braithwaite right on all that nonsense about that hairdresser fellow and her tenant. Of course we didn't believe any of it, not for one moment, did we, Joan?' Turning to reassure their heroine of this fact, Reg and Joan found themselves facing an empty space. They looked about the shop, hoping to unearth Charlotte from behind the rotating rack of thrillers and bodice-rippers. They were disappointed.

Hurrying away from the shop, Charlotte was already turning left into Daisy Bank and making for Acacia Lane. She wanted very much to scream. Coming back to Hulme Welford was supposed to have had a calming influence on her life. It was to have been a return to all that was comfortingly familiar, like the sisterly irritation between herself and Hilary, and the lack of understanding on her mother's part; even the interfering Iris Braithwaite was supposed to have been a necessary part of her rehabilitation. But in less than forty-eight hours she had somehow destroyed the steady equilibrium she had deliberately chosen to return to.

On her first night at Ivy Cottage she had experienced the sensation of having the silky edging torn away from her comfort blanket – now, she had practically unravelled the entire thing.

'And I certainly didn't speak to her, David, not after what

she's done,' Hilary said, slamming the dishwasher shut as though underscoring the seriousness of her words, but all it did was make her wince at the sound of crashing crockery within.

'Why are you so cross, Mummy?' said Becky, her head bent over a colouring book on the kitchen table. 'I hope you haven't smashed my Peter Rabbit plate.'

Philip, who was sitting on the back doorstep scraping the mud from yesterday's match off his football boots, laughed and said, 'Serves you right if Mum has, after you deliberately smashed my Manchester City mug.'

Becky threw a yellow crayon at her brother through the open door. In return she got a wedge of dried mud flicked back at her. She set up a high-pitched wail.

'Stop it, you two,' said Hilary, ramming the remains of breakfast down the waste-disposal unit. Turning on the tap, she set off the loud chomping and churning. Above the noise she shouted at David, who was leaning back against the Aga reading the colour supplement. 'I don't know how she had the cheek to even be there.'

'What?' David said without looking up.

'I said . . . Oh, what's the use?' Turning the waste-disposal unit off, Hilary said, her voice still raised, 'If we had the next model up, we wouldn't have this trouble. They're much quieter, the more expensive ones.'

David was lost. 'What on earth are you talking about?' He gathered up the papers and headed off to the sitting-room for some peace and quiet. He knew from experience that it wasn't wise to hang about when Hilary was in one of these moods. Quite frankly, he didn't believe a word of what was being said about Charlotte. He wondered though whether this was because he didn't want to believe it, didn't like to imagine Charlotte capable of such a thing.

Hilary pursed her lips, got hold of a wooden spoon and started to push yet more discarded crusts and congealed cornflakes down the disposal unit.

'Mummy?'

'*Yes*, Becky,' Hilary snapped, before reminding herself that it wasn't her daughter's fault that Charlotte was bringing such shame on the family. 'What is it, dear?'

'Mummy, you know Auntie Charlotte?'

'Yes.' Well, I thought I did, she said to herself.

'Why doesn't Auntie Charlotte wear jim-jams like me?'

'What a strange question. Why do you ask?'

Becky looked up from her colouring book. 'I heard someone at church saying that Auntie Charlotte needs two men in bed with her to keep her warm.'

When Charlotte got home she rushed upstairs and screamed, long and loud, her head inside the airing cupboard where she hoped the sound would be confined. As a form of therapy it fell way short of working. She shut the door and went downstairs to the kitchen where she found Mabel chewing on a squeaky toy bought by Charlotte and her father yesterday, along with tins of food and a lead. Seeing Charlotte, the little dog scuttled over to her. Charlotte smiled and instantly felt better.

She fed Mabel and walked her about the garden wondering what she should do for the rest of the day. She ought to go over and apologise to Hilary but she really couldn't face her sister at the moment. And there was nothing in the house for her to do, not until tomorrow when the removal van would be arriving, and besides it was far too nice a day to be stuck inside.

Seeing the potting shed, with its duck-egg-blue-painted door, Charlotte remembered there was supposed to be some garden furniture stored in there. She went back into the house and found the large, clearly labelled, rusty key.

While she fiddled with the key in the lock to make it work, Charlotte could feel the warmth of the sun on her back. It was quite a suntrap, this corner of the garden, with its overgrown flower beds of London Pride, forget-me-nots and tiny wild purple pansies spilling over on to the path and along the bottom of the brick wall of the potting shed, which was mostly hidden beneath a flourishing wisteria. Against this wall was an assortment of cracked and chipped terracotta pots, some lying haphazardly on their sides. Charlotte thought they looked sad, as if they were still waiting for the Cliffords to come back for them.

Charlotte finally got the key to work. Without any resistance the door swung open. David's particulars of the property had informed Charlotte that not only did Ivy Cottage 'offer a surprisingly capacious potting shed' but that a 'selection of charming, rustic garden furniture could be found within'.

At first glance, this did not seem to be the case. All that Charlotte could discern in the suffused light and cobwebs was that the Cliffords must have forgotten to look in here before they moved. There was an old lawnmower, a collection of brooms in varying degrees of fatigue, a pair of mud-caked gardening gloves adopting a chilling posture on the floor – as though waiting to pounce on their next victim – along with some shears and a trug full of dead-headed roses. It was stiflingly warm, with an oppressive smell of baked soil and fertilizer.

Charlotte stepped inside and realised that the potting shed was much larger than she had at first thought. Beyond the lawnmower she could see a wheelbarrow and what looked like a selection of old garden furniture.

With Mabel trotting behind her, Charlotte carried two white-painted, rickety folding chairs across the lawn, one to sit on and one for her feet. Placing them beside the sprawling fig tree on the left-hand side of the garden, she carefully prised the chairs open. They were filthy, covered with dead insects and patches of flaking paint. She went back into the house and reappeared with a bowl of water and a cloth. A window cracked open behind her and the sound of Bach's Mass in B Minor flooded out, followed by the unmistakable smell of somebody else's lunch being cooked, along with the accompanying clatter of crockery. This reminded Charlotte that not only had she not given a thought to what she was going to eat that day, but that here, clearly, was one of the disadvantages of sharing her house and garden. Should she turn and acknowledge Alex Hamilton, who doubtless was standing in his kitchen watching her, or should she be circumspect and pretend she hadn't heard the window?

She remembered how nice Alex had been to her and that she owed him an apology, so she turned around, ready to give a signal of a peace offering. But there was no sign of him.

She went back to the chairs and started cleaning them. Eventually satisfied that she had done all that she could, she sat down cautiously. The flimsy chair creaked a little, but as it gave no other indication that it was about to collapse, she relaxed into it, clasped her hands at the back of her head, stretched her feet in front of her on the other chair, and turned her attention to the garden.

It was lovely, in need of some work admittedly, but lovely all the same. The lawn was covered with a sprinkling of daisies and dandelions and swept down some hundred feet or so towards a windbreak of high conifers, spruces and silver birches and a variety of rhododendrons on the point of bursting into flower. To her right was a deep, neglected border, and behind this, screening her from In The Pink, was a tall copper beech hedge.

Charlotte couldn't help but think she was going to need something more effective than a beech hedge to keep Derek Rogers out.

To her left, on the other side of the fig tree, was more copper beech hedging, but there was nothing beyond it, only a dense thicket.

She closed her eyes, listening to the tranquil cooing of doves in the trees around her, accompanied by the more fortissimo passages of the Bach that managed to reach this far down the garden. With this peace around her, together with the warmth of the sun, Charlotte soon found herself slipping into sleep.

She started, and sat bolt upright at the sound of barking. Mabel. She had forgotten about Mabel. Where was she? Looking towards the house, she saw the little dog lying on the grass in front of the conservatory being stroked by Alex, who was crouched down beside her.

'Hello,' he said, looking up at Charlotte.

She nodded, got up from her chair and walked over to him.

'I just came out to ask if you'd like to join me for lunch.'

'Oh,' she said, surprised. 'I've just eaten,' she lied.

He looked disappointed, squinting his eyes a little against the sun. 'I thought I'd eat out here. Seemed a good idea, on such a lovely day.'

He was right, Charlotte thought, it was a good idea, and she was starving. Why had she just lied to him?

'Roast beef and Yorkshire pudding,' he said. 'Are you sure you won't join me?'

She pushed her hands down into her trouser pockets. 'Oh, go on then, why not?'

Between them they fished out the cast-iron table from the potting shed and whilst Charlotte cleaned it up, Alex brought out two trays of food, along with a couple of glasses and a bottle of red wine. Mabel danced attendance, getting in their way.

'You knew I was lying, didn't you?' Charlotte said, when at last they sat down.

'Let's call it intuition.' He handed her a knife and a fork. 'I bet you haven't eaten a proper meal since Friday night.'

'Have you been spying on me?' Her voice sounded slightly accusing.

'It's hard not to, living so close.' He passed her a glass of wine and raising his own in the air, said, 'Here's to . . .' he paused, smiled and said decisively, 'here's to a good summer.'

'Yes, a good summer,' Charlotte repeated unconvincingly. She took a sip of her wine.

'Bulgarian, cheap and cheerful,' he said, watching her. 'I'm afraid I don't believe in expensive wines.'

'So what do you believe in, then?' The cynicism in her voice was undisguised.

He placed his glass carefully down on the table. 'Good question, that.'

'I'm sorry, that was uncalled for. I promised myself yesterday I'd stop doing that – being cynical, that is.' She put a piece of fluffy Yorkshire pudding in her mouth and then looked away, down to the silver birches, where she could see a pair of magpies building a nest.

Taking the opportunity to look at Charlotte unobserved, Alex decided that the first thing anyone would notice about Charlotte was her shoulder-length hair; it was so dark and without a hint of grey. She was wearing it, as she had on Friday night, loosely round her face, and it framed a mouth that could be described as large, but for his taste was perfect – full and sensuous – and when she smiled, two dimples appeared. He had noticed this the other night, along with the colour of her eyes that he now realised seemed to change depending on the light. At dinner they had seemed dusky, almost violet; here, sitting in the sun, he was struck by the dazzling gentian-blue colour they had become. He was also aware that she looked worn out. More than this, she looked uncomfortable with herself, there was an awkwardness about her. Was that suppressed anger, he wondered, anger with life for having dealt her such a rough hand? She certainly deserved to feel that way . . . hadn't he himself once?

'Some magpies are building a nest up there in the tallest birch,' he said, 'can you see? Their first nest was in one of the conifers but it got raided by a crow.' He smiled as Charlotte looked at him. 'Life's hard all round, isn't it?' he said softly.

'This is wonderful,' she said, a piece of beef poised on her fork. 'When did you learn to cook like this?'

'A legacy of my student days,' he said, noting the ground on which she wasn't prepared to walk, 'when I lodged with the redoubtable Mrs Holroyd, sadly no longer with us, but out there,' he cast his arm about him as though presenting the world to Charlotte, 'there's a multitude who carry her memory with them. Actually, she was a formidable landlady who taught generations of scruffy students the stuff of life – how to cook, wash and iron.'

Charlotte smiled. 'So where did all this take place, which university? No, don't tell me, let me guess. I'd say you were a Cambridge man.'

He laughed, then took a sip of his wine. 'My parents wanted me to go there, to follow in my father's footsteps and my older brother's. I was even offered a place.'

'So why didn't you go?'

'Lots of eighteen-year-old reasons: I didn't want to conform and I didn't want the hassle and all the pressure, so I opted for Leeds instead.'

'Then what, what did you do next, start a commune out on the Yorkshire moors?'

'Guess what? I conformed. As soon as I graduated, I joined up with Henderson and Wyatt and before I knew where I was, I was a fully paid-up member of everything I had always despised. Disappointing end to an encouraging beginning, wouldn't you say?'

'If it had stopped at that, maybe, but you're here in Hulme Welford. Why?'

Alex told Charlotte how he had ended his career with Henderson and Wyatt, how he had simply sold up and done as he pleased. 'It suddenly became important to me to prove to myself that in the big scheme of things it all meant nothing, all that status, all that supposed power and wealth, it was all a nonsense. I knew perfectly well that my leaving the company meant no real difference in the long term to those individuals concerned. In the short term they were all tripping over themselves to find the right replacement for the dynamic Alex Hamilton, but I bet you now they'll all be saying Alex who? And that's fine, because that's what they would have been saying in the end when I retired with my slippers by the fireside.'

Charlotte frowned. 'It's strange that, isn't it? Most people like to feel that they're important, indispensable even. It's what gives them their sense of identity, their name tag, if you like.'

'It takes courage to be yourself and to know that you're

a significant person in your own right, with something worthwhile to offer, without having to acquire all those labels of self-justification.'

Charlotte thought about this for a moment. 'How about marriage,' she said. 'Is that a label you don't need either?'

He looked at her and then placed his knife and fork together on his now empty plate. 'I was very nearly married,' he answered. *Very nearly married* – how glib he sounded, almost as though his time with Lucy hadn't meant anything. Not so long ago he wouldn't have thought it possible to refer to that period in his life without experiencing some degree of pain. Now here he was, living proof of what his friends and family had told him: *Time is the great healer*. It had taken a while, but eventually they had been proved right. 'More wine?' he said.

'Not for me, thank you. After my behaviour at Hilary's I think I'd better be careful. What does "very nearly" mean?'

A blackbird above their heads in the branches of the fig tree began to chirp. Mabel, in response, got to her feet and barked loudly at it. The bird squawked indignantly and flew off.

'She didn't fall for my understated charm and kept turning me down,' Alex said with a light laugh, and changed the subject. 'So tell me, what's St John's like?'

'Better than when I grew up here,' Charlotte replied, acknowledging that, like most people, Alex Hamilton had his own Achilles' heel. 'It's a bit Low Church for Iris Braithwaite's taste though.' Suddenly she was back in the churchyard, seeing the terrible look on Iris's face.

Sitting here in the garden having lunch with Alex, she had managed to forget what had happened earlier that morning. Thinking of it now, she felt the colour drain from her face, wondered whether Alex himself had heard the gossip that must have touched all corners of the village. But if he had, surely he would have mentioned it?

'What's wrong?' he asked.

'I . . .' This was awful. How was she supposed to tell him? She cleared her throat. 'I probably ought to tell you something before you find out from someone else.'

Alex raised his eyebrows. 'What have I missed?'

Charlotte sighed and told Alex what she was supposed to have been up to with him and Derek.

She watched Alex cross one leg over the other and then pull his foot up towards himself. He was trying hard not to smile, she could tell, but she pressed on, telling him about her mother's visit, Derek's son Barry cross-examining her in church, her exchange with Iris Braithwaite and finally the scene at Ted the Toup's.

'So surely that's an end to it,' Alex said, when she had finished. 'Iris Braithwaite apologises and everyone forgets all about it. You've been exonerated.'

She shook her head. 'No I haven't, and I never will be. Don't you see, they all believed I was capable?'

'Well, to a certain extent, we're all capable.'

'And Hilary ignored me in church this morning, snubbed me. There she was standing by the font with some ridiculous toilet seat in her hands and she turned away when I smiled at her. So much for Christian forgiveness!' She lowered her head, her hair cascading over her face, hiding the tears welling up in her eyes.

Alex leaned back in his chair. He looked thoughtfully across at Charlotte. After a moment's quiet, he placed a hand on her shoulder. She jerked her head up, looked at him and then got to her feet.

'I'd better be going. I'm not very good company at the moment, I'm too busy feeling sorry for myself.' She shook her head. 'And do you know, I was feeling sorry for Iris earlier.'

'Now you've really thrown me,' he said, confused. 'Come on, stay a bit longer and explain that one to me.'

She sat down again, surprising herself that she did so, and willingly. 'You know, I challenged Iris this morning because I truly believed it was the right thing to do, like I thought it was the right thing to come back here to Hulme Welford. Now none of it makes sense any more.'

'Tell me,' Alex said, slowly. 'Tell me about your life in Brussels with Peter, what was it like?'

She kicked off her trainers and played her bare feet lightly over the grass. She thought about Alex's question. Nobody had ever really asked her what *her* life had been like. Assumptions had been made – she had been the wife of a 'bright young thing', they had always been going places, geographically as well as figuratively. They had been well off, comfortably placed, a good future ahead of them and she had tried hard to make a life for herself, always adjusting it to suit Peter, until she had realised she could not cope with knowing that her husband loved his work more than her; that she had become an unwelcome interruption to what really excited him. She then saw herself as just another acquisition, picked up by Peter along the way. She was a necessary part of his portrayal of the perfect corporate man, so long as she was prepared to remain a bit player, with hardly any lines to speak.

Waiting in the wings of her mind now was her programmed response to Alex's question – *it was fun, lots to do and see, all that food and culture* – but she found herself looking Alex in the eye and saying, 'It was empty and cold and I hated it.'

Chapter Thirteen

'Hello, not interrupting, am I?'

David's arrival, crashing into the garden of Ivy Cottage so unexpectedly, blasted away the tableau effect that Charlotte's words had just created in the soft, dappled sunlight beneath the fig tree. His entrance was marked by a confusion of noise and activity, with Mabel barking and the blackbird – who had been frightened away earlier and had since returned – flying off once again to the safety of the beech hedge, squawking noisily as it went.

'Of course you're not interrupting,' Charlotte said, grateful that her brother-in-law had saved her from any further revealing disclosures. What had made her say such a thing? She would have to be careful in future, to ensure no further slip-ups like that, for it would only open up the floodgates of confession. *Why did you hate Brussels so much?* would be the next logical question. *Because my husband stopped needing anything in his life, other than work; because my husband made it impossible for me to love him in the way I wanted to.* Oh no, that line of conversation could only lead in one direction, to that dreaded, final denouement – that she was to blame for Peter's death on that icy road to Luxembourg.

'I'll go and get another chair,' she said.

As he watched his sister-in-law walk away from him, David was reminded of the first time he had seen

Charlotte. He had met Hilary in his first year at Oxford Polytechnic and during the Christmas vacation he was invited to stay a few days with Hilary and her family. On New Year's Eve Charlotte had turned up from London in a smart little racing-green MG with a boyfriend called Clive. It had snowed for the best part of the evening, and late that night, coming back from the village after a festive drink to Louise and Neville's half-timbered cottage, Charlotte had started laughing, saying she felt like dancing barefoot in the snow. They thought she was joking, but snatching off her thick overcoat and shoes, she had done just that, cavorting like a nymph in the moonlight. Hilary had, of course, disapproved. 'Oh for goodness' sake, Charlotte, stop showing off.' But he and Clive had watched, mesmerised. As the church bells chimed the passing of another year, they had cheered loudly and kissed one another. He remembered wanting to give Charlotte a long, wet, open-mouthed kiss, but had made do with an impetuous collision of their lips.

Three years later he and Hilary were married. By then he had become like a brother to Charlotte, and kisses were a mere respectable brush of the cheek.

Watching Charlotte now as she walked barefoot across the grass, David wondered whether she had ever, since that night, danced barefoot in the snow again.

Alex looked at Charlotte's retreating figure and wondered at what she had just told him – *It was empty and cold and I hated it*. It was a stark and disturbing image she had given and only a fool would think she was referring to Belgium's low population and inclement weather. But something else was disturbing him.

How about marriage, or is that a label you don't need either? Lucy. Twice now in one day he had been forced to unwrap and touch the memory of her. Sat here in the sun listening to Charlotte he had tried to dismiss Lucy from his mind, to relocate this dislodged memory to the back of his brain where for so long it had been treasured and, like so many treasures, rarely touched. She had been a lively, forceful girl, and so was her memory, even after seven years.

'Alex, if I've told you once, I've told you a hundred times. I'm not going to throw myself away on you, not when there's the hope of marrying someone who doesn't spend his every waking moment in front of a computer.'

'I don't really want to marry you,' he had laughed, catching her hand in his as they walked along the footpath towards the waterfall at Haworth. 'I just want to get you into bed every night, that's all.'

'Well, you do that often enough anyway.'

Kissing her, he had pulled her down amongst the heather and ripening bilberries despite the presence of a coach party of Japanese tourists, their sunhats bobbing, their cameras swinging.

'You're a lout, Alex Hamilton, and I love you!' she had shouted at the top of her voice, just as the last of the tourists had tried to scuttle discreetly by.

There had been other women in his life since Lucy, but without really trying he had succeeded in keeping any subsequent relationship on a purely superficial level.

'Anything to drink, David?' he said abruptly, getting to his feet.

David looked at the bottle of wine on the table. 'A glass of that would be nice, thanks.'

As Alex went into his side of Ivy Cottage to fetch a glass, Charlotte returned with a chair.

'I see you found the garden furniture. It's old, could almost be antique,' David said.

'Very old, I should think,' Charlotte said, giving the

chair a rub with the cloth. 'Back to Noah's cruising days I shouldn't wonder.'

Reappearing with another glass, Alex poured the wine. Charlotte refused any more. 'So David, why aren't you over at The Gables, hard at whatever it is fathers do on a Sunday?'

'If you must know, I've had it up to here.' He pointed to his unshaven chin. 'Hilary's got one on her today. I think it's got to do with . . .' He paused and took a fortifying sip of his wine. 'Well, you know, about . . .' Again he paused and nodded his head in the direction of In The Pink and then back at Alex.

Alex smiled. 'But you don't believe any of it, do you, David?'

'Good heavens, no!' David said, stretching his legs out in front of him and resting his glass on his slightly domed stomach.

'Liar,' said Charlotte suddenly. 'You're just as bad as the rest of them.'

'No, really, I don't. It's just, well, you know what it's like, you can't help but fall back on the old maxim, no smoke without fire and all that.'

'So,' Charlotte said, her eyes narrowing slightly, 'Hilary's mad as hell, is she?'

'Tell me about it,' David said, puffing out his cheeks. 'She's in a right lather.'

'Well, the day's not been a complete waste then, has it?'

'Oh that's great, just great,' David said loudly, tossing back a large mouthful of wine. 'This is what I've got to look forward to from now on, is it? You two sisters winding one another up the whole time and yours truly caught in the crossfire?'

'You know who's really caught in the crossfire, don't you?' said Alex, leaning forward in his chair.

Both Charlotte and David looked at him. 'Who?' they said together.

'Cindy, of course. Has anyone been round to see her and tell her the truth?'

Charlotte pulled a face. 'I'm afraid I haven't had the nerve. Do you think I ought to?'

'How about we go together?' Alex said. 'From what I understand of Derek's reputation, she's going to need some pretty good convincing that nothing did actually happen between you two.'

'I'll think about it,' Charlotte said, avoiding Alex's eyes. She had no desire to rush headlong into Cindy.

Apart from Barry, Cindy was alone in the house. She could hear music coming from behind his door: monks singing the same thing, over and over again. Uplifting, Barry had called it the other day, on one of his rare excursions out of his room.

Every day was the same. As soon as Barry got in from school he went straight up to his room, music on, head in a book. And today, Sunday, was no exception. He had been there since he got back from jogging this morning, only coming out briefly for his lunch and hardly saying a word at the table, just forking food into his mouth absentmindedly, keeping his eyes firmly on the book he was reading. Boys she had known at eighteen had never been like Barry. They had been more like Derek, she thought with a rueful smile. But Barry was a strange boy, so quiet, so preoccupied, and recently even more so. She had tried searching his room while he was at school one day, but had come up with nothing. She had hated doing it, but those leaflets from school had told you what to do if you noticed a change in your child's behaviour. She couldn't imagine Barry getting mixed up in anything like that, not drugs. Tiffany, yes. Like a shot. She winced at this unfortunate pun and put the thought of her children aside. She went through to the en suite bathroom and looked in the large illuminated mirror above the his-and-hers basins.

She stared critically at her face, then gently smoothed the skin under her right eye with a perfectly manicured forefinger. The shaded hue of the slightly loosening skin beneath her lashes was warning enough that her favourite lemon and apricot eye care pack was needed. *Grief can have a devastating effect on your skin* – the irony of her words to Charlotte on Friday night was not lost on her. But she didn't feel in the mood for an eye care pack, and anyway, it was Sunday. Surely even her skin was allowed a day off?

No, she told herself emphatically, don't let yourself go, don't let it get to you. You've survived countless meaningless affairs before, this is just one more. Let it blow over, let him get her out of his system and then that will be that.

She was very calm, really. She had taught herself to be that. Even when she had heard the juniors in the salon, Tracy and Lorraine, tidying up the linen cupboard late yesterday afternoon, she had stayed calm.

'He's at it again,' Lorraine had sniggered.

'But he's got competition this time, hasn't he?' Tracy had replied. 'That good-looking bloke, just moved in.'

Cindy scraped her hair back into a tight ponytail and secured it with a scrunch band. First she cleansed and toned her skin, then carefully applied the sweet-smelling, creamy paste around her eyes.

With ten minutes to wait for the eye pack to do its work, she walked through to the bedroom to get a magazine. Passing the full-length mirror at the other end of the pale peach room, she caught sight of herself, and for a split second she saw a gaunt, white face that looked nothing like her, but like a hideously deformed old woman. Derek would never love a woman like that, a voice inside her head whispered. She stood looking at this terrifying image and then, slowly, it passed, became the face she was accustomed to seeing and the face she hoped Derek loved . . . in his own way.

She went back into the bathroom with the magazine, sat down on the small cane settee by the bath and started to flick through the pages of life-enhancing recipes for sex and filo pastry, trying desperately not to think of Derek and what he was doing to her.

She didn't hate him for what he did, he couldn't help himself half the time – it was habitual. And for reasons she couldn't make sense of, she loved him, always had, and she knew that this would always be there between them . . . but then, so would all the affairs.

By most people's standards she felt that she was still an attractive woman. Her skin was smooth and firm, her bust hadn't drooped, nor had her buttocks. She worked out, ate the right things, rarely drank alcohol and always kept herself well dressed. And she had never once, in all their years together, refused Derek in bed. So why wasn't that enough for him, what more did he need?

And why did that wretched Charlotte Lawrence have to come and live next door?

Chapter Fourteen

'I know it's my fault,' Hilary said down the telephone. 'It was stupid of me not to put it on the calendar, but Tiffany can't manage it tonight – apparently it's Barry's birthday – and David's got one of his tedious Rotary evenings, and would you believe it, Mum and Dad are out as well? So I just thought, Charlotte, that maybe, and I do appreciate what a busy day you must have had, but do you think you could babysit for me, tonight?'

Babysit! Charlotte looked at the mayhem all around her in the hall and wondered whether her sister had any idea just how busy a day it had been for her.

At eight-thirty that morning rowdy voices, English and French, had added to the noise of the Belgian removal van as it tried to position itself to reverse up the drive of Ivy Cottage. Having already got the huge pantechnicon tangled up in Hilary's terracotta pots at the end of The Gables' driveway, the driver had then endeavoured to squeeze his load through the metaphorical eye of a needle, bringing with it the lower overhanging branches of a rowan together with a good deal of forsythia.

Charlotte had viewed the approaching removal van with apprehension, knowing that coming towards her, with reversing siren wailing, was the past eight years of her life – approximately thirty-two cubic metres of marital souvenirs. Up until this point, Ivy Cottage had been neutral territory, had been devoid of anything to do with Peter. Now it was about to open its doors and embrace eight years of the man, and Charlotte wasn't sure how she was going to feel about this.

'Any chance of a brew before we get started?' the foreman had said, giving her no further time to be squeamish about what was to be spilled out of the lorry.

Five hours later the team of tea- and coffee-swilling men had filled Ivy Cottage and departed, leaving behind them a house full of randomly emptied boxes. With no one to help sort out the chaos, Charlotte had worked on alone until her father arrived.

'Hello,' he called from the open front door.

'In here,' she called back.

He came hesitantly into the cardboard box havoc of the sitting-room. 'Need any help?'

Charlotte bobbed up from behind the sofa. 'Does a fish need water?'

Together they pushed, lifted, emptied and filled until eventually, exhausted, they retired to the crockery-splattered kitchen for a respite.

'I had no idea you'd be all alone. I thought Hilary would have been here to help you,' Neville said, accepting a mug of tea from Charlotte.

Charlotte slumped down into a chair. 'No, she's off on a school trip with Becky's class. Chester Zoo, I think, back about five.'

'I'm surprised no one else offered to help,' Neville said quietly.

She noticed the inclination of her father's head. 'I heard his car leaving just before eight this morning, Dad, unless of course you were thinking that Derek and Cindy might have liked to help.'

Neville looked deep into his mug of tea. 'Well, I wasn't being specific, I just meant . . .'

'Come on, Dad,' she laughed, 'finish your tea and get off home. I need to take Mabel for a walk.'

Charlotte had just said goodbye to her father, closed the front door and was stepping over boxes of books and piles of unwrapped pictures when Hilary had telephoned.

'I shan't be long, it's a PTA meeting,' Hilary was saying. 'Patricia Longton's away, so I'll be stepping out of my role as Secretary and be acting as Chairwoman for the evening. And anyway, seeing as you've not even seen the children since you moved in, I thought it might be nice for you to have them all to yourself for a while. What do you say?'

Hilary held her breath. She was conscious of the silence at the other end of the telephone. She knew that she was pushing her luck, that she had, since Friday, acted a little harshly towards her sister, as David had gone to great lengths to inform her yesterday when he got back from Ivy Cottage. She had been taking a batch of cup cakes out of the Aga for the school trip when David had breezed in and said, 'Hilary, you're a bloody fool and you're going to have to apologise to Charlotte.'

Concentrating on mixing pink icing in a bowl and searching for the hoard of hundreds and thousands that she kept hidden from Becky, Hilary had let David have his say.

'How you could have thought your own sister capable of such a thing! Hasn't she got enough on her plate without you and all the other old biddies in the village making her out to be some kind of insatiable . . .' She had listened to the silence while he seemingly searched his mind for a suitable word. ' Slut!' he said at last.

She had looked up at him at this point. 'David, that's not a nice word.'

'Too bloody right, it isn't.'

'What's a slut, Daddy?'

Together they had spun round to see Becky standing in the doorway, practising a few wobbly demi-pliés. 'Don't stick your bottom out,' Hilary had said quickly, bustling about the kitchen and giving David one of her see-what-you've-done-now looks.

'So what do you say, Charlotte?' Hilary repeated. 'It'll only be a few hours.' She wondered whether she ought to mention anything about letting bygones be bygones: after all, this telephone call was by way of an apology, surely her stubborn sister could see that? Then she heard what she thought sounded like suppressed crying at the other end of the telephone. 'Charlotte,' she said anxiously, 'do you want me to come over?'

'No.'

'But you're upset, you're crying. I'll come over and put the kettle on. I'll make us a nice cup of tea.'

'I wasn't crying.'

'Charlotte, it's all right, really it is, tears are all part of the grieving process, you must . . .'

'I wasn't crying, I was laughing, Hilary.'

'Laughing!' What on earth did her sister have to laugh about, for goodness' sake?

'I had forgotten what a persistent pain you are.'

Hilary sighed with relief. 'So you'll do it. See you in about an hour then.'

Still laughing to herself, Charlotte put down the receiver, located Mabel's lead and then found Mabel, curled up inside a knocked-over packing box.

She locked the front door behind her and set off along the drive. Halfway down she noticed a red Citroën come up the parallel driveway. She saw Alex and because the sunroof was open she could hear the sound of Mozart's Requiem. He waved across the front lawn to her and parked the car.

'How did the unpacking go?' he called out.

'Ongoing,' she said, pulling a face.

He came over. 'Sorry I wasn't around to help. Is there anything I can do now?'

'I've stopped for the day, too exhausted to do any more. But thanks for the offer.'

Bending down to Mabel, who was straining on her lead to reach him, Alex said, 'Have you seen Cindy yet?'

'No,' Charlotte said awkwardly, glad at least to have the perfect excuse. 'I haven't had time today.'

He stood up and looked at her. 'How about now? I could come with you. We ought to put her mind at rest . . . and yours.'

Charlotte looked away, wondered why this man was so concerned about everyone else's feelings.

'What's the problem? Are you worried she's not going to believe us?'

'No, it's not that exactly, it's more . . . oh, I don't know, it's sounds silly really, only I don't think Cindy and I are ever going to be the best of friends. I've a feeling she's already condemned me as one of Derek's trophies. Even if I'm found innocent this time, in her eyes it's only a matter of time before I really am guilty.'

Alex shook his head. 'You're right,' he said, 'it does sound silly. Come on, let's just go next door, say what we've got to say and let the poor woman make up her own mind.'

'Do you always bully people like this?'

He smiled. 'Yes, all the time, never stop.'

'Is it possible to see Mrs Rogers please?' Charlotte asked

the young receptionist, who immediately pouted her lips in irritation at being delayed at getting off home.

'Have you got an appointment?' she said, pulling on her jacket.

'No, but . . .'

'Well, I'm very sorry but we're just about to close and Mrs Rogers is in a hurry. She needs to get off on time tonight, it's her son's eighteenth . . .'

'Thank you, Tracy, I'm sure I can spare my neighbours a few minutes.' It was Cindy, elegantly poised on cerise high heels and wearing a white uniform which gave her slim arms and legs the appearance of being even more tanned. Her hair, unlike last Friday night, was pinned back and showed off a flawless complexion. She was a walking advertisement for In The Pink, what Charlotte suspected all their customers aspired to.

'We don't actually allow dogs on the premises,' Cindy said looking down at Mabel, 'but Tracy will look after it for you.' Ignoring Tracy's look of annoyance at being delayed even longer, she carried on, 'We'll go through to the office where we won't be disturbed.' She turned and started clicking her way down a corridor. As Charlotte and Alex followed behind, Cindy turned and said, 'Derek's busy with Mrs Jeffs at the moment. She's one of his regulars. She comes in three times a week.'

'Really,' said Charlotte, not missing the point of the statement.

Cindy opened a door. 'Mrs Jeffs' husband plays for Manchester United. Maybe you're a fan of football? I'm not.'

Or of Mrs Jeffs, thought Charlotte looking about her and being surprised by the austerity of the room in which they were standing. What they had seen so far of In The Pink was a frothy concoction of pink frilly blinds and flowery wallpaper; here the walls were a cool grey and the office furniture was uncompromisingly black, modern, angular, and shouted no-nonsense business acumen. Charlotte thought Cindy looked more at home hovering by the large desk than she had in the reception area.

'Please, sit down,' Cindy said. 'Would you like a cup of coffee?'

Nobody sat down. Alex spoke first. 'No thank you, Cindy. We shan't keep you long. Your receptionist told us you were in a rush to get away. All we've come to say is that, well, to try and explain that what . . .'

Cindy smiled for the first time.

Charlotte took over. 'Nothing happened, Cindy. Iris Braithwaite got some silly idea into her head, and went round making a fool of herself and us.'

'I know,' Cindy said softly, though there was little warmth to her voice. This was a new experience for her – one of Derek's women actually protesting her innocence. 'Mrs Braithwaite came to see me last night. She did manage to apologise in the end.'

'I'm so glad it's all been sorted out,' Charlotte said, visibly relaxing.

'Yes,' agreed Cindy, picking up a paperclip from the desk. She turned it over in her hands as though examining it for any possible defects. She looked at Charlotte. 'Except for one thing of course.'

'What's that?' Charlotte said nervously.

'Well, it's only a small thing, but what exactly was my husband doing at your house with a bouquet of roses?'

'I knew it, I just knew it!' Charlotte said, as they walked away from In The Pink. 'I knew this would happen. You see what you've done?'

'Cindy would probably have said that to you anyway.

Better it was done there in private. At least nobody else was there to hear her.'

'But what was I supposed to say? How could I have answered her question? Oh yes, Cindy, your husband came to see me with the biggest bunch of red roses I've ever seen and kissed me up against the kitchen sink.'

'She didn't expect an answer. She knows perfectly well what Derek had in mind when he turned up on your doorstep. It was a warning shot she was firing, that was all. She needs to convince herself that she's doing all she can to prevent Derek from hurting her any more.' Alex pushed his hands down inside his trouser pockets. 'So . . . he kissed you, did he?'

Charlotte groaned. 'It was just some stupid kind of grope thing,' she said, exasperated. 'I didn't take much notice of it at the time.'

Alex looked at her and then started to laugh. Charlotte smiled and then she too laughed as she realised how implausible her words had sounded.

Opening Philip's bedroom window, Hilary heard the sound of laughter. She looked across the road and saw Charlotte and Alex walking towards Ivy Cottage. Things were going very nicely.

Chapter Fifteen

Barry walked blindly behind his sister, allowing her to guide him through the house and out on to the driveway.

'Now stand there,' Tiffany told him, 'and keep your eyes closed, until I tell you to open them.' He felt her hands fumbling at the back of his head, undoing the knot she had tied in the bandana and then he felt the material slip away. 'Open your eyes, now – *surprise*!'

He blinked in the low evening sunlight and then stared unbelievably at a brand new Peugeot 205.

'Well, what do you reckon to that then, Bas?' his father said, leaning against the car. 'Bit of all right I'd say. The most I had at your age was a pushbike.'

'It's great, Dad,' Barry said, still staring at the metallic-grey car. 'I never expected anything like this, I don't know what to say . . . thanks.'

'Nothing like a flash motor to help you pull. You'll have no worries on that score now.'

Barry turned to his mother. 'Thanks,' he said. 'It's a great present.'

'Just make sure you drive carefully,' she said.

'Now all you've got to do is pass your test next week,' said Tiffany, 'and then we can hit the road, just you and me, kid.'

Barry frowned and ran a hand through his hair. 'I might not pass.'

'Muffin 'ell, 'course you will. It's not as if Dad's been teaching you.'

'Less of that,' said Derek. 'Anyway, I don't know about you lot, but my stomach feels like it's been cut off from my throat.' He tossed a key over to Barry. 'Come on, Bas, you can get the feel of it by driving us to the restaurant.'

'We can't possibly go yet,' said Cindy.

'Why ever not?'

'Tiffany can't go looking like that, look at the state of her. They won't let her in the restaurant in those disgusting clothes.'

'Give up, Mum!' shouted Tiffany.

'Don't you dare shout at me for all the neighbours to hear. Just get back in the house and change into something decent.'

Glaring at her mother, Tiffany stood her ground and didn't move.

Barry sensed his mother's anger giving way to bitter disappointment. He felt sorry for her, felt he knew the sense of frustration and disillusionment that filled her life – firstly his father, then himself, and to top it all, Tiffany. It was quite simple really: all his mother had ever wanted in life was a faithful husband and a real daughter.

'Look, Mum,' he said, 'I know it's a pain, but that's how she likes to dress. She's not doing anyone any harm.'

'If you could just quit with all the philosophy crap,' Derek said impatiently, 'we could get a move on.' He shook his head. 'Families, I ask you, who the bloody hell needs them?'

We do, thought Barry, as he walked over to unlock his birthday present.

'I think they must have given me the wrong cassette in the

shop,' Derek said, jabbing a finger at the cassette player on the dashboard and ejecting a tape. 'I thought I'd got you the Four Seasons.'

'You have, Dad, it's great, thanks,' Barry said, keeping his eyes firmly on the road.

Derek made a play of reading the label. 'Yep, I knew they'd made a mistake, this isn't Frankie Valli at all. It's that Nigel Kennedy bloke.'

'Muffin 'ell, Dad,' shouted Tiffany from the back of the car, 'you're a plonker, you really are.'

Derek turned round and grinned at Tiffany. 'I can still fool you though, can't I?'

'Idiot!'

'Don't speak to your father like that,' Cindy said.

'Yes,' agreed Derek, smirking, 'it would be nice to see some respect in this family for a change.'

Barry looked in the mirror and caught his sister's expression of explosive retaliation.

'Good evening, sir,' said the maître d' at the White Swan. 'I'm sorry but there are no tables free, perhaps you'd care to wait in the bar, I'm sure . . .'

'That's all right, pal, you're new here, aren't you? Rogers is the name. We've got a booking.'

They watched the *maître d'* move off with his air of grandiose superiority to check the list of reservations.

'If you'd like to come this way, Mr Rogers,' the maître d' said, sliding back to them, 'your table is over here. You ordered a bottle of champagne on the telephone. Shall I open it right away for you, sir?'

They sat at a fussy blue-and-white-trimmed table and were handed four over-sized menus. Barry watched his father make a great show of tasting the champagne and declaring it adequate. They raised their glasses and set about playing happy families for the evening – an evening which for Barry stretched ominously ahead.

As a family they rarely spent any time together, and on occasions like this when they were forced to act out the part, it was usually a strain. Barry could already see the strain showing on his mother's face. Ever since he could remember, he had sensed a detachment, almost an estrangement, between himself and his mother. For years he hadn't understood what was going on, but more recently he had come to know that no matter what he did, he could not please his mother, could not make her happy. Tiffany had managed it effortlessly when she was small, but then she had grown up, and almost overnight had destroyed the illusion their mother had so carefully created.

'Happy birthday, Bas,' his father said, chinking his fluted glass against Barry's own. 'Now get this down you, and don't worry about driving home, I'll drive.'

'Cheers,' Barry said, taking a small sip. He had no intention of getting drunk. He had far too much work to get through with his exams only a few days away.

'I still don't get it though, Bas. Why the hell didn't you want a night out with your own mates? You could have gone into Manchester, picked up a few girls, had a party? We'd have paid for it, you know.'

Barry shook his head. 'Wasn't what I wanted.'

'And this was?' Tiffany said, looking about her.

'We don't often sit round a table together and talk, do we?' Barry started to say.

'Just as well,' Tiffany interrupted.

'Maybe Barry's right.'

Barry looked at his mother, searching her face for signs of cynicism. He found none. Perhaps tonight he would be able to broach the subject after all.

'Hey, this is all getting a bit serious, isn't it?' Derek said, draining his glass. 'Come on, another glass of champagne.' He reached for the bottle behind him in the wine cooler. At once, a young waiter, about the same age as Barry, appeared at his side and took over. 'Don't worry, pal,' Derek said. 'I wasn't about to get you kicked out of a job.'

'No worries there, mate. They're understaffed as it is. Even if I gobbed in your soup, they couldn't afford to sack me.'

Derek roared. In response, a few heads bobbed up from their plates around the White Swan.

The waiter was just his father's kind of man, Barry thought, someone as brazen as himself with a take-me-as-you-find-me attitude. If he were more like that, Barry knew he would get on better with his father.

'Nice bloke,' Derek said, when they'd ordered their meal. 'Will probably do well in life.'

Tiffany sniffed loudly. 'Hope it's your soup he gobs in, then.'

When they had finished their desserts and coffee and Cindy had gone off to the ladies' room, Barry knew he had lost his opportunity. His father was now regaling the young waiter with his life history – his rags to riches saga. 'You see, lad, your life's all before you. What are you – seventeen?'

'Eighteen,' the waiter replied, stifling a yawn.

'So's my lad, look, the one there sitting like a stuffed Henry. Wouldn't think it was his eighteenth birthday today, would you? He should be out celebrating with his mates, shouldn't he, not stuck here with us? I bet you celebrated.' He poked the young waiter in the ribs and gave him a wink.

The waiter looked at Tiffany. 'Too right I did.'

'I've paid the bill, Derek, it's time we were going.' It was Cindy coming back to the table, looking far from pleased.

Outside in the poorly lit car park Cindy and Barry guided Derek towards the car. 'Now you'd better let me drive, Bas,' Derek said. 'Don't want you losing your licence before you've even got it, do we?'

'He's pathetic, he really is,' Tiffany said with disgust, dragging behind.

'Shut up, Tiffany,' hissed Cindy, 'just remember, he's your father.'

'Oh please, how can I ever forget?'

They drove home, listening to Derek singing 'Ooh What a Night' to Vivaldi's 'L'Autonno'. For Barry, the evening had turned out just as he'd known it would. He had been a fool to think that anyone in his family would be interested in what he had to say. After all, to his father he was nothing more than a 'stuffed Henry' – not a very pleasant revelation that, on his eighteenth birthday. But he was used to it, like he was used to all the jokes and innuendoes. Well, he would just have to wait until the right time presented itself.

Chapter Sixteen

Hilary had come deliberately early, before Iris Braithwaite and the others arrived to help set up the St John's spring jumble sale. At least this way it gave her a chance to get things done the way she liked, and not the way Iris wanted. It seemed a dreadful shame to Hilary that one woman could so easily put a blight on the community. She knew for a fact that more people would volunteer to help out in the village if Iris Braithwaite wasn't already there on practically every committee. 'Sorry,' people would whisper when asked to help, 'no can do, not with *her* to answer to.'

Hilary hadn't seen or heard from Iris in the past week, which was unusual in the run-up to an event such as today's, but Iris's low profile probably had a lot to do with what Charlotte had said to her last Sunday. Even though Hilary couldn't help but admire her sister, she still felt a pang of jealousy that Charlotte had had the courage to stand up to Iris, and she did not. She wished that she had been there to witness it, instead of rushing off home to clear up the breakfast things and get the Sunday roast in the oven. A shame no one had told her at the time what had taken place; it would have saved an awful lot of misunderstanding between her and Charlotte. Luckily though, Kate Hampton, the PTA Treasurer, had told her about it at their Monday evening meeting. 'Your sister was quite magnificent. There was more drama in that church porch than in a week's worth of *EastEnders*. Perhaps we'll see a few changes round here from now on. Belgium's loss is certainly Hulme Welford's gain. She's become quite the local hero.'

Hilary had tried to clamp down on her disappointment at her sister suddenly getting all the attention. It wasn't quite how she had envisaged things. True she didn't want Charlotte to be miserable, but on the other hand, she didn't want her to come striding back into the village and take over – grieving widows weren't supposed to behave like that. Demure, quietly tearful and in need of a friendly shoulder to lean against was more the mark, surely?

She started setting up the tables, which Brown Owl and her pack of Brownies were supposed to have organised last night, and then she moved on to the boxes of clothes, sorting things out by gender and then by size. She was just holding up a red, lacy G-string – the kind of thing she would never contemplate wearing – and wondering who on earth in the village had donated it, when in walked Iris Braithwaite, followed by Mrs Haslip and Mrs Bradley, each weighed down with several large Tupperware boxes.

'Mrs Parker! I trust you have no intention of offering *that* for sale?'

Hilary flushed. 'Of course not, Mrs Braithwaite. I was just wondering . . .'

'Well don't. Put them, I mean it, in the bin and let's get on, we've lots to do. Mrs Haslip, you get to work in the kitchen, and for heaven's sake make sure the kettles are clean and the coffee urn doesn't have anything untoward inside. I know what those ghastly Cubs are like.'

Philip was a Cub and Hilary wanted very much to rush to his defence. But instead she bent down to the next box of jumble and started sorting through it. It wasn't fair: it was *she* who had done most of the work; it was *her* house that had been used as a collecting point; *their* computer that had prepared all the posters to advertise the event – it was all her time and effort and now, at the very last minute, in came Iris Braithwaite and took command.

It hadn't always been like this. Before she had had the children she had been a teacher, and quite a good one, in her opinion. She knew when it had all changed – it was having the children and being at home. She had read once that each time the afterbirth was ejected from a woman's body, so was a piece of her self-confidence, taking away her sense of freedom and her courage. Hilary didn't normally believe such fanciful theories, but since having the children she had indeed grown afraid of more and more things: heights, flying, deep water – and Iris Braithwaite.

'Now Mrs Parker, I suggest Mrs Bradley helps you so that we ensure no other unsavoury items end up on the tables. Good gracious, just look at the state of this floor. Mrs Haslip, is there a broom in the kitchen? If so, fetch it here this minute.'

As they worked away under Iris's tyrannical directives, Hilary couldn't help but begin to feel a perverse sense of satisfaction. It looked as though Charlotte's brave words after church last week had had no great effect on Iris after all. So much for being the local hero.

At a quarter to eleven Malcolm Jackson, Charlotte, and the other press-ganged helpers turned up, and under Iris's baleful eye stood ready to receive the flood of bargain hunters.

Jumble sales in Hulme Welford were always well attended, and due to the eagerness of the queue outside, the doors were generally opened early. Today was no exception.

'Right, ladies,' announced Iris Braithwaite, 'are you

ready?' She stood poised between the locked door and a small table, which had on it an embroidered tablecloth and a battered Quality Street tin ready to receive the twenty pence entrance fee. She turned the key and addressed the crowd. 'Ladies and gentlemen . . .' But her voice was lost as a loud cheer went up and she very sensibly moved back to her Quality Street tin.

Charlotte and Hilary stood together behind the ladies' clothes stall, ready for the onslaught. Charlotte's initial reaction, when her sister had asked her if she would like to help out, had been to say no, but then, why not, she had asked herself, what else had she to do?

It had been a quiet, pleasant week at Ivy Cottage, apart from Hilary popping over every few hours 'just to see how she was getting on'. She had continued with the unpacking and made rather an expensive purchase – a new car. With Peter's words ringing in her ears, she had tried to convince herself that she need not feel guilty about this: '*It's a false economy to buy second-hand,*' he had always said. And as the smartly dressed, Polo-scented salesman in the showroom had said, there was always her own personal safety to consider; statistically she was less likely to break down in a new car than an old one. It still hadn't felt right, though, picking out a car with money she believed did not rightfully belong to her.

The subject of Peter's money was one she tried hard not to think about. If she had gone ahead and divorced him, she would have expected nothing. As it was, he was dead, and because of his well-planned insurance policies, she was now reasonably well off.

'How much is this?'

Charlotte looked at the sharp-faced woman in front of her and at the Marks & Spencer blouse in her hand. 'Forty pence,' she replied.

'Forty pence, luv, you've got to be joking. This is a jumble sale, not bleeding 'arrods!'

Hilary had warned her about the hard-nosed professionals of the jumble sale circuit. She stuck to her guns. 'It's definitely forty pence. It's in very good condition. Look, you can see, it's barely been worn.'

'How do you know that? And anyway, it's only polyester. I mean, it's not silk or anything, is it?'

Charlotte was beginning to enjoy herself. It was good to be arguing on this irrational basis, and over something as trivial as a second-hand blouse. Too much of her married life she had been unable to argue with Peter, who had never liked confrontations. He had always walked away from her whenever she had tried to argue a point.

'Come back and fight with me!' she would shout at him.

'Fight?' he replied once. 'But I'm your husband,' or another time, 'Charlotte, you really do say the strangest of things.' His logic had been irrefutable which had had the effect of suppressing her anger, and in turn had made her angrier still.

'You know how polyester can sometimes bobble up after it's been worn a few times?'

'Yes,' said the woman, screwing her eyes up to look at the cuff Charlotte was showing her.

'Well, look, there's not a bobble in sight.'

'Mm . . .' said the woman, 'perhaps you're right, maybe it's never been worn, but the first time I wear it, it'll probably bobble up something rotten. I'll give you twenty pence.'

'Sorry, it's forty,' Charlotte said firmly, 'and the money does go for a good cause, a replacement stained-glass window in the church.'

'Go on, then, give it here, there's your money, and I'll

want a plaque by the side of the bleeding window with my name on it.'

With a triumphant toss of her hand, Charlotte threw the coins into the tin. This was going to be more fun than she had thought.

'However did you manage that?' whispered Hilary at her side. 'I've never been able to hold my ground with that wretched Mrs Barret. Oh look, Malcolm's getting into his stride now.'

Over by the kitchen counter the Reverend Jackson was drumming up interest in the refreshments. 'Teas and coffees now being served, everyone,' he shouted above the din of eager bargain hunters, 'and don't forget the delicious home-made cakes.'

'Hello, you two.'

'Alex!' said Hilary. 'How nice of you to come and support us.'

Charlotte noticed the extra width to Hilary's smile and the hand raised to pat her hair in place.

'How much is this, luv?' It was Mrs Barret again with a navy-blue cardigan in her hand. Charlotte leaned forward, but the old woman said, 'No, I'm not asking you, I'm asking her.' And she thrust the cardigan towards Hilary.

'I see you've already snapped up a few purchases,' Charlotte said, looking at the pile of detective novels in Alex's hands.

'Too good an opportunity to pass by,' he said. 'Five murders for a pound and a book on trees, though I think my ribs have suffered into the bargain.'

'You'll have to get some serious training in before the next jumble sale and wear protective clothing.' Charlotte lowered her voice. 'It's the old women you have to look out for. They're the worst, elbows like skewers.'

'They show no mercy, that's for sure.'

'Come on now, Mrs Lawrence, no shirking. There are customers waiting to be served.' Iris Braithwaite was on the prowl. 'Good to see you participating, Mr Hamilton,' she said. 'May I suggest you try men's clothing just a little further along. There are some rather nice pullovers in your size I think.'

Alex winked at Charlotte and moved off, not to the gentleman's outfitters, but to the miscellaneous junk department.

Charlotte watched him go, at the same time trying to stop the twisted pile of cardigans, blouses and dresses – which seemed to have a life of their own – from falling off the table. She could hear her sister faltering at her side with the indomitable Mrs Barret, who was still haggling.

Smiling to herself, Charlotte observed Alex pick up a revoltingly garish picture of a little boy with a tear trickling down his cheek. To her amazement, he bought it. He started to walk away, but turned back to the table. Something else had caught his eye. Fascinated to see what other rubbish he was about to waste his money on, Charlotte watched him pick up a small spoon. He turned it over in his hands, examined the back of it closely, and then working his fingers down to the bowl he caressed it gently. Charlotte shivered.

'How long do I have to stand here before I'm served?'

'I'm sorry?'

'I want these two skirts, how much?'

'A spoon.'

'I beg your pardon?'

Charlotte flushed deep crimson. 'I mean, a pound. They're fifty pence each.'

The customer handed over her money and moved

away. Her place at the table was immediately filled by another. 'Hello Charlotte, heard any good gossip recently?' It was Derek.

'Wouldn't have thought there'd be anything to interest you here,' she said. Looking at Derek's tight faded jeans, pink polo shirt, gold bracelet and cream jacket tossed casually over his shoulder, she added, 'Don't suppose there's anything flash enough.'

He grinned suggestively. 'You'll do for starters.'

Charlotte knew she shouldn't laugh. Men like Derek Rogers needed no encouragement. She tried to sound as businesslike as she could. 'Well, seeing as you've come, you might as well buy something.'

'What a good idea. I could try buying Cindy a present. I hear you came to see her. Did she give you a hard time? She's a real Satan in slingbacks, isn't she?' He put his jacket down on the edge of the adjoining table and started poking around amongst the clothes. 'Oh, what's this I've found?' From the bottom of the pile he pulled out the red lacy G-string. 'Now this is more like it.'

'Oh, go on then, tell me you recognise it,' Charlotte said derisively.

'Now you come to mention it, it does look familiar.' He twanged the garment playfully at her.

At that moment Hilary joined them at the table. 'For goodness' sake!' she said. 'Give that to me, Derek.'

'Certainly not. I want to buy it.'

'Don't be silly. Just give it to me before Iris catches sight of it.'

'Why, is it hers?'

Charlotte burst out laughing. Hilary still looked serious. 'I was supposed to get rid of it, but I forgot. She'll go mad if she sees it.'

'Go on, Derek, hand it over,' Charlotte said, seeing the

discomfort on her sister's face. Poor Hilary, she could never see the funny side of things.

'Hand what over?' It was Alex, half hidden behind his ghastly picture.

Derek waved the lacy item in front of him. Alex raised an eyebrow. 'What exotic jumble sales you have in these parts.'

'Hilary won't let me buy it.'

'Perhaps she wants to see the colour of your money first.'

'Well in that case, let me get my wallet.' Derek reached for his jacket and then looked about him. 'It's gone!'

Seeing the G-string abandoned on top of all the jumble, Charlotte made a surreptitious grab for it and passed it to Hilary.

'Come on,' Derek said, his voice beginning to rise, 'a joke's a joke.'

Hilary and Charlotte exchanged worried looks. Rule number one of any jumble sale – *never* put anything down.

'Look. I put my jacket just here. It's cream, it's Armani and it's bloody well gone!'

'Hi Dad, what's all the commotion?'

Derek turned round at the sound of Tiffany's voice, and then fell back against the table, both hands clasped over his gaping mouth. 'Bloody hell, Tiffany!'

Tiffany's hair was immaculately coiffured into an amazing one-foot-high beehive, and it was shocking pink.

'The trouble with you lot is that you can't take a joke!' Tiffany screamed at her parents in their kitchen.

'Some joke,' Cindy said faintly, her face and lips almost as white as her uniform.

'Right now, girl, you can start by telling us what kind

of product it was they used, then we can think how to change it.'

'How the hell should I know, Dad? I just asked for it to be pink. Anyway, I've had enough of this, I'm going out.'

'Oh no you're not, young lady,' shouted Derek. 'I don't want people seeing you like that.'

'Not you as well, Dad.'

She slammed the door after her and stamped off down the drive without a clue or care where she was going. Willing back hot angry tears, she muttered to herself, 'Fifteen-year-old girls don't cry.'

'Thirty-six-year-old women do though,' said a voice.

Hilary Parker's sister was standing in front of her.

'Are you okay?'

Tiffany sniffed. 'Don't know,' she said sulkily.

'Your parents giving you a hard time?'

Tiffany sniffed again.

'Why don't you come and have a boring old cup of tea with me. I'm exhausted after all that sales pitch talk down at the hall.'

'You're not going to tell me I've been stupid as well, are you?'

Charlotte laughed. 'Come on, come and tell me what it's like to be a teenager again. I've nearly forgotten what a miserable time it was.'

At Ivy Cottage they were greeted noisily by Mabel at the back door.

'Let her out, will you?' Charlotte said. 'She must be desperate by now. What do you want, tea or coffee or something cold?'

'Coffee please, lots of milk and two sugars.'

'I remember those days.'

Tiffany frowned. 'Why do you make yourself sound older than you really are?'

'Probably because that's the way I feel at the moment. Where do you want to sit, inside or out?'

'The garden would be nice. It looks lovely from my bedroom window.'

They sat on the dry grass beneath the fig tree. With Mabel on her lap, Charlotte kicked off her shoes and looked at Tiffany's heavily clad feet. 'Are those boots as uncomfortable as they look?'

'No, though you have to break them in.' She set to work undoing one of the laces, giving the boot all her concentration. Suddenly she looked up. 'Aren't you going to ask me why I did it?'

Charlotte took a sip of her tea. She looked thoughtfully at this model-thin, fifteen-year-old girl in front of her, with her pale skin, black eyes, dangling earrings and incredible candyfloss hair. 'That depends,' she said at last.

'Depends on what?'

'Depends on whether you really want me to ask you why you did it.'

'I suppose that's it. Mum and Dad didn't even bother to ask me. I really wanted them to ask so that . . .'

'So that you could have a good go at them?'

Tiffany smiled. 'You see, you do remember what it's like to be a teenager.'

Charlotte lay back on the grass. 'Go on then, tell me all about it.'

With both boots off now, Tiffany rubbed her sweaty white feet, then she too stretched out on the lawn. 'Two reasons really,' she said, looking up at the leaves on the tree above them. 'Firstly I thought it would be a laugh to turn up the same disgusting colour as our house. After all, if they can do it to our home, I can do it to my hair.'

Charlotte smiled, recognising the logic she might well have employed with Peter had he done something so outlandish. 'Go on,' she said. 'What's the other reason?'

'I just wanted to shock the hell out of them!'

Honesty. How refreshing, thought Charlotte. 'Good for you,' she said. 'Though don't quote me on that, will you?'

'Dad's face was good, wasn't it?' Tiffany said, placing a tentative hand on her rigid hair.

'I don't know who was more shocked, Iris or your father.'

'Ma Braithwaite looked great, didn't she?'

'She looked something all right.' Charlotte sat up to finish her tea. 'I don't know your dad well, but I should think that's one of the rare times in his life when he's been left speechless.'

'You're right there. By the way, what happened to his jacket, did you find it?'

'Alex tracked it down. Ted the Toup had bought it from Mrs Bradley and Alex had to barter to get it back again. Ted said he'd paid two pounds for it and that he wouldn't let it go for anything less than three. So tell your father that he owes Alex three pounds.'

Tiffany smirked. 'Dad'll be furious – he paid nearly four hundred for it.'

Chapter Seventeen

She allowed Alex to lead her upstairs. At the foot of the bed he kissed her, slowly, tentatively, like a faint summer breeze blowing over her. He stood back, held her arms outstretched towards him and entwined his slender fingers through hers. Loving it and loving him, she closed her eyes, capturing the moment for ever, never wanting it to end. She heard a rustle of movement and opening her eyes she found herself staring into the carnal gaze of Derek. His hands reached out for her and pushed her down on to the bed. She turned away and closed her eyes again. She wanted Alex. She called out to him and opened her eyes once more, expectantly. This time, coming towards her was Peter. He lay on top of her and moaned, then she felt his body, hot and wet against her own. He started to scream, violent screams of agonising pain as his body started to open, revealing a shattered ribcage and a pulsating heart. She pushed him away and cried out as she felt herself covered in the wetness of his blood.

Charlotte pushed back the twisted duvet and stumbled to the bathroom. She leaned against the cold sink and stared into the mirror. Covered in sweat, her heart pounding, she ripped off the cotton T-shirt she was wearing and went and stood under the shower, letting the powerful jets of water stab and prick at her. When at last she had stopped shaking, she turned off the water and dried herself roughly with a towel.

In the darkness of the bedroom, she looked at the clock on the bedside table. Half past three, the luminous hands told her.

She opened the window and breathed in the scent of dew-moistened grass and earth. Above her a bulging moon illuminated the garden, picking out in brilliant, magical whiteness the bark of the silver birches at the end of the lawn. It was all so peaceful out there, so undemanding, and it contrasted dramatically with the all-consuming terror she had just experienced.

Resting her elbows on the sill, Charlotte looked down at the tendrils of wisteria trying to reach inside the window. Peter would never have tolerated anything as untidy as wisteria. Peter.

She shuddered. It was the first time since the accident that she'd dreamt of him. She clasped her arms around her body, protecting herself against the thought of that blood. Why had she dreamt of that? It was odd. When she had been taken to identify Peter's body there had been very little blood. She had thought at the time that even in death Peter had been unwilling to give away any of himself. She wasn't proud of that thought now.

She wasn't proud either of the first part of the dream she had just experienced. Just what was happening to her?

She drew the curtains across the window and got back into bed, carefully so as not to disturb Mabel who was curled up, fast asleep, on what had once been Peter's side of the bed.

With a Hulme Welford jumble sale now under his belt, Alex decided it was time to give St John's a try.

He was met at the porch by Mrs Braithwaite and a woman whom he recognised from yesterday in the village hall. Mrs Braithwaite handed him a hymn book and an order of service. 'Glad to see you finally putting in an appearance, Mr Hamilton,' she said.

He gave her a nod of his head.

'Good morning,' said the other woman with contrasting friendliness. She sounded a little breathless. 'I'm Mrs Bradley. I do hope you'll enjoy your visit and come again. It's very old, you know, the church dates back to . . .'

'Really, Mrs Bradley,' interrupted Iris, 'we're working for the Lord, not the National Trust.'

'Thank you,' Alex said. 'I'm sure I'll find it most interesting.'

'Edifying, I should hope, Mr Hamilton. Reverend Jackson's theme today is following God's plan.'

'Ah yes,' said Alex. ' "And he has showered down upon us the richness of his grace – for how well he understands us and knows what is best for us at all times".'

'Quite so,' said Mrs Braithwaite dismissively. 'Now come along, Mr Hamilton, there are other people behind you trying to get in.'

Alex chose to sit where he always did in any church, at the back and in the left-hand pew, and without even looking about him, he bowed his head.

A few moments later when he raised his head he found Charlotte was sitting next to him. She seemed startled when he looked at her. 'I didn't know it was you,' she said, and appeared to back away from him.

'What's wrong?' He noted the deep shadows around her eyes and her pale complexion. 'Am I *persona non grata* all of a sudden?'

She looked down, and he watched her turn her gold wedding band on her finger.

Charlotte felt Alex's gaze and knew she should answer his question. But what could she say? That he was the last person in Hulme Welford she wanted to be sitting next to that morning; that twice in twenty-four hours she had desired him, consciously and subconsciously. 'I'm surprised to see you here this morning, that's all,' she said at last.

'You're not the only one. Mrs Braithwaite has already given me a grilling. A little of that woman certainly goes a long way. Ah, I see we're off.' And picking up his hymn book, he got to his feet as the organ started up jauntily with 'Come Sing the Praise of Jesus'.

They were halfway through the second verse when a third person joined Alex and Charlotte in their pew. It was Barry Rogers. Charlotte recognised the now familiar jogging suit and flushed face, and once again noticed that he was positioned behind the stone pillar. Then, as the service was drawing to a close, he disappeared as furtively as he had arrived, just as he had last week.

'I wonder why?' Charlotte said to Alex after she had explained this to him. 'Why does Barry sneak in and out of church each week? It's a bit odd, don't you think?'

Alex shrugged his shoulders. 'Maybe he's a late riser and has to get away early each time.'

'No, there's more to it than that. I bet you . . .'

'Gambling in the Lord's house, Mrs Lawrence, shame on you.' It was Iris Braithwaite looming large behind them both. 'And Mr Hamilton, I trust the sermon served you well?' Not expecting any kind of reply she was quickly off and moving towards her next prey. 'Now Mrs Haslip, I really must question the suitability of orchids in the altar flowers. Their costliness bothered me throughout the entire service. Reverend Jackson needs serviceable fauna, not exotic frippery.'

'Can't say I'd even noticed the flowers,' Alex said to Charlotte as they inched their way towards Malcolm Jackson.

'All I could think of,' Charlotte said, smiling for the first time. 'Kept thinking, what a lot of exotic frippery about the altar.'

'Hello Charlotte,' Malcolm Jackson's voice cut in. 'Good to see you again. How are things?'

'Fine,' she lied, and parrying with the kind of ease she despised, she said, 'Have you met my tenant, Mr Hamilton?'

'Always good to have new blood sitting in the pews.'

Charlotte flinched.

'Wouldn't be interested in ushering, would you?' Malcolm asked as he shook Alex's hand. 'It would give the congregation someone new to criticise,' he added, laughing.

'Why not?' Alex said.

Malcolm Jackson was amazed, for his sales pitch seldom worked. 'Right you are. I'll call round during the week with a copy of the rota for you.'

'You didn't have to, you know. You could have said no to Malcolm, most people do,' Charlotte told Alex as they waited to cross the road outside the church.

'Well, I'm not most people.'

Charlotte looked at him closely. 'You're not, are you, but then who or what are you?'

'That sounds like the corniest of lines from an old movie.'

'You're right,' she said, 'but the question still stands.'

'Tell you what, let me cut the grass for you this afternoon and then I'll tell you.'

'Okay. How about I do some lunch for us first?' She frowned and looked away from him, staring hard at the ground as they turned into Acacia Lane.

'That would be nice.' Alex was conscious of Charlotte's wariness. 'But only if you really want to.'

She stood still and looked up at him. 'Maybe we shouldn't. I wouldn't want people to . . . after all, Peter's only been dead a short while.'

He stared into her eyes which, in the leafy shade of the trees, were that same dusky violet he remembered so well from their first meeting. 'I presume it was only lunch you were offering.'

'For goodness' sake, you're beginning to sound like Derek now,' she snapped back at him.

'That's better, you don't look so . . .'

'Go on, what don't I look?'

He hesitated before speaking. It had struck him from the moment he had met Charlotte that there was something wrong about her grief; he didn't know what it was, but knew only that something jarred. He felt at times that he forgot to treat her as a woman who had recently lost the man she loved, because she didn't behave like one. He said, 'I just feel that sometimes you're your real self and at other times it's as if you're trying to become the person you feel others expect you to be.'

'And what might that person be?' Charlotte said coolly.

'The grieving widow,' he said softly, still looking straight at her.

Charlotte said nothing, but walked on ahead, fast. Alex let her go, then, after a moment's thought, he caught her up at the entrance to his part of Ivy Cottage. 'I'm sorry,' he said. 'Perhaps I shouldn't have said that.'

She turned on him and he braced himself for her anger. Instead she looked quite calmly at him. 'Can we carry on with this conversation over lunch?'

'How do you think Charlotte is coping?' Neville Archer asked his wife, as he pulled slowly away at the lights in Wilmslow. He was aware of the impatient Range Rover behind him, practically climbing into the boot of his tired old Volvo, but he would not be hurried. Moving into second gear, he added, 'I mean, really getting on.'

Louise looked up from the Royal Worcester teapot on her lap – the rest of that Sunday morning's car boot sale pickings were in the back of the car, but not this dear little teapot. Despite the small crack in the lid, it was a beauty, a real find. Stroking the spout, she said absentmindedly, 'How do you mean?'

Neville knew his wife wasn't listening. Louise's mind was on, around and inside that piece of china on her lap. Funny that something as small and insignificant as a piece of china should arouse such passion within his wife. Nothing else seemed to.

With him, of course, it was his gooseberries. Now that really was something to get excited about. The endless search to produce the ultimate berry, to nurse it through those first precious days of its infancy, watching it grow, until that exciting, poignant moment when it was time to pick it and give it up to be judged. Rather like children really – nurturing and sheltering them and then giving them up to life. Which reminded him: Charlotte.

'I was just wondering whether we should be doing more for her.' What he really wanted to say, but couldn't, was how inadequate he felt, how helpless he thought himself to be in matters of personal grief. He had been a GP all his working life, had coped admirably with gall bladders, chicken pox, herpes, chest infections and piles, but when it had come to Mrs Jenkins having a breakdown because Mr Jenkins had left her, or when he had had to tell Mr Forbes that his pretty young wife was dying of ovarian cancer, he had been useless, and he'd known it.

For no good reason that he could think of, he was convinced that Charlotte was hiding something. Whether it was from him specifically, or from everyone, he was not sure. Which was why he was now probing his wife. Had Charlotte discussed with her mother something she couldn't possibly tell him? He doubted this. He and Charlotte had always been so close.

'Look out!' Louise's voice crashed unexpectedly into his thoughts. He saw the brake lights of the car in front and pushed down hard on the brake pedal. The Volvo performed a splendid emergency stop, jerking Louise forward in her seat so that her nose almost tipped the glove compartment.

'I don't know what's the matter with you these days,' she said, straightening herself up, at the same time checking her precious teapot. 'You're so . . .'

Neville knew what she was going to say.

' . . . slow!' she said vehemently.

In response, he gripped the steering wheel tighter, his arms at a perfect ten-to-two position. 'You haven't answered my question,' he said holding back the desire to say, and you're so vague these days, you don't listen to a word I say.

'I don't know why you keep harping on about Charlotte. She's old enough to look after herself.'

He indicated to overtake a crawling refuse van, then pulled out. 'Don't you think that's being a little harsh? It was her husband who died, not a family pet. It was hardly an everyday occurrence for her.'

Louise glanced at the driver of the refuse van as they drew level. He gave her a crude wink. She looked away. 'For goodness' sake, Neville, can't you hurry up? And yes, I am well aware of the fact that it was Peter who died and not some nibbling hamster, but this is something Charlotte has got to sort out for herself.'

Neville pushed down hard on the accelerator, imagining for one delicious moment that Louise's cherished little teapot was under the pedal. A smile cracked his face and he pushed down harder. Speeding down the A34 towards Hulme Welford, he made up his mind to ignore his wife. He would go and see Charlotte and get her to talk to him. He would go tomorrow, when Louise was busy at the shop.

Chapter Eighteen

She was gulping the wine down, much too fast, she always did when she was nervous. But why was she nervous? Alex was the least intimidating man she had ever met.

They had started their meal sitting on Alex's patio, then when the May sun had proved too hot, they had retreated to Charlotte's favourite spot in the garden, to the welcome cool shade offered by the drooping branches of the fig tree. Each having eaten two helpings of spaghetti carbonara mopped up with chunks of garlic bread, they were now sitting back in their chairs, enjoying the feeling that only a pleasantly satisfied stomach can bring. Alex reached out for a grape from the Tuscan pottery bowl on the table between them.

Charlotte tried not to watch him, but she couldn't help it. His hands fascinated her, which was probably one of the reasons why she was drinking too much. Before the spoon incident at the jumble sale she hadn't given Alex's hands a second glance; now they seemed to be constantly on her mind. She shuddered involuntarily and looked down at Mabel at her feet. She lifted the little dog up on to her lap so that she had something to occupy her own hands.

'Are you cold? We could move back into the sun if you want?'

'Sorry? Oh I see, no, no I'm not cold, not at all.'

He smiled. 'Do you want to carry on that conversation now?'

Throughout the meal, they hadn't said a word about what Alex had said to her after church. It hadn't been a matter of skirting round the issue, it just hadn't cropped up. They had talked about all sorts of things: of Alex's love of small silver knick-knacks – hence the spoon; and the game that he and his brother played – who can find the most disgusting birthday present for the other – hence the tearful boy. And then he had told her about the book on trees he had bought.

'Did you know that the name rowan is believed to be derived from the Norse word *runa*?'

'Heavens, is it really?' she had said playfully, pretending to yawn.

'It means charm,' he carried on undeterred. 'Apparently rowan trees were planted outside churchyards and houses to ward off witches.'

Then she had seen the twinkle in his eye.

'I only mention it because I notice there's one at the end of your drive. With a bit of luck it should keep Mrs Braithwaite off your doorstep.'

She had laughed at that and at herself for momentarily accusing Alex of being dull.

But the issue had now been raised. What was she going to do, or say? What on earth had made her think that she could talk to Alex about her failing marriage? Why him? Why not Hilary? Why not her parents? Was it because Alex had never known Peter and she thought he would not sit in judgement of her?

'I . . . I'm not sure, to be honest,' she said. 'I don't think I can. I thought I could, but now I can't.'

He looked at her with a steady gaze, then turned away. 'You have a lovely garden. In London it was something I always wanted.'

'That's stupid,' she said, grateful for the reprieve. 'Why didn't you just buy a house with a garden?'

He leaned back in his chair and glanced up at the drooping wisteria that covered the back of Ivy Cottage. 'Sometimes,' he said slowly, 'dreams are better than reality.' He picked at another grape. 'And anyway, the reality at the time was that I didn't have a free moment to indulge my fantasy. Work was the number one priority then.'

'Peter was like that. He would never admit it though.'

'Most men don't realise they're doing it. It's like falling in love, you don't mean to do it, it just happens. But it must be hard for a wife to accept.'

'It is, or rather, it was,' Charlotte said thoughtfully. 'But somehow you come to terms with the fact that you're no longer your husband's *numero uno*. It hurts though, and there's always a danger that . . .' But her voice trailed away. Should she tell him? Would he understand? Would he understand that eventually being second on the list makes you hate yourself and hate those around you, especially the one you once loved. 'But is work still your number one priority?' she asked, turning the conversation away from herself.

He laughed and rolled a grape between his thumb and forefinger. She wished he wouldn't do that. No she didn't. She wished he'd keep on doing it.

'I think that my very sitting here in my landlady's garden, drinking cheap supermarket Hungarian wine, proves that it isn't that important to me any longer. My eighty-hour weeks have long since gone, but then so has my company car, along with my smart address.'

'So you don't think Acacia Lane is grand enough for you?'

He laughed again and once more stretched forward to

pluck a grape. Charlotte watched him carefully remove its small stalk and she shuddered again.

'Come on,' he said, getting to his feet. 'Let's get you back in the sun, you're obviously freezing.'

She tried hard not to laugh, and putting Mabel down on to the grass, she got up and started gathering up the lunch things. 'I've kept my side of the bargain,' she said, 'now it's your turn. The mower's that way.'

'Coo-ee, only me, all right if I come in?' Hilary appeared through the open conservatory door. Stepping into the kitchen, she joined Charlotte at the sink. 'I'm selling tickets for the fork supper next Saturday. I was supposed to be selling them after church this morning, only I couldn't because I wasn't there. I had to take Philip to an away match in Macclesfield – he scored the winning goal. He's really very good, you should come and see him play some time.' She put down her bundle of supper tickets and envelope of money, looked for a tea towel and automatically started drying the plates Charlotte had just washed. 'You've missed a bit,' she said, slipping one of the plates back into the soapy water. 'So, where was I?'

'Selling tickets for the fork supper, I think,' Charlotte said, smiling to herself.

'Oh yes. Well, I've just been trying next door,' she nodded her head towards the kitchen wall that backed on to Alex's part of the house, 'but there was no answer, so I thought that maybe Alex was here with you.'

'Did you now?' Charlotte fixed her attention on the pan she was rinsing under the hot tap.

'This tea towel isn't very clean. Have you got another?'

'In the drawer over there.'

Hilary began rummaging through the chaotically filled drawer. 'Charlotte . . .' she said, but got no further as she was interrupted by the sound of a powerful lawnmower starting up. She joined her sister and looked out of the window. 'It's Alex,' Charlotte said unnecessarily, as a lawnmower appeared from behind the potting shed followed by Alex, stripped to the waist and now wearing shorts.

'I can see that,' Hilary said pressing herself hard up against the sink. 'Just look at him.'

'Hilary!'

Hilary slapped a hand over her mouth, as though to prevent any other impure thoughts from slipping out. 'I didn't mean, I only . . .'

Charlotte laughed. 'I know exactly what you mean and I happen to agree with you.'

'You do?' Hilary said, her hopes rising. Her sister was falling for Alex after all. Smiling to herself she stared out of the window as Alex pushed the mower towards the bottom of the garden. 'He's well tanned, isn't he?'

Charlotte tilted her head to one side as though looking at Alex's naked back from a better angle. 'Mm . . . I suppose he is.'

'Looks good in shorts.' Hilary decided to push the point home. 'Good-looking altogether, wouldn't you say?'

Charlotte was about to respond when Alex reached the far end of the garden, turned the mower round and looked straight up at them. He waved nonchalantly.

They acknowledged him, then moved away from the window. 'Put the kettle on, shall I?' Hilary said, awkwardly.

They sat with their drinks at the table, Hilary just managing to keep one eye on the garden, but Charlotte with her back to it. 'It's a long time since we did any serious ogling, isn't it?' Hilary said.

Charlotte made no response. Hilary decided to be

brave. 'You are allowed to, you know . . . just because you're a widow, it doesn't mean you're no longer a woman. You're going to have to try and remember what it was like in the old days, before Peter.'

Charlotte reflected on this, taking a sip of her tea. Pre-Peter. In those days Hilary had accused her of having a lascivious nature, but that was only because Hilary had been so taken up with David.

Hilary sensed Charlotte wasn't going to say anything more on the subject. She picked up her bundle of tickets. 'You'll come, won't you?'

Charlotte shook her head. 'I don't think so.'

'Why ever not?' Hilary's disappointment was obvious. She had been so sure that she could lure Charlotte and Alex together for the evening at the village hall.

Charlotte banged her mug down. Splashes of tea spilled over the table. 'I know exactly what you were thinking. One ticket to Alex and one to Charlotte. Do you really think I'm that naïve?'

Charlotte could feel her face colouring, her skin prickling with irrational hot rage. Suddenly she wanted to cry, to cry great sobs of . . . she didn't know what. Yes she did. Remorse. Guilt! It was there all the time, baiting her day and night. It had been there when she and Alex had had lunch together. A perfectly innocent lunch, but all the time she had felt it was wrong, wrong to have enjoyed Alex's company. And damn it, she had. She liked being with him. He was nice, amusing, attentive, and what's more she found him attractive. And now here was Hilary egging her on even further. Well, it wouldn't do. She would have to put a stop to it, here and now. It was time for her to take control. There would be no more 'Alex and Charlotte' because then there would be no more guilt . . . and no more dreams.

Common sense told her it was too soon. No woman in her right mind would let herself get caught up in another relationship only months after the death of her husband. It was madness. It was disrespectful. Yes. That was it. There had to be a decent period of mourning to be honoured. It was her duty. She may have failed Peter in marriage but she could at least do the right thing in death. She owed him that much. She almost sighed with relief, knowing she had hit upon infallible justification for not getting involved with Alex Hamilton. She had found the right weapon with which to fight off any temptation he offered.

Hilary peered over the top of her mug. She said quietly, 'You could always come on your own.'

'I know that,' Charlotte said calmly. 'Or I could bring a friend with me.'

Hilary looked crestfallen. 'You could.' She decided to force her sister's hand. 'So that's two tickets, then.' She peeled off two orange cards from her bundle. 'That'll be five pounds.'

Charlotte went in search of her bag and wondered at what she had just done. Who on earth could she ask to go with her? She walked back into the kitchen and handed over a five pound note.

'So who are you going to bring?' Hilary said, putting her things together but not daring to look Charlotte in the eye.

For a split second Charlotte hated her sister. 'You'll just have to wait and see.'

Hilary had the grace not to push her sister any more. She headed for the door. 'Tell Alex I'll catch him later, will you? Bye for now.' She left.

Charlotte looked out of the window. Alex was halfway through the lawn now, deep in concentration. He had the look of a man completely at peace with himself.

Charlotte envied him.

Alex switched the engine off and pushed the mower into the potting shed. He noticed Charlotte standing at the kitchen window again. He noticed too the way she instantly turned away the moment she realised he had seen her.

He bent down to the mower and started to clean off some of the stuck-on bits of grass. But his thoughts remained on Charlotte. There were times when he felt sure that there was something she wanted to tell him – maybe not him specifically, just someone. There were other times though when she treated him as if he were Jack the Ripper.

He smiled to himself as he thought of Lucy's words, spoken to him so often: *Alex, I do believe you're a frustrated agony aunt, always trying to sort out other people's problems.*

'There's no need, you know.'

Charlotte was silhouetted in the doorway and Alex knew from the stilted tone of her voice that he had once again taken on the guise of Jack the Ripper.

'I can clean it myself,' she said.

He stood up. Sidestepping the mower, he moved towards her. 'It's no problem,' he said. What had suddenly happened between lunch and now? What had caused her to change? Was it something he had said? 'Perhaps I could become your full-time gardener,' he quipped. 'I could move in here, into the potting shed.'

'And I could be your Lady Chatterley, I suppose.' Her words were heavy with sarcasm.

They stood in silence, each staring at the other, until Charlotte could bear it no more. She felt overwhelmed by the heady earthiness of the stifling shed, together with the sweet smell of fresh grass cuttings and petrol. She stepped back towards the sunshine and fresh air. As she moved Alex picked up his T-shirt which was hanging on the hook on the door. 'I'm sorry I upset you,' he said. 'It was only a joke.'

Charlotte wanted to apologise, but she knew she mustn't. She knew too that standing as she was, barely inches away from Alex and the warmth of his glistening body, she wanted very much to pretend she was Constance Chatterley. She swallowed hard and tried to cling to her objective. 'I've a message for you from Hilary,' she said.

His face was unreadable.

'It's about the fork supper at the village hall next Saturday. Hilary wondered if you'd be wanting a ticket. Of course she realises that you've probably got better things to do on a Saturday night.' She forced herself to add a casual laugh.

Alex managed a laugh as well. 'What, and have Mrs Braithwaite commenting on my absence? No fear. You can tell Hilary I'll have a ticket. In fact, you can tell her I'll have two. I suppose it's okay for me to take a friend along?'

'The more the merrier,' Charlotte said, surprised. 'Actually, I'm taking someone as well.'

Throwing his T-shirt over his shoulder, Alex turned and walked away.

Damn! thought Charlotte, watching him stroll across the lawn. What on earth was she going to do now? Not only was Hilary expecting her to turn up with a man, but Alex was also bringing a partner. Hell!

Chapter Nineteen

What was happening to her? She never had sugar in her coffee. It was Peter who had sugar.

She had dreamt of him again last night. This time he was lying in a hospital bed, not in a normal ward but in a room that had been made into an office: a fax machine in one corner, an array of potted plants in another, a desk in the middle with Peter's attaché case, and Peter himself, lying on a bed beneath his faithful laptop computer. All this she was seeing through a glass window as she was trying to make an appointment to see her husband. But the attractive nurse was telling her that Mr Lawrence was too busy to see her right now, and could she come back later? 'But he'll be dead later,' she had screamed at the nurse. Then two policemen had led her away, saying they wanted to question her about the death of her husband.

Was she cracking up? Charlotte shook her head. Getting up from the table, she tipped her coffee – Peter's coffee – down the sink. She heard the sound of the letterbox being pushed open and went through to the hall.

She made herself another drink, and taking the letters upstairs to read she found Mabel curled up on the bed. The first letter was from her solicitor, something about investments Peter had made. She put this back in its envelope. The next was a handwritten letter with a Brussels postmark. She knew straight away who it was from. Christina Castelli.

Scanning through the first page Charlotte was not surprised by the lack of 'hope you're settling in' platitudes – that was definitely not Christina's style. Instead it was a full account of a fat German industrialist and an Irish diplomat who had spent an entire evening singing in Gaelic to her. At the bottom of the second page was '. . . and so, Carlotta, I have booked a flight to Manchester and shall come to stay with you next month.' The letter went on to explain the exact date and time that Christina would be arriving, along with '. . . no need to meet me, I shall arrange for a taxi and arrive in time for cocktails.'

Charlotte laughed out loud. 'Cocktails!' she said. 'In Acacia Lane, just imagine.' She laughed again and tried to imagine Christina here in Hulme Welford: Christina and Iris Braithwaite . . . Christina and Derek Rogers! Lying back on the pillow, she reread the letter, squeezing it for more contact with her friend. Her thoughts were interrupted by the shrill ring of the telephone at the side of the bed. She picked up the receiver. 'Hello.'

'Charlotte?'

'Yes.' Her brain automatically ran through a list of possible male callers she might get at eight o'clock in the morning.

'It's me, Jonathan.'

'Jonathan!'

'I'm over in England on Friday, business, Birmingham, okay if I buzz up to see you, Saturday, about lunchtime, a bed for the night wouldn't go amiss?'

Yes, it was Jonathan all right, he always did speak like a telegram. 'Yes of course, I'll look forward to it,' she lied.

'Okay, see you.' The phone clicked and Charlotte was left with a droning sound in her ears and a stupefied expression on her face. She put the receiver down and nudged Mabel. 'So, we're to have the pleasure of Jonathan's company, how fortunate we are. Jonathan, King Kong of Hong Kong. Bet you'll dislike Peter's brother as much as I do.'

In eight years of marriage, Charlotte had only met her brother-in-law on a handful of occasions. The first time was by coincidence, at a party in London, not long after she and Peter had met. At the time she had no idea Peter had a brother, and coming out of their hostess's kitchen with two glasses of wine she had found Peter in the hall, admiring a large painting. Handing him his glass, she had kissed him lightly on the cheek, only to realise he was not Peter, and have it confirmed by the look of wonder on the man's face. Embarrassed, she had simply stood and stared, completely taken aback by the extraordinary likeness between this man and Peter. Peter had then appeared and he too, for a moment, had simply stood and stared.

'Surprise!' the man had said, taking a large mouthful of wine from the glass Charlotte had just given him.

'Another one of your passing-through visits, is it?' Peter said coldly.

'Needs must, when the devil drives. Aren't you going to introduce me?'

Peter turned to face Charlotte, his eyes narrow and dark. 'This is Jonathan, and as you've no doubt worked out for yourself, he's my brother.'

Driving home in the car afterwards, Peter had barely said a word, his tight-lipped expression telling Charlotte all she needed to know – that despite the striking resemblance there was no love between the two brothers.

Another occasion when they had met was in Singapore. It was then that Charlotte began to get a clearer picture of the intense rivalry between the two men. Jonathan was the elder brother by four years and neither of the two seemed able to forget this. 'As older brother, I insist on taking you two out for dinner,' Jonathan had said, when he arrived at their apartment, having just flown in from Hong Kong, where he lived and worked lucrative deals of gigantic proportions.

'I've already booked us a restaurant,' Peter had said, 'where the manager knows me personally.'

And so the evening had continued, with each brother trying to outdo the other, oblivious to Charlotte.

Now, after all these years, Jonathan wanted to come and see her. Why? Was it so that he could have one last shot at Peter – 'You see, little brother, I've got more staying power than you.'

The thought suddenly occurred to Charlotte that she could make good use of Jonathan while he was here.

It was just after twelve o'clock when the door bell rang and Mabel started to bark.

'Hello.' Neville Archer was standing on the doorstep. He bent down to stroke the little dog. 'Have you got time to see your old dad?'

'Come in,' Charlotte said, kissing his cheek.

He peered into rooms as he walked through to the kitchen. He could see that his daughter had got things more or less straight since Monday when he had helped her with the unpacking. A few pictures were hanging on the walls now, though there were still some propped up on the floor against the wall. Perhaps he should offer to help Charlotte put them up, or would she think he was interfering?

'How about some lunch? I haven't been out to the shops yet but I've got the remains of a bit of Cambazola and some crackers.'

He nodded and sat down at the table. 'Don't tell your

mother. I haven't been allowed Cambazola for six months – too many calories.'

They laughed conspiratorially. Neville felt reassured. She was still his ally after all. He waited until Charlotte had sat down with him at the table before embarking on what he had to say. 'Charlotte,' he helped himself to some cheese, 'I know you could tell me to mind my own business, or you could of course throw me out, or simply lie, but just how are you really feeling? I know I'm not much good at this kind of thing, as I'm sure your mother would be the first to agree . . .'

'Has Mother sent you here?' Charlotte wondered at her father's words which had come out like a well-prepared speech.

'No. As a matter of fact, she thinks I've gone to see Ron Wicklow about the gooseberry show.'

'You lied to Mother. Why?'

Neville shrugged. He felt like a small boy caught with apples in his pockets. 'I . . . I was worried about you and wanted to know . . .'

'Oh Dad.' She reached out and touched his arm, finding comfort in the feel of his old tweed jacket – he had always dressed like a country doctor and still did. With a sudden surge of emotion she remembered vividly waiting outside his surgery, as a child, listening to two elderly women discussing her father: 'He's such a dear man, I'd love to take him home and put him on the mantelpiece.'

'I've been worried about you,' Neville pressed on. 'Losing Peter like that, so suddenly, must have been awful. I just want you to know that I'm here if you need me.'

She felt tears welling up, but she battled against them and passed him the plate of crackers. 'We've always been close, haven't we?'

He nodded his head. They were on uncharted territory now and he didn't trust himself to speak.

'We've always sort of known what the other was thinking.'

Again he nodded.

'At the moment though, you couldn't possibly guess what's going on inside my head . . . I wouldn't want you to.'

Still he said nothing, convinced now that there was something his daughter was holding back. If he waited long enough she'd talk to him, it would all come out.

'Do you want some more cheese?' she said, pushing the plate towards him.

He shook his head.

'You see, it's not as everyone thinks. Everyone thinks that I . . .' She got up from the table and started fiddling with the kettle.

It was no good. He couldn't take it any longer. He had to say something. 'Charlotte . . .' But he got no further because the telephone rang. Was that relief he saw on his daughter's face as she went out to the hall to answer it?

He watched Charlotte through the open door as she picked up the receiver. 'Hello Mum,' she said. He shook his head and then pretended to hold a gun to his temple. Charlotte tried hard not to smile. 'What, here, you think Dad's here?' She put her hand over the mouthpiece of the receiver and whispered, 'Ron Wicklow's just been on the phone asking for you.'

'Oh heavens,' groaned Neville.

Charlotte packed her father off to meet his fate, cleared up the lunch things and went outside. She collected a few tools and the wheelbarrow from the potting shed, and headed off towards the bottom of the garden.

The flower beds had not been tended in a long while; the death of Mrs Clifford senior must have put the garden very low on the list of priorities for the Clifford family. Death was like that. Or was it? Another person might have absorbed themselves into a regime of digging, weeding and pruning, worked all hours so as not to think of their loss. Perhaps that was what she should do. Throw herself into something, so that she didn't have time to keep blaming herself, would not keep feeling the need to confess. She had almost told her father, had been so close to telling him everything. She dug deep and vigorously into the heavy clay soil. 'Ashes to ashes, dust to dust,' she suddenly said out loud.

Alex put the phone down and made some hurried notes on the pad on his desk – a company over in Knutsford wanted to update their current stock control system.

He looked out of the window. At the bottom of the garden he could see Charlotte with a fully loaded wheelbarrow. Immediately he was working out what excuse he could use to go and talk to her. He smiled to himself. He was off again.

He went through to his small kitchen and put the kettle on. He would take her a cup of tea.

He made his way down the garden and stood some twelve feet away from where Charlotte was digging. She was talking to herself. No, not talking, it was more like a chant: 'Ashes to ashes, dust to dust,' she was repeating over and over again. He stood still, not knowing what to do. It was obvious she had no idea he was there. He felt like an intruder, and was about to step slowly backwards when from behind him came the sound of yapping. Mabel was scuttling across the lawn.

Charlotte turned round sharply. 'How long have you

been there?' Her faced flushed and he noticed a long smudge of earth across her right cheek. He wanted very much to wipe it away for her.

'Thought you'd like a tea break,' he said, ignoring her question.

'Oh, thank you.' She dropped the spade and pulled off her gardening gloves. 'I was miles away, I didn't hear you coming. Have you been working?' Her words were rushed in a conspicuous attempt to overcome her embarrassment. He handed her the mug.

'Yes,' he said, thankful that for the time being he didn't seem to be Jack the Ripper. 'I think I've just gained a new client, over at Knutsford. How long do you think it will take me to get there?'

'Not long,' she said, flicking her hair out of her eyes. 'About thirty minutes. Parking can be a devil though. I should give yourself an extra ten minutes to be on the safe side.'

Glad to be able to talk to her, Alex carried on. 'So what's Knutsford like?'

'Nice, but very twee. Black and white like Hulme Welford, except more upmarket. They've got Mrs Gaskell while all we've got is Iris Braithwaite.'

He laughed.

Charlotte drained her mug and handed it back to him. 'Thank you, I enjoyed that.' He noticed her looking over his shoulder. 'It looks like one of us has a visitor,' she said.

Alex turned and saw Barry Rogers coming towards them.

'Congratulations!' he said. 'I hear you passed your driving test on Wednesday. Well done.'

Barry pushed at his glasses. 'I think I was just lucky.'

'Nonsense,' said Charlotte. 'No such thing as luck.'

'I hope there is. I had my first physics exam this

morning.' He pushed his hair back, which like his glasses slipped straight back to its familiar place.

Charlotte groaned. 'How did it go?'

Barry smiled, which had the effect of altering his earnest face completely. 'It was okay actually, easier than I thought it might be.'

'Good for you,' Alex said. 'What else are you doing?'

'Chemistry starts tomorrow, next comes biology and then economics. They're spread out over three and a half weeks.'

Charlotte groaned again. 'You poor boy. But what brings you here? You've not come to me for private tuition I hope?'

As suddenly as the smile had appeared so it vanished. Barry looked awkwardly at them both.

Alex could see how tense he was, and thinking it might be to do with the Charlotte and Derek incident, he said, 'I'll be off then.'

'No, no, don't do that.'

Again a nudge of the glasses and a hand pushing fruitlessly at his hair. 'I'd like to speak to both of you, if that's all right.'

'Sounds ominous,' Charlotte said, leading them towards the chairs which she now kept permanently by the fig tree. 'It hasn't got anything to do with your parents, has it?' she added cautiously.

'No, certainly not, well, not directly anyway. I suppose I should apologise for what I said to you in church that morning. I don't normally go around . . .'

'I'm sure I'd have done the same if I'd been in your shoes.'

'Well,' said Alex, setting the empty mugs down on the table, 'how can we help you?'

'It's a bit difficult.' Barry squeezed his large frame into

one of the flimsy chairs. 'I'm not sure where to start, and please don't say at the beginning.'

'I'm tired of clichés myself,' Charlotte smiled. 'Carry on, just as you want.' Her words were warm and sincere and Alex realised that here was the real Charlotte, relaxed and eager to help. Barry posed no threat to her. It was he himself who somehow caused her to smell danger. Why?

'You see, it's true, isn't it?' Barry was saying. 'Most people at some stage in their lives feel something, experience something, that they know will change their lives for ever.' He turned his earnest face up at them both, seeking confirmation of this statement.

Alex nodded and Charlotte leaned forward in her chair, as though willing Barry on.

'Well, I guess I've just reached that point in my life and I'm not sure what to do about it.'

Alex rubbed his chin thoughtfully and for a split second Charlotte's attention was drawn away from Barry and was absorbed in Alex's hands.

'So what you're saying,' Alex said, causing Charlotte to concentrate again, 'is that something has happened to you recently, something that has changed your understanding of your life?'

'Yes, that's exactly it.' Barry looked visibly relieved. 'I felt sure you'd understand. That's why I came to you.'

Charlotte thought about this for a moment. What was it about Alex that had this effect on people? What made people want to confide in him? First her, now Barry. She couldn't understand it, nor this conversation. What were they talking about? Was it a girl? Had Barry fallen in love? She took her courage in both hands. 'So what's her name?'

At first Barry looked confused, then he smiled, again a smile which transformed his serious teenage face into that of a dazzling young man. 'I think, Mrs Lawrence,' he said politely, at the same time making Charlotte feel like Old Mother Hubbard, 'that perhaps I've misled you.'

'Oh,' said Charlotte, 'but I thought . . .' And then another idea came into her head. 'Oh,' she said again, 'you mean it's a . . .'

Alex cut in swiftly. 'I think Barry should spell it out for us.' He looked at Barry and smiled encouragingly.

Chapter Twenty

Barry felt better for having talked it through with someone else. Now all he had to do was tell his parents.

It certainly wasn't going to be easy. Bewilderment would come first with his father, then it would be ridicule. Tiffany would be okay. She'd tease him for a while and then get bored with it all. His mother he wasn't so sure about. It was difficult at times to know what she thought.

He could hear his parents down in the kitchen, not talking to one another, just moving about. He decided the time was right, breathed in deeply, got up from his desk and went downstairs.

They started supper in silence. Tiffany's chair was typically empty. Without her, Barry didn't want to say anything. But the longer he waited the more he could feel his nerve going. Perhaps he could tell them tomorrow, after his chemistry exam? He ran his hand nervously through his hair. 'I had my first physics exam this morning,' he said.

His mother looked up from her plate of salad. 'Oh, I'm sorry, I forgot all about that.' She looked genuinely pained at this parental oversight. 'How did it go?'

'Cost of the fees at that school, he'd better have done all right,' his father said, reaching for the jar of mayonnaise. 'Only joking, Bas. How was it?'

'Okay, I think. I was lucky, I'd revised the right bits.'

'You're late,' Cindy said, looking over Barry's shoulder as Tiffany sauntered into the kitchen.

Still cyclamen pink, Tiffany ignored her mother and pulled a face at the sight of the salad on her plate. She sat down and smiled at Barry. 'So, how was it?'

'If you'd been here when you were supposed to be,' Cindy snapped, 'you would have heard.'

Still ignoring her mother, Tiffany said, 'Tell me later, Barry.'

'Actually,' Barry said carefully, putting his knife and fork down on his plate, 'I've got something I want to tell you all.'

His father viewed him speculatively and then a broad smile covered his face, and, brandishing a large radish on the end of his fork, he said, 'You sly old devil, you've gone and got yourself a girl, haven't you? I told you that car would do the trick.'

'Give it a rest, Dad,' Tiffany said. 'Let Barry speak.'

'Watch your step, young lady. You're not so—'

'Look,' Barry interrupted, raising his voice slightly, 'this is hard enough for me to say without you lot arguing as well.'

Cindy looked up sharply. 'Hard enough?' she repeated. 'Why, what have you done?'

'Oh my God,' Derek said slowly looking at his son across the table. 'You've gone and got a girl pregnant, haven't you? All that crap about not being interested in girls and studying like mad was just to fool us. Bloody hell! I'd have expected even you to know about safe sex.'

'What, like you?' Cindy's voice was as brittle as the look she gave her husband.

Barry got up from the table, scraping his chair noisily on the tiled floor. A silence followed as everyone looked up at him. 'Look, Dad,' he said, 'this has absolutely nothing whatsoever to do with a girl.' He had their attention now and so pushed on, trying to gain confidence through momentum. 'I've recently discovered something about myself that I feel I need to share with you, something that may surprise you.' He paused as he sought the right words.

His father threw down his knife and fork on the table. He too stood up and looked Barry straight in the eye. 'Well, you can pack your bags now. You can bugger off somewhere else, anywhere, so long as I don't have to set eyes on you.'

Three pairs of eyes stared at Derek in astonishment. 'Not only,' he said, looking at his wife and then back at Barry, 'not only is he a stuffed Henry, but he's a bloody great screaming poofter.' He turned away from them all. 'I need a beer,' he said, reaching for the fridge.

Cindy's eyes filled with tears as she pushed her plate away and bent her head down over the table. Tiffany got to her feet and stepped towards Barry. She put her arm around him. 'If he goes,' she said dramatically, 'so do I.'

'Good!' shouted Derek, slamming the fridge door shut and yanking at the ring pull on his can of beer. 'Good bloody riddance to the pair of you.'

'But Dad . . .' It was Barry, his voice strangely calm and assured.

'Don't "but Dad" me anything,' Derek rounded on him. 'You've betrayed us all. You filthy . . . homosexual!' He almost spat out the last word.

'But Dad, I'm not a homosexual.'

'Not a homosexual? Then what do you call yourself, got some other bloody fancy name for it, have you?'

'My sexuality doesn't come into this at all,' Barry said.

'Then what the hell does?'

'God does.'

'God!' shouted Derek. 'And just what is that supposed to mean?'

'It means I've become a Christian.'

Frothy bubbles spurted across the kitchen floor as Derek choked on his beer. 'A what?' he gasped.

Barry was fully in control of himself now. 'A Christian, Dad. You know, someone who believes in Jesus Christ as his personal saviour.'

Derek suddenly looked very pale and dazed as he slumped back heavily against the worktop, speechless.

'Muffin 'ell, Barry,' said Tiffany, 'that really has shut Dad up.'

'Perhaps we could all sit down again,' Barry said quietly, aware how drawn his mother looked as she sat completely motionless at the table. Dutifully his father and sister sat down. Feeling better than he had for weeks, Barry picked up his knife and fork and said, 'Anybody want to say anything?'

'So, um . . .' Derek said at last, 'so what exactly does this mean – orange dresses and tambourines?'

Barry laughed and nudged his glasses on his nose. 'Dad, I'm not about to create a Fort Waco here in Acacia Lane.' His words were light, almost flippant, in an attempt to lighten the mood around the table.

'But you haven't been confirmed or anything,' Tiffany said.

'I know. More importantly, I haven't even been baptised.'

'I wanted you both baptised,' Cindy said, her first words in more than ten minutes. 'I wanted you both baptised when you were babies.'

'Only because you wanted a new dress and a party out of it,' Derek fired at her, tossing back the last of his beer.

'I did not!'

'Well, I think it's brilliant,' Tiffany said, sensing a row about to start up again. 'At least now we might get some much needed morality in this house.' She fixed her eyes on her father.

For the first time in his life, Barry saw his father flinch.

By eight o'clock they had finished their meal, which, on reflection, Barry thought, must have seemed like an eternity for his parents, sitting there as though the Archbishop of Canterbury had just dropped in. They both seemed relieved when he said he was going out for a short while.

Barry knocked on Alex's door.

'How bad was it?' Alex led him through to the small uncluttered sitting-room.

'I'm amazed you didn't hear all the shouting. Poor Dad, he thought I was trying to tell him that I was gay.'

'Oh Lord,' Alex said. 'But then, parents have such a tough time of it. I suppose it's only natural they jump to the wrong conclusions, which are usually their worst fears.'

'I hadn't thought of it like that, but you're right. To Dad, sexuality is all.'

'So, what happens next?'

'I go home and get myself ready for my chemistry exam tomorrow morning.'

Chapter Twenty-One

'Left you nicely, didn't he?'

Charlotte swallowed hard, not for the first time in the two hours since her brother-in-law had turned up, driving an over-sized hired Mercedes and carrying his Ralph Lauren garment bag and matching leather briefcase.

She looked across the sitting-room at Jonathan in his expensive, crisp suit, his long legs sticking out from the sofa, and felt repelled by his air of being entirely at ease, wherever he was. But what had really taken her by surprise was the shock of being with such a tangible reminder of Peter. She hadn't prepared herself for that, hadn't thought how disturbing it could feel to be face to face with a man who looked so similar to her dead husband. Even the way Jonathan picked minuscule specks of fluff off his jacket sleeve put her in mind of Peter.

'Lucky old you.'

Charlotte looked up at Jonathan. 'Lucky old me,' she repeated. 'How's that exactly?'

Jonathan crossed his legs. 'All that money Peter must have left you.'

Charlotte got up from her chair, trying to keep a rein on her anger. How typical, how bloody typical that Jonathan should show no sign of missing his own brother, but only show a keen interest in how well off Peter had left his widow. And why? Why the hell should Jonathan care about how much money she had, when he himself had bank accounts scattered far and wide? Did he feel cheated? She breathed in deeply, determined to stay calm. She had to keep Jonathan sweet until tomorrow morning, then she could tell him what she really thought of him. If she blew it now, she would lose her 'date' for the evening down at the village hall.

'Nice place you've got yourself, Charlotte. An expensive but worthwhile investment, I shouldn't wonder.'

She nodded. How dare he! How dare he talk to her like this. What right did he have to make these assumptions? Or was she angry because it was almost as though Jonathan knew the truth: that Peter's death had left her better off – in all ways. She looked out of the window trying to take her mind off this dreadful man sitting a few feet away from her. 'I can't dispute that Peter has left me comfortably off, so I suppose, as you say, I am indeed lucky.' She turned to face Jonathan once more. 'But you know, there's more to life than how much money is involved. Wasn't it John Ruskin who said "The only wealth is life itself"?'

He smiled, like a weasel. 'Helps though.'

Charlotte pushed her nails hard into the palm of her hand. 'Coffee?'

'Black, no sugar.'

She escaped to the kitchen and vented her anger by rattling mugs and spoons until she realised that she was no longer alone. Jonathan was standing in the doorway. He came towards her. She suddenly felt uncomfortable.

'You'll soon marry again of course, won't you?' he said.

She could feel his hot breath on her neck and moving away from him she wondered at this statement. The very idea was preposterous. Why would she want to replace one man with another, who in the end would probably do exactly as Peter had done – turn her into second best. No. The answer was no. She would not marry again.

She looked out of the window and saw Alex walk across the lawn in front of his part of the house. He was carrying a glass of beer in one hand and a book in the other. She watched him settle himself down on the grass. Why wasn't that man ever at work? she thought angrily to herself. She turned round sharply to face Jonathan.

'No, I have no intention of remarrying,' she said, smiling sweetly up at him. 'Just in case that was a proposal from you, Jonathan.'

Derek switched off the lights in the salon. It had been a busy Saturday and they had finished late, leaving him no time for a session in the gym and a sauna before going out for the evening. A village hall jamboree was far from his idea of a good night out, but it would do no harm for the business for him and Cindy to be seen socially in the village. And of course, there was always the prospect that Charlotte would be there.

He hadn't seen Charlotte since that farce of a jumble sale last Saturday and what with the ridiculous number of problems at the Wilmslow and Altrincham salons, he hadn't had any free time during the week to slip next door. What really bothered him, though, was that her tenant might be doing more than his fair share of '*slipping next door*'.

Going up the stairs in the main part of the house, Derek could hear Tiffany's hi-fi playing loudly in her bedroom – The Doors, yet more revival music. A spark of annoyance flickered within him as he stood and listened to 'Come on Baby Light my Fire'. He hated nostalgia. It served no purpose other than to remind him he was getting older.

He moved further along the landing and paused outside

Bas's room. Silence. Probably down on his knees, Derek thought caustically. Immediately he regretted this thought. He didn't know why, but he did, and that disturbed him. He never regretted anything. He remained standing outside his son's room, half tempted to go in. But what would he say? What could he say? He shook his head. Just what was happening to his family? He didn't understand any of it. Tiffany running around like a liquorice allsort and now Bas turning into some bloody kind of monk! Brother Bas! He shook his head again, it was all beyond him. Religion was for weirdos, for those cranks and loonies too weak to get through life without some kind of mental crutch. So where did Bas fit in?

'Hello Dad.'

Derek started and turned round to see Barry standing behind him. 'Bas,' he said, feeling unaccountably pleased to see his son, all six foot two of him and looking anything but a crank or a loony. 'I thought you were in your room.'

'No, I've been down at the village hall helping to get things ready for tonight. I went to see Malcolm Jackson earlier and he kind of roped me in.'

Derek looked uneasy.

'I went to see him about being baptised. He said he could do a service later in the summer.'

'I see,' was all Derek could think to say. He could sense that his son had something else to tell him. He watched him push his glasses up on to the bridge of his nose.

'Dad, I'd like you and Mum to be there, Tiffany too.'

Derek gaped. 'Oh no, I don't think . . . I mean, we can't . . . not Tiffany, not the way she looks.'

'Dad, it really doesn't matter what she looks like. But you don't have to come if you don't want to. I . . . I don't want to embarrass you. I understand.'

Derek looked at his son. All at once he felt like the biggest shit that had ever walked the earth. Unable to meet his son's gaze, he pushed his hands deep into his pockets and looked down at his shoes. At last he raised his head. 'Okay, if you want us there, we'll be there. But you'll look a right prat in a christening gown. I'll buy you a decent suit.'

'Thanks, Dad, that's great.'

They stood facing each other, suddenly not knowing what else to say, with the noise of thumping music invading the silence between them.

The moment was broken by the sound of a door opening followed by Tiffany. 'You look dead serious,' she shouted above the music. 'Been arguing again?'

Derek and Barry exchanged looks and both laughed.

'What's got into you two?' Tiffany said.

Inexplicably, Derek felt an unfamiliar rush of warmth run through him for his children. Wondering where Cindy had got to, he said, 'Where's your mother?'

'She was having a lie down earlier, said she had a headache,' Tiffany answered.

'Well, you can turn that bloody din off then,' Derek said. 'How do you expect her to rest with all that noise going on?'

Baffled, Barry and Tiffany looked at each other. Consideration – from their father?

'Oh Lord, where have I put it?'

'Put what?' David asked Hilary, as she pushed past him like an express train.

'The key,' Hilary shouted. 'The key for the hall, for tonight.'

David always knew when his wife was panicking. She seemed to grow six inches taller and her nostrils flared imperceptibly. Experience had taught him that in these situations there was usually very little he could do. Years ago he had been stupid enough to think that it was his job to take control of the situation, but now he knew better. He stood back patiently watching, while Hilary gave the oak chest of drawers on her side of the bed a ruthless body search.

'I had it earlier when I came back after setting up all the tables,' she said.

David cleared his throat and decided to risk it. 'What did you have on this afternoon?'

'Oh don't be so stupid, David. Of course I've already thought of that. I'm not that daft.' She let out a cry of frustration as she slumped down on to the bed, sitting heavily on the dress she had just spent ten minutes ironing. 'I was so looking forward to tonight,' she moaned. 'I thought for once I had it all carefully organised: the tickets, the food, the drinks. Everything. And now I've gone and lost the wretched key and no one will be able to get into the hall. What *will* everyone think of me?'

David took a cautious step towards the bed. 'Can't we borrow Brown Owl's key?'

Hilary sniffed dismissively. 'No. She's gone rambling in the Peak District this weekend.' She reached for a tissue and blew her nose. 'I've got exactly one hour to find this key,' she said, determination rising in her voice, 'and find it I will.'

Knowing there was nothing he could say or do, David sat down on the small boudoir chair in the corner of the bedroom, at the same time being careful to move to one side Hilary's jeans. He remembered having seen her wearing them earlier. Wouldn't do any harm to check, he thought. Fumbling furtively so as not to alert Hilary that he had doubted her, he searched all the pockets. To his relief he touched cold metal, but there was something with it, something lacy. 'Hilary,' he said, 'what's this?'

'For goodness' sake, David, don't bother me now,' she replied tersely, rushing past him and heading full tilt for the en suite bathroom.

He followed her in and closed the door behind him. 'I've got something for you.' He held up a large key and waved it in front of her.

'David, you wonderful man! Where was it?'

'Your jeans.'

She looked puzzled, at the same time seeming to shrink back to her normal size. 'But I checked the pockets,' she said, 'truly I did.'

'The back pockets?'

She shook her head and reached out for the key. But David snapped his hand away. 'Not so fast.' With his other hand he dangled something red and lacy in front of her. 'What's this, darling?' he said. 'Something you've been hiding from me?'

Flushing as red as the G-string in David's hands, Hilary blurted out, 'It's not mine. I found it at the jumble sale. Derek Rogers wanted it and I wouldn't let him.'

David laughed. 'Well that wasn't very sporting of you, was it?'

'You don't understand.' She was flustered. 'Iris told me to get rid of it and I forgot and somehow it ended up on the table with all the other clothes and I . . .'

David looked at his wife. 'Ah, and there was I thinking you'd got me something special.' He pulled Hilary to him and kissed her, leaving her in no doubt what was in his mind.

'The children,' she said.

'They're watching the telly.'

'We haven't got long . . . Tiffany will be . . .'

He kissed her again. 'I'm claiming my reward for finding the key.'

Chapter Twenty-Two

For the third time in five minutes, Charlotte looked at the broken lock on the bathroom door. Jonathan was taking a shower in the guest bathroom, but there was something about the way her brother-in-law had been acting during the day that had seriously unnerved her. In the eight years she had been married to Peter, Jonathan had never once paid her the slightest bit of attention; now suddenly he seemed overly attentive.

Sitting in the bath, she wished fervently that she was one of those glamorous women you see on television who always have froth-filled baths, so that if a surprise guest just happens to drop in only a pair of perfectly tanned shoulders peep seductively above the bubbles. As it was, her own stark, white nakedness was all too apparent in the clear bathwater.

She lay back and tried to relax, wondering how to control the events of an evening that seemed to stretch dauntingly ahead of her. She had finally dared to ask Jonathan – while sitting out in the garden – if he would mind taking her to the fork supper. From the look on his face, at first she thought he was going to turn her down. Then he had smiled and said, 'How quaint. What time?'

Resting one foot on the hot tap, Charlotte considered her objective for the evening: to throw her sister off the scent and to convince Alex she was in no need of his attentions. To this end, she would have to achieve the impossible – to appear thoroughly at ease with Jonathan at the supper and to remain at his side throughout the entire evening. Tonight, she had to be seen as a woman who needed no outside help in re-establishing her life.

She closed her eyes and doused her face with the strawberry-shaped sponge. She shook the water off her face and tried harder to relax. Smiling was supposed to be helpful here. It struck her that it might be a good idea to practise thinking of Jonathan and smiling at the same time – after all, she would have to do plenty of that at the village hall this evening. She parted her lips and grinned inanely. She caught sight of herself at the end of the bath in the reflection of one of the shiny chrome taps. The distorted convex image made her smile more naturally. She covered the tap with her foot and thought how tonight she was going to prove to herself that she could handle not only Jonathan, but all the rest of them who seemed so intent on organising her life. She breathed out deeply, having convinced herself that all would be well.

Then all hell broke loose.

'God dammit, what the bloody hell's been going on here? I leave my room for ten minutes . . .'

Charlotte sat up at the sound of Jonathan's angry voice on the landing. She heard barking followed by a sound that had her springing out of the bath and reaching for a towel. It was Mabel, yelping.

She threw open the bathroom door. There was Jonathan, a towel around his waist, holding up in one hand a mangy-looking tie, and in the other hand Mabel, grasped firmly by the scruff of her neck, eyes bulging, teeth bared.

Charlotte acted without thinking. She kicked Jonathan in the shin, twice, and then she reached out for the little dog. Hugging the whimpering animal to her, she pushed past Jonathan and slammed her bedroom door shut. Only then, as she sat down on the bed to look at Mabel, did she realise that her towel had gone.

'Now remember, Neville, avoid all the dishes with mayonnaise.'

'Yes dear.'

'Did you remember to lock the back door?'

'Yes.'

'I hope Malcolm doesn't make a long speech like he did last year. I seem to remember hearing your stomach rumbling throughout most of it. Just look at that.' Her hands full of quiches, Louise nodded towards David's Volvo. 'You'd think they'd have walked, wouldn't you? Did I tell you that Hilary said Charlotte would be coming tonight? Apparently she's bringing a friend. I wonder who. I mean, she doesn't really know anyone here, does she? Neville, are you listening to me?'

'What?'

'Oh never mind. But remember what I said about the mayonnaise.'

'Mrs Parker, the music is far too loud, turn it down. If I've told you once, I've told you a hundred times, my shattered nerves just won't take that kind of volume.'

'But I don't know how to, Mrs Braithwaite. There are so many switches and dials.'

'Well, don't just stand there in the way. Let me through.'

Easing herself out of the small boxed-in area that contained Malcolm Jackson's state-of-the-art CD player and amplifier, Hilary escaped to the safety of the kitchen at the back of the hall. Within seconds the sound of Mantovani – Iris's own personal choice – was blaring through the hall. Then there was nothing, just an awkward silence, leaving people stuck mid-air in unfinished sentences.

'Mrs Braithwaite, allow me,' said a worried Malcolm Jackson moving swiftly across the wooden floor to ensure that no further harm came to his most prized possession. 'This knob here, the one marked volume, you have to make sure that the needles are both synchronised, that way you avoid overloading the . . .'

'Quite so, I'm sure, Vicar. But I can't stand around here all evening discussing synchronised needles. I have work to do in the kitchen.'

Malcolm sighed with relief and moved off to greet more of his parishioners at the door. 'Ah, Louise and Neville, good to see you.'

'Hello Malcolm,' Louise said. 'Excuse me if I don't hang around. I must get these quiches on the tables.'

'Evening Malcolm,' Neville said as the two men shook hands. 'Anything I can do?'

'That's kind, but I think everything's under control now. Between your daughter and Mrs Braithwaite, we all seem to be more or less whipped into shape.'

'That's our Hilary for you.' Neville moved off to get himself a drink. He could see his son-in-law behind the drinks table, acting as barman. He joined the queue. 'Need any help?' he called out above the rumblings of conversation ahead of him.

'No thanks,' David called back. 'I think I can manage.'

Eventually it was Neville's turn.

'What can I get you? I've got red wine, white wine, some dreadful non-alcohol stuff, lager, beer, orange juice, Seven-Up, or mineral water?'

'I'll have some red wine, please. Are you sure I can't help you?'

David smiled. 'No, that's all right. You go off and enjoy yourself.'

Seeing the queue of people waiting behind him to be served, Neville paid for his drink and wandered away. He stood beneath a curling photograph of the Queen and tried hard not to allow his sense of isolation overwhelm him. He was no good in a large gathering such as this, unable to march in step with the rest of the parade. He looked at his watch and wondered where Charlotte was.

Alex and his guest entered the hall and were greeted by Malcolm Jackson. 'Ah, I see you've brought some liquid refreshment. Put it on the table at the back there where David Parker looks like he's being mobbed.'

Pushing through the crowd of villagers, most of whom he had never seen before, Alex guided his guest through to the bar. 'David,' he said, 'these bottles any use to you?'

'Hello Alex. Yes, they'll do nicely, thanks.' David took the two bottles of white wine from Alex and added them to his stockpile. 'Hilary mentioned you might be coming,' he said. 'And with a friend.'

David's eager eyes rested predictably on his guest's face, so Alex made the necessary introductions. 'David, this is Heather; Heather, this is David, one of my neighbours and my landlady's brother-in-law.'

'You're not from around here, are you?' David said. 'I'm sure I would have remembered you if I'd seen you before.'

Alex smiled to himself at this hackneyed line which David had delivered with true conviction. For indisputably it was true. With her young, willowy figure, powder-blue eyes and curly blonde hair, Heather fitted neatly into that category of female that was all things to most men. He had met her only a few days ago in Knutsford, where she worked as a receptionist at the company which had approached him earlier in the week about some consultancy work. While handing in his visitor's badge on his way out of the building he'd asked her out for lunch. They had eaten in a crowded wine bar in King Street and he had let her do most of the talking, while he sat and questioned his motives for being there at all. He had never once used a girl before and yet here he was doing exactly that. And all because of Charlotte.

When he had told Charlotte he would be taking a friend to the fork supper he had said it as a knee-jerk reaction to her sudden change in mood towards him. That evening, though, he had regretted his words. But following their conversation in the garden with Barry later that week when he had seen how relaxed she was in somebody else's company, the thought had occurred to him that if he backed off she might feel more comfortable in his presence. He had reasoned that if he was to take someone else to the supper, there was a chance he would still be able to enjoy Charlotte's company without causing her to feel threatened in any way. The one question in all of this he hadn't asked himself was why he was prepared to go to such lengths to be with Charlotte.

By the end of the meal his plan was fixed. 'A fork supper,' Heather had repeated. 'I've never been to one of those. What should I wear?'

'Casual,' he had answered, feeling almost sorry for her. A nightclub in Manchester was probably more what she was used to.

'What can I get you?' David asked Heather.

'I'd love a 20-20.'

'Ah,' David said, looking at his supply of bottles. He didn't have a clue what he'd just been asked for. 'Try again.'

'Malibu and Coke?'

'How about a glass of white wine?'

'And a beer for me please.' Alex looked around him. So this was a village hall fork supper. He'd never been to such an event before. It was busier than he had imagined it would be, with people appearing to enjoy themselves – more than he thought might be the case. He tried to pick out a few familiar faces. There was Hilary over by the kitchen hatch looking flushed and agitated; Louise Archer chatting to a middle-aged woman whom he didn't know; Ted the Toup being told in no uncertain terms by Iris Braithwaite not to smoke and Neville Archer standing on his own looking up at a gaudy photograph of the Queen. 'Come on,' Alex said, taking their drinks from David and leading Heather by the arm. 'Let me introduce you to my landlady's father.'

They inched their way through the crowd. 'Hello Neville.'

He swung round. 'Good to see you again, Alex.'

'This is Heather.' Alex hesitated before adding, 'A friend.' They shook hands. 'No sign of Charlotte, then?' Alex said lightly, looking up at the Queen.

'No. And to be honest, I could do with her here. I'm not much good in these situations. Never know what to say to people. I find it difficult to make small talk with those I've seen without their clothes on.'

Alex laughed. Seeing the look of surprise on Heather's face, he said, 'Neville's a doctor.'

'*Was* a doctor,' Neville corrected him. 'Now I'm just a . . .'

'Just a what?' It was Louise, with a handful of peanuts.

'Nothing, dear,' Neville said, looking longingly at the nuts.

Louise turned to Alex. 'How are you, Alex? I hear you've taken up gardening.'

'Are you ready, Jonathan? It's time we were going.'

The question, called through the guest-room door, sounded ludicrous. But Charlotte could think of nothing else to say to this man for whom she cared so little and whom she had just physically assaulted, not to mention cavorted naked in front of.

The door opened and she offered a smile. 'Look, Jonathan . . .' she started to say.

'Thirty-six pounds, that tie,' he said.

She breathed in deeply. 'I can write you out a cheque if you like, or perhaps you would prefer cash?'

He ignored her and turned back into the bedroom.

He reached for the jacket which completed his dark navy Yves Saint Laurent suit. He looked at himself in the full-length wardrobe mirror before stooping to pick up a towel from the floor. He handed it to her. 'Yours, I believe?'

She coloured and took it from him. 'Thank you.'

His garment bag lay packed on top of the bed. He picked it up. 'A hotel for the night is the best thing.'

'No,' she said, 'don't do that.'

He looked at her closely.

'There's no need, Jonathan,' she said, and biting back every instinct within her, she added, 'I'm sorry, I shouldn't have kicked you like that. I don't know what came over me.'

He continued to stare at her in silence, as though assessing her, and then suddenly his face broke into that familiar weasel-like smile. With a patronising shake of his head he said, 'God, Charlotte, you're going to need a man in your life again, and soon.'

She didn't trust herself to say anything to this preposterous remark, so she turned away and moved towards the stairs. 'We'd better go,' she said. And with each step she took, she prayed, Please God, just get me through this evening.

It was still light as they walked the short distance to the village hall, Jonathan being careful just where he placed his expensive shoes. They were silent until they had almost reached the hall, when Charlotte, conscious that Jonathan looked dressed more for dinner at the Ritz than a village beanfeast, said, 'You'll find it all terribly simple, Jonathan, not at all what you're used to.'

He said nothing.

She laughed brightly and slipped her arm through his. He looked taken aback. Her public performance had begun.

Inside the hall, Charlotte saw Alex straight away, and knew too that he had seen her. Automatically she smiled up at Jonathan. 'Come on,' she said, 'I need to . . . I mean . . . I want to introduce you to someone.'

For a moment, the two couples stood facing each other, like four advancing pawns on a chess board. 'Hello Charlotte,' Alex said. She nodded back at him and placed her hand on Jonathan's arm. 'I'd like you to meet Jonathan. He's stopping the weekend with me.' Was it her imagination, or did she detect a slight lift of the eyebrow?

'Hello,' Alex said, taking in the contrast between his own jeans and plaid shirt and the immaculate suit in front of him.

'And you are?' Jonathan enquired.

Alex couldn't help himself. 'Alex Hamilton. I live with Charlotte.' He felt Heather stiffen at his side, saw the horrified expression on Charlotte's face, but most of all, the look of surprise on her companion's.

Charlotte laughed, a little too loudly. 'What Mr

Hamilton is trying to say is that he's my temporary tenant in the granny annexe.' She emphasised the word 'temporary' and threw Alex a wait-till-I-get-you-home look.

'But you can't be his landlady?'

Charlotte looked at Heather, twenty-two at the most, she reckoned, and with a waist to match. 'Why ever not?' she asked.

Heather looked at Alex accusingly. 'You told me your landlady was bad-tempered and rude. I was expecting someone much older.'

Alex felt Charlotte's eyes blazing at him. He laughed awkwardly. 'No, no, that was Iris Braithwaite I was describing.'

'So,' said Jonathan, obviously bored with the conversation, 'what are you in?'

That did it. Now Alex knew for certain that he didn't like this so-called friend of Charlotte's. 'The village hall actually,' he replied. 'Can I get you and Charlotte a drink?' Alex noticed Charlotte biting her lower lip. Was that a slight smile she was trying to hold back?

'I'll get them,' Charlotte said. 'White wine do you?'

'A well-chilled Chardonnay would be out of the question, I suppose?'

Alex tried not to laugh and followed quickly behind Charlotte as she moved off to the bar. 'I'll give you a hand,' he said.

'There's no need,' she hissed back at him. 'I can manage.'

'Of course you can,' Alex said, as they joined the queue. 'I know that. Who's your friend?'

She smiled. 'Oh, we go way back.'

Alex pushed his hands into his pockets. 'Nice suit he's got on.'

'And what's that supposed to mean?'

'Nothing, nothing at all,' he said innocently. 'Nice suit in the right place, that is.'

'As a matter of fact he's just flown in from Hong Kong and that's all he had with him.'

'Oh,' Alex said, nodding his head in an exaggerated fashion, 'that explains it.'

'So what time do you have to get your little friend home?'

'*Touché.*'

They took the glasses of wine back to where they had been standing, only to find that both Jonathan and Heather had disappeared. 'Ah well,' Alex said, 'that just leaves you and me.'

'So it does.' Charlotte looked anxiously round the hall for Jonathan.

'And what was all that about me being a temporary tenant?' Alex said.

'Well, you are. You'll be wanting to buy your own house soon, won't you?'

Alex frowned. That of course had been the original plan, but now he wasn't so sure.

'And how dare you describe me as being bad-tempered.'

'And rude,' he added helpfully.

'I've a good mind to evict you.'

'Hello you two.' It was Hilary. 'Having a good time? Don't tell me your dates have stood you up, then?'

Charlotte glared at her sister.

'We seem to have lost them,' Alex said. 'They're here somewhere.'

'What do they look like? I might have seen them.'

'His,' Charlotte said, 'looks as though she ought to be home in bed by now.'

'And hers looks like he's lost his briefcase.'

'Oh well,' Hilary said brightly, not really listening, 'I'm

sure they'll pop up. We're just about to serve the food, but whatever you do, don't touch Iris's lentil dip. I was on the loo for days after it last year. Oh look, Derek and Cindy at last.'

Following behind Cindy was Derek, pushing an ostentatious hostess trolley. 'Coming through,' Derek yelled, scattering people in his wake as he steered the trolley at full speed through the crowded hall.

'I'd better go and see what they've brought,' Hilary said. 'It looks a lot, whatever it is.'

Left alone again, Alex said, 'Your father was looking for you earlier. He's a nice man. I like him.'

Charlotte smiled. 'I'm still going to evict you though.'

'Come on, let's get some food. I'm starving. You can serve me notice while I'm eating.'

'I think, everybody,' Malcolm Jackson shouted, turning the music down, at the same time halting the raised cutlery over the bowls of rice salads and quiches, 'that we should now take this opportunity to bow our heads and give thanks . . .'

From nowhere, a loud scream filled the obediently drawn silence. Alex saw Hilary slump against Louise, who in turn gasped loudly. Wide-eyed and staring, both women looked as though they had been turned to stone. He followed their gaze and found himself looking at Charlotte's friend Jonathan, standing next to Heather.

'Damn!'

He turned to Charlotte at his side.

'Damn,' she said again.

'For goodness' sake Charlotte, why on earth didn't you tell us?'

'Yes, Mother's right, why didn't you?' Hilary said, as they stood in the hall kitchen. 'He's family, after all.'

Charlotte bristled. 'No, he's not. None of you know him, and anyway, you wouldn't want to know him, he's a pig.'

'Charlotte!' Hilary remonstrated with predictable horror. 'He's Peter's brother.'

Charlotte pursed her lips.

'Well,' said Neville, feeling he ought to contribute to the conversation in some way. 'He's certainly the spitting image of Peter, isn't he?'

Hilary shook her head. 'I couldn't believe it when I saw him. I was so convinced it was Peter . . . a ghost . . .' Her voice trailed away. 'I feel a bit of a fool now.'

'Seeing as we've all recovered from the shock,' said Louise, 'I suggest we all go out there and at least introduce ourselves to Peter's brother.' She threw Charlotte one more reproving look and led the way, followed by Hilary, then Neville and finally Charlotte, who dragged disconsolately behind. Her plan had misfired because she had failed to take into account the simple fact that anyone who had known Peter would be struck by Jonathan's likeness. But she hadn't thought that anyone would go so far as to think he was Peter's ghost. Silly Hilary. And how typical of her to jump to such a ridiculous conclusion.

She chewed unhappily on her lower lip, knowing she had made rather an idiot of herself. How on earth had she thought she could get away with such a half-baked scheme? Convincing Alex that Jonathan was an old flame from way back was one thing, but thinking she could fool her family was another.

In the main part of the hall the other party-goers seemed to have forgotten about the commotion. Frank Sinatra had replaced Mantovani and the general ambience indicated that everyone was having a jolly good time.

'Suddenly I don't feel hungry,' Charlotte said despondently to her father.

'Come on, you'd better try something. Tell me which dishes have got mayonnaise in them. I want to try them all.'

Over at the bar, David was pouring out a glass of wine for Derek.

'You mean Charlotte's husband looked just like that jerk in the suit?'

David tried not to smile as he handed Derek his drink. 'Pretty much like him. But how about the blonde piece? She came with Alex, but seems to have abandoned him now.'

Derek laughed. He looked about the hall, trying to track down Alex. He found him eventually, balancing a plate of rice and an empty glass in one hand and a fork in the other, listening attentively to Iris Braithwaite. 'Looks like our Alex prefers older birds,' Derek said. He took a gulp of his wine. 'That's disgusting,' he shuddered, 'like gnat's pee. What the hell is it?'

David looked at the bottle. 'I'm sorry. I've given you the non-alcoholic wine by mistake. Iris Braithwaite insisted we have some, says alcohol is the way to hell.'

'Well, don't just stand there, give me a one-way ticket,' he said. 'No, on second thoughts, make that two tickets to hell.' And taking the glasses from David, he sauntered in the direction of Alex and Iris Braithwaite.

'Evening, Mrs Braithwaite,' he said sidling up to her. He nodded to Alex. 'Thought you'd like a drink.' He handed her a glass. 'I must say, this non-alcoholic wine is very good. I could become quite an addict.'

Alex looked at Derek, wondering if he'd heard right.

'I'm pleased to hear that,' Iris said. 'Alcohol is the way to—'

'Hell,' Derek finished for her. 'That's so true, Mrs Braithwaite.'

Again, Alex wondered if he'd heard correctly. 'Well, if you'll excuse me, I'll just go and help myself to some more food.'

'Try some of my lentil dip. There's lots left,' Iris said after him. She raised her glass and drank from it. She winced, drawing in her lips like a cat's bottom.

'Quite dry, isn't it?' Derek said smiling. 'It's an acquired taste.'

Helping himself to a slice of spinach quiche, Alex found himself standing next to Cindy. 'Hello,' he said. 'I've just left Derek extolling the merits of alcohol-free wine to Iris Braithwaite.'

She looked at him as though he were mad. 'I doubt that somehow.'

'I should go easy on that lentil dip,' he said. 'Hilary told me earlier it has rather a lethal effect the next day. How's Barry?'

'Barry? He's fine, why?'

'I was thinking about his exams. He seems a bright lad, he should do well. I expect you'll miss him when he goes off to university?'

Cindy picked up a stuffed tomato which she added to her sparsely filled plate. 'I suppose I will. Though to be honest with you, even when he's at home, we hardly ever see him. Just shuts himself away in his room mostly.'

Moving away from the tables of food, they located a couple of chairs and sat down. Over on the other side of the hall, Alex could see Derek at the bar again. He watched with interest as Derek carried two full glasses of wine in Mrs Braithwaite's direction. He turned back to face Cindy and was surprised to see her with her hand over her mouth. Her eyes were watering. 'Lentil dip?' he asked.

At about half past ten, when Charlotte was helping her sister to make sixty-two cups of coffee, she realised that something was wrong. Iris Braithwaite had a distinct pink edge to her. An election-winning Margaret Thatcher sprang to mind as Charlotte watched Iris bobbing about the hall, talking animatedly to everyone as though they had just returned her to high office. Even her handbag was swinging from her arm *à la* Maggie. Charlotte decided to go and investigate.

Armed with a cup of coffee, she caught up with Iris as she laid a hand on Alex's shoulder. 'Mrs Braithwaite, cup of coffee?'

Iris spun round at the sound of Charlotte's voice. 'Certainly not,' she announced. 'I want some more of that delicious alcohol-free wine that nice Mr Rogers has been giving me. Kindly fetch me some while I talk to your lovely young man.'

Charlotte took a discreet sniff at Iris's powdered face. She looked at Alex and mouthed the incongruous words, 'I think she's drunk.'

Alex thought fast. 'There's none left, Mrs Braithwaite,' he said.

'What!' shrieked Iris, causing those around to look at them. Alex and Charlotte moved closer to Iris, trying to shield her from view.

But Iris was having none of it. 'I want a drink,' she said like a determined four-year-old. 'Where's Mr Rogers?' And turning away from them, she hurried off to look for Derek. Charlotte and Alex saw her track him down by Malcolm Jackson's hi-fi, sorting through the selection of CDs and cassettes. He seemed alarmed at her approaching figure and quickly moved away.

'Oh, oh, you naughty man,' giggled Iris, increasing her step. 'Running away from me, are you?'

Derek looked genuinely horrified and sped off. Then disaster struck. Iris, in her haste to catch up with Derek, tripped over an electricity cable running from the hi-fi to the main power socket. She reached out to hold on to something secure, only to plunge the hall into complete darkness by pulling the fuse box off the wall.

Amongst the general crashing about that followed – the screams of mock horror, the giggling, the sonorous tones of the vicar requesting everyone to remain calm and one ridiculous voice calling out 'Let there be light' – there was one very loud crash, accompanied by an even louder cry and an expression that was quite out of place at a church fund-raising event.

Neville, who had been hiding out in the kitchen at the time of the black-out, managed to find a box of candles and some matches on a shelf above the coffee urn. It wasn't long before a procession of candle bearers, somewhat akin to acolytes, miraculously emerged from the kitchen and streamed out into the main body of the hall. And a voice, presumably the same one that had said 'Let there be light', called out, 'And then there was light.'

The air of wreckage everywhere was surprising. Chairs had been knocked over, along with one of the tables that had been heavily laden with rice salads. In the flickering candlelight, the floor looked as though it was covered with a thousand stunned maggots. A ripped curtain, complete with track, lay in a bedraggled heap on the floor.

'I think I've broken something!' came a cry from the semi-darkness. Recognising her husband's voice, Cindy carefully made her way over to Derek, lying sprawled out on his side. She bent towards him, then stood up again. 'What's that all over your back, Derek?'

'I think it's dog crap!' he shouted, wincing with pain. 'I bloody well slipped on it.'

Somebody laughed. 'I think you'll find that's Mrs Braithwaite's lentil dip.'

Chapter Twenty-Three

'Start spreading the news, I'm leaving today . . .'

'Please, Mrs Braithwaite, be quiet, someone will hear you,' Charlotte pleaded with the older woman who was held firmly between Alex and herself as they slowly made their way, in the dark, from the village hall towards Acacia Lane.

But Iris was not to be put off. ' . . . I want to be a part of it, New York, New York . . .'

'Come on, Mrs Braithwaite,' coaxed Alex, 'we're taking you home.'

Iris beamed back at him, and then kissing him on the cheek continued with ' . . . These vagabond shoes are longing to stray right through the very heart of it, New York, New York . . .'

Charlotte started to laugh. Iris at that moment slipped away from Charlotte's grip and swung round to face Alex, and staring him in the eye she sang at him, her deep contralto voice wobbling just slightly off key, her pronunciation, though, surprisingly clear for one so drunk, ' . . . I want to wake up in a city that doesn't sleep and find I'm king of the hills, top of the heap . . .' And in a moment of inspiration, Alex threw his arms round Iris and started to tango with her, skilfully edging her towards The White Cottage.

Charlotte followed behind as best she could. Tears were rolling down her cheeks, she was helpless with laughter. 'I don't think I can take much more of this,' she groaned, bent double and with her legs crossed. 'I think I'm going to wet myself.'

'Well, before you do, see if you can find her key,' Alex called over his shoulder as they approached Iris's gate. 'It's probably in her handbag.'

Charlotte reached forward but Iris pushed open the gate and, dragging Alex behind her as though *she* were leading the way home, she marched him up the path. She rummaged in her handbag and pulled out her door key. She snapped the bag shut and promptly pushed the key through the letter box. She turned and looked at them both, her eyes wide with surprise. 'The keyhole's grown,' she said, and rocking from side to side as if on a tilting ship, she sang out, '. . . I'll make a brand new start of it in old New York and if I can make it there I can make it anywhere . . .'

'Now what do we do?' Charlotte said. 'Break a window?'

'Certainly not, Mrs Lawrence,' said Iris sharply, breaking off from her singing, 'not when there's a perfectly good key hidden in the back garden.'

'Come on,' Alex said 'let's go a-hunting.'

Iris was off again. 'A-hunting we shall go, a-hunting we shall go . . .' she sang as she led the way, almost breaking into a jaunty little skip as she cornered the house.

'Mind my pelargoniums, Mr Hamilton, I believe you're perry close to them, I mean, peril, peril, perilously close to them. Who's that hiding in the dark?'

'It's me, Mrs Braithwaite, Charlotte Lawrence.'

'Well, what on earth are you doing in my herb garden at this time of night?

'Mrs Braithwaite,' Alex interceded patiently, 'can you find the key?'

'Well of course I can, young man, but you'll have to close your eyes while I get it, and you, Mrs Lawrence, you too.'

Amazingly Iris not only found the key, but managed to insert it into the lock and open the back door. They stepped into the kitchen, Alex fumbling blindly for a light switch. He found it at last and steered Iris towards the hall. Charlotte said, 'I'll get her up to bed, you make her some coffee.'

'I'd better find her a bucket, or something,' Alex said. 'She's likely to be as sick as a dog at some stage in the night.'

'Did somebody mention my dog? Where is Henry?'

Alex and Charlotte looked at each other. It was a good question. Where was Iris's spaniel? Surely he should have barked the house down by now with all the din they had just been making outside in the garden.

'Come on, Henry,' Iris cooed, 'come to Mummy.'

'Get her upstairs,' Alex said. 'I'll look for him.'

'Let's look upstairs for Henry, shall we, Mrs Braithwaite?' Charlotte said, taking her by the hand. 'I expect he's waiting for you up there.'

Iris looked pleased. 'Henry,' she called out with each stumbling step, 'Henry, Mummy's coming.'

Alex found Henry in the sitting-room, curled up in his basket. He knew straight away that the dog wasn't asleep. He was dead.

'Oh my darling Henry,' wailed Iris. 'He was my only real friend, the only one who truly loved me . . . even Sidney didn't really love me. Poor little Henry, he was only eleven years old, he should have lived until he was at least fourteen. Why has he died?' Her grief was enormous, she was inconsolable.

'I wish Henry hadn't chosen tonight to snuff it,' Charlotte whispered downstairs in the kitchen, when they had at last got Iris off to bed. 'For just a few moments Iris seemed . . . well, sort of happier than I've ever seen her. It seems like a particularly cheap and nasty trick on God's part, don't you think?'

Alex shook his head. 'I'll dig a hole in the garden tomorrow for him. I suppose that's what she'll want.'

'Alex?' Charlotte suddenly said. 'Why are we here?'

'What, you mean planet earth and all that?'

'No. I mean, why did *we* get Iris out of the village hall and bring her home?'

'You mean why didn't we just abandon her to the public humiliation that everyone thinks she probably deserves?'

'Yes, that exactly.'

'Because we're nice people, I suppose.'

'Are we?'

Alex laughed. 'Charlotte, I'm too tired for this, go home. I'll stay on here in case Mrs Braithwaite is ill in the night.'

Charlotte looked hard at Alex. 'What is it with you and vomiting women?' she said. 'Anyway, shouldn't you go and see what's happened to your little bit of moorland Heather?'

He laughed again. 'I don't think I'll bother. I expect she's being well looked after by your . . . by Jonathan . . . do you mind?'

Charlotte shook her head. 'No.' She decided to come clean. 'I guess you got the gist of all that fuss earlier in the evening, didn't you?'

'That Jonathan is Peter's brother? Yes, I did. Does he look very much like Peter?'

'The first time I met him, I thought he was Peter.'

'But that must be so . . .' he paused, making sure he used the right word, 'difficult for you.' He knew from experience how painful it was to be physically reminded of someone you'd loved and lost.

Charlotte picked up the mugs on the green Formica-topped table and carried them to the sink. 'I didn't think it would be, but you're right. It was quite a shock seeing him coming up the drive this morning.' She rinsed the mugs out, and then turning round, she found Alex standing behind her. Only that afternoon, Jonathan had been standing behind her in much the same way, and only a couple of weeks ago, so had Derek.

She looked up into Alex's face. Blue eyes. She hadn't noticed their colour before, nor that there was a small white scar just below his left eyebrow. His lips were parted and she felt he was about to say something. Her heart began to beat faster.

'Charlotte—'

'No, please don't say anything.' And with the slightest of movements she leaned towards him, knowing what it would mean, knowing also it was what she wanted. He reached out to her and the touch of his fingers against her cheek made her turn and kiss his hand. He kissed her and she held him tightly, frightened he might stop, thinking only how much she wanted him.

But from upstairs came an unmistakable sound.

'Another time perhaps,' Alex said calmly, looking into her eyes and tracing the outline of her cheek with his hand.

Charlotte swayed slightly. She felt anything but calm. She swallowed back her disappointment and followed Alex out of the kitchen.

It was three o'clock in the morning when they finally

settled Iris Braithwaite. They collapsed on the sofa in the sitting-room – Henry and his basket having been moved to the dining-room as his makeshift chapel of rest.

Charlotte said, 'You know, I don't understand how all this happened. How on earth did Iris end up drunk? She never drinks alcohol.'

'I think you'll find that Derek had a lot to do with it,' Alex said, yawning and putting his arm around Charlotte.

She kicked off her shoes, tucked her feet under her and snuggled up to him. 'How stupid I've been. Of course, that's what Iris said, didn't she? She wanted some more of that lovely non-alcoholic wine Mr Rogers had been giving her. Poor Iris. She's lost her dignity, her reputation and her little Henry all in one night.'

She looked up at Alex. His eyes were closed. She didn't know whether she was feeling lightheaded from being so tired or was still reeling from the shock of what she had instigated in the kitchen, but she was aware of an added frisson of pleasure and expectancy running through her. 'Alex?'

'Yes.'

'What would have happened in the kitchen, if Iris hadn't . . . ?'

He opened his eyes. 'You mean, would I have made love to you there and then on the kitchen table?'

'I didn't mean . . . well yes, okay then, is that what you would have done?'

'No, Charlotte. I wouldn't have made love to you.'

She sat up straight. 'Why?' She felt affronted. 'Why not? she repeated.

'Come on, Charlotte, it's late. Can't we talk about this tomorrow?'

'No. I want an answer. Would you now, for instance?'

He looked at her, confused. 'Am I dreaming this conversation, or have I missed a huge chunk of it?'

She moved away from him and went and sat in one of the armchairs. 'It seems Iris is not the only one to have made a fool of herself tonight.'

Chapter Twenty-Four

Derek lay awake in the strange bed. The injection he'd been given had wiped out the excruciating pain, but not his anger and the humiliation he had felt lying on the village hall floor. He shuddered at the memory of all that revolting muck he had lain in – nobody was ever going to convince him that it was something edible he had slipped on. Thank God there had been a 'doctor in the house'. Neville Archer had never struck him as a particularly competent man before, but he had certainly shown his mettle, clearing away all those gawping onlookers and sending someone off to call for an ambulance.

A broken leg was his reward for showing up at the village hall jamboree, but that wasn't all – that fool of an ambulance man had ripped his trousers! Eighty quid those trousers had cost him last month. Fine bloody evening it had turned out to be and not even a moment of it spent with Charlotte. And where was she when he was lying on the floor in agony? Bloody scarpered with that Alex, that's where. He'd seen them leaving together.

And now here he was alone, three-thirty in the morning and surrounded by stale bodies in striped flannelette. Thank heavens he'd had the presence of mind to make Cindy pick up a pair of decent boxer shorts on the way to the hospital. He eased himself upright and craned his neck forward to see if any of the nurses were about. Ah yes.

There she was, sitting at her illuminated desk, the pretty young blonde one, Nurse Wilkins, who earlier had helped him into bed. She was bent over a book with her hands around a mug in front of her.

Derek pressed the green button just above his plastic jug of water. 'Nurse,' he called out. Hurried squeaking steps sounded out across the thick linoleum floor.

'Yes, Mr Rogers, what is it?'

'Hello,' he said brightly, as though she were a wine bar waitress coming to take his order.

'Ssh . . . you'll wake the others. Now what's the matter?' Though young and recently qualified, Nurse Wilkins was already astute enough to know what her newest patient was up to.

'Come and sit here,' Derek said, patting the side of his bed, 'and I'll tell you.'

Nurse Wilkins smiled and turned to go, but Derek let out a loud groan, which had her instantly bending over him, giving him a closer inspection.

'That's better,' he said. 'Come and talk to me, I'm lonely.'

'It's very late, Mr Rogers, you should get some sleep.'

A smile spread across Derek's face. 'I can't. I'm not used to sleeping on my own.'

'Somehow that doesn't surprise me,' Nurse Wilkins said, contemplating her healthy-looking patient, with his bare tanned chest and roving eyes.

'So, now that I've thoroughly captivated you, tell me your name. Mine's Derek.'

'It's Rosemary and I really should be getting back to my desk now.'

Satisfied that he had made a sufficient enough impression, Derek said, 'I'll see you in the morning, then, before I'm wheeled away to meet my fate on the operating table.'

'Sorry. Tomorrow you'll be in the capable hands of Nurse Baker. You'll like Nurse Baker.'

'I will?'

'Nurse Baker's very nice, very accommodating. Goodnight.'

'Goodnight Rosemary.' At last Derek was beginning to feel the onset of sleep as the lingering humiliation he had experienced earlier began to fade.

'I tell you I'm right,' Hilary said. It was ten minutes past eight the next morning and she was looking out of the bedroom window across the road towards Ivy Cottage. 'Charlotte didn't go home last night, none of the curtains have been drawn and that Mercedes has gone as well.'

'What?' David said, peering out from beneath the corner of the frilled duvet cover, which had wrapped itself around his head making him look as though he was wearing a baby's bonnet.

Hilary appeared from behind the curtain. 'Come on, David, it's perfectly obvious what happened.'

David tried hard to think. It was Sunday morning, the one day of the week when he was sure of a lie-in; most Saturdays he was in the office persuading people to buy their dream house – nightmares, more like it, as some of them discovered. Nightmares, that rang a bell. Yes, last night, chaos down at the village hall. He turned over, pushed his head under the pillow and thought about Derek Rogers lying there on the floor. While Neville had been sorting Derek out, he had made himself scarce and hidden in the kitchen so that no one would see him laughing.

It had been a funny old night, one way and another. That business with Charlotte and Peter's brother had triggered events. Fancy Charlotte not telling any of them

Jonathan was coming. On the other hand he was a complete jerk – bit like Peter really – maybe that was why she had kept him quiet.

He certainly had a condescending way with him, David thought. 'Real estate,' Jonathan had said, shaking his head dismissively, when David had introduced himself after the furore of Peter's 'resurrection' had calmed down. 'What's your turnover?' he had gone on to ask. Mind your own business, David had wanted to tell him, but instead he had plucked an astronomical figure out of the air and then quadrupled it. Even that had been pushed aside as Jonathan went on to explain in detail why, in general, the British made such lousy businessmen. 'No balls,' seemed to be the long and short of it.

Finally he had been rescued by Neville appearing at his side, and he had escaped to man the bar once more. Then later on he had hardly been able to believe his eyes as he watched Old Ma Braithwaite chase Derek round the hall, until they were all plunged into complete darkness, only to discover, when some candles had been found, Derek lying on the floor clutching his leg.

As though picking up on his thoughts, Hilary said, 'Funny that when the ambulance came there was no sign of Charlotte or Alex. That's why I'm so sure—'

'You can't be sure of anything, Hilary,' David said grumpily from beneath the pillow, 'but wherever Charlotte is, I hope she's getting more sleep than I am.'

Giving up on David, Hilary got dressed and went downstairs, to find Philip and Becky in their pyjamas at opposite ends of the sofa, imbibing their weekend diet of brain-wasting pre-breakfast television. 'How long have you been down here?' she asked.

'Only ten minutes,' Philip said, never taking his eyes off the screen.

Becky unplugged her thumb from her mouth. 'We've seen *Sonic the Hedgehog*, *Disney Club* and *Scooby-Doo*.'

'That's an awful lot just in ten minutes.'

Philip scowled at his sister. 'Bigmouth,' he said. 'When's breakfast, Mum?'

'When you're both dressed you can get your own. I'm popping over the road to see Auntie Charlotte. I'll be back in a moment and then it won't be long before we're due at church.'

'Ooh, can I come?' Becky asked, bouncing off the sofa. 'I want to see her little dog. She didn't bring it when she came to babysit.'

'No,' Hilary said. She wanted to go and snoop about in private, to prove to herself that she was right and that Charlotte had spent the night with Alex. But then a thought struck her. Supposing her sister was there after all? If she took Becky with her at least she had a perfect excuse for calling so early – to see if Charlotte would let Becky play with Mabel. She smiled at her daughter. 'All right then, but hurry up and get yourself dressed. I'll wait for you in the kitchen.'

As they crossed the road, Becky ran on ahead to ring the door bell. To her dismay she found she was too small to reach the button. While she waited for her mother to come up the drive she pushed open the brass letter box and peered inside. Mabel came yapping towards her. Becky poked a small finger in, then seeing that Mabel could jump quite high, she withdrew it quickly with a high-pitched squeal.

Hilary pressed the door bell, which in turn brought on a further burst of yapping. Hilary looked pleased. Here of course was her excuse – she had been worried about Charlotte's dog, she had heard it barking.

'Do you think Auntie Charlotte's still in bed, Mummy?'

'Quite likely,' she said and brought out a bunch of keys from her pocket.

'Will one of our keys work in Auntie Charlotte's keyhole?'

'Ssh,' Hilary said, turning the key in the lock, suddenly realising that if her sister was with Alex, they were, after all, only next door. 'No,' she whispered in answer to Becky's question. 'This is an Ivy Cottage key.'

'Did she give it to you?'

'Yes,' lied Hilary. She knew her sister would never get around to giving her a spare key, so she had taken the precaution of having an extra key cut, just in case . . . just in case of an emergency such as rescuing a small dog, she thought, absolving herself of any accusation Charlotte might throw at her.

'Shouldn't we come back later if she's still in bed, Mummy?'

'Just be quiet, Becky.'

Hilary pushed against the door and was immediately confronted with Mabel dancing excitedly around her feet. 'You play with Mabel while I nip up and see Auntie Charlotte.'

She went slowly up the stairs, calling Charlotte's name quietly as she went, then crept along the landing, checking the bedrooms. All were empty. With a smile on her face she went back down the stairs. As she reached the bottom step she heard Becky say, 'Oh, you naughty little dog. Look at all the puddles and splatter-pies you've made.'

Hilary grimaced at the scene in the kitchen. She stepped cautiously across the floor as though tiptoeing through a minefield. She made it to the back door and let in some much needed fresh air, then opened the cupboard under the sink where only a couple of weeks ago she had put a selection of cleaning fluids.

'Let me help you, Mummy,' said Becky, bored with Mabel and liking the look of one of the aerosol cleaners. She made a grab for it.

'Watch where you put your feet!' shouted Hilary. But it was too late. Becky skidded on a wet patch, sending her legs in different directions, until she lost her balance altogether and ended up sitting down with a bump in one of Mabel's puddles. She started to wail.

Sensing some excitement after a night on her own, Mabel pattered across the floor and climbed on top of Becky.

'Get away,' Becky squealed, 'get away from me, it's all your fault.'

Mistaking Becky's pushing for playfulness, Mabel sank her teeth into the sleeve of Becky's sweatshirt and with her tail waving in the air like a high-speed windscreen wiper, she started to pull, shaking her head from side to side and giving off an occasional growl. Becky pulled sharply in the opposite direction and tipped backwards with Mabel still attached. Hilary made a desperate attempt to prevent her daughter's fall but she wasn't fast enough. She watched helplessly as Becky's head landed in the inevitable with a soft splat.

Hilary and Becky retreated from the mayhem of Ivy Cottage to the relative quiet and hygiene of The Gables. Becky was hysterical by now and Hilary was only seconds away from slapping her daughter as she stripped off Becky's sodden leggings and sweatshirt. She was throwing the clothes in the washing machine, when David appeared in the kitchen.

'What the hell's going on?' he shouted above the noise of Becky's screaming.

'Daddy!' she shouted. 'I fell in Mabel's—'

'We had a little accident,' Hilary said, trying to sound

quite calm, knowing that David would never understand what she had been doing over the road at Ivy Cottage.

'I'm never, never, ever going over to Auntie Charlotte's again,' whimpered Becky.

David looked at Hilary and noticed that she was looking anywhere but at him. 'What were you doing over at Charlotte's? I seem to remember you saying something earlier about knowing that she wasn't there.'

'I was worried about her dog, if you must know.'

David laughed, not with humour. 'You were snooping, weren't you?' Not expecting an answer, he turned to go, but then looked back at his wife. 'Well, was she there or not?'

Chapter Twenty-Five

When Charlotte woke up in Iris's sitting-room, she was stiff and cold. Alex was still asleep on the sofa. Seeing him she remembered how angry she had felt last night, not so much with Alex, but with herself.

After all her resolute determination not to get involved with Alex, she had allowed herself to do a complete U-turn. Kissing him and being in his arms had made her want him more than she would have imagined possible. Had the circumstances been right last night she knew she would have made love with Alex. But then later he had made it only too clear that he wasn't interested. She had fallen asleep stinging with hurt pride and the decision firmly resolved in her mind that it was not going to happen again. His rejection had, once and for all, established their relationship. From now on he was merely her tenant.

She drew the heavy velvet curtains and looked out over Iris's front garden, trying to decide what she was going to say to Alex. When she turned round he was sitting upright and rubbing his face. 'Good morning,' he said.

She walked over to the fireplace and rested one hand on the mantelpiece. 'Alex . . .'

'You're not going to give me a lecture on snoring, are you?'

'Alex,' she started again, conscious that the tone of her voice was at odds with his. 'What happened last night was . . .'

He looked at her for a moment, then stood up. 'Charlotte. Do I take it you're referring, and stop me if I'm wrong, to us kissing each other last night? Because if you are, I have to tell you, from where I was standing it was pretty enjoyable. I don't know what went through your head afterwards, but I was left with the distinct impression that yet again I had done something wrong. For the life of me I can't think what.'

'That's rich. It was you who said . . .'

'Said what?'

'Oh nothing. Forget it.'

'No, go on. Tell me.'

'You said you didn't want to make . . .' she moved away from the mantelpiece, over to the window, 'so on the basis of that it would be better all round if . . .'

'My God, I don't believe it, you think . . .'

'Alex, will you let me finish? I acted without thinking last night.' She took a deep breath. 'I can't handle being on this emotional roller coaster any more, so I would prefer it if we got things sorted out between us. You're my tenant. Let's just keep our relationship on that level from now on.'

'This is ridiculous. I only meant . . .'

'Please, Alex.'

He shrugged his shoulders. 'You don't give me much choice, do you?'

Alex pushed hard on the spade, forcing it down into the soil as he began digging Henry's grave. Charlotte bloody Lawrence! What was she doing to him? *She* was tired of being on an emotional roller coaster? Well, so was he for that matter. Enough was enough. But how could she be so dense? He hadn't meant that he didn't want to make love to her. He'd said those words, yes, but only because he didn't want her to think he would take advantage of her when she was still so vulnerable. Why couldn't she see that? He pushed on the spade again. And who in their right mind would want to make love in Iris Braithwaite's kitchen? Instantly some of his anger vanished at the thought of Iris catching him with his trousers down.

Charlotte watched Alex in the garden, to convince herself that she could now regard him quite dispassionately. She found she could, and picking up the kettle from the cooker, she filled it at the enamel sink. She placed it on the gas ring and struck a match. Last night she had done exactly the same, but then she hadn't noticed her surroundings. This morning though, with the early morning sunlight pouring in through the spotlessly clean window, the kitchen was picked out in detail like a 1950s film set. Everything about it was cluttered and unfitted, with bulky appliances which Charlotte could remember from her own childhood along with the same green and cream colour scheme – where others had moved on, Iris had not.

As she waited for the kettle to boil, Charlotte picked up the mugs she had rinsed out last night and looked around for some tea. There was no sign of a tea caddy on the green Formica worktop between the cooker and sink, so she slid back one of the plastic doors on the freestanding unit. Coffee, but still no tea. She noticed a door off the kitchen and pulled it open. As she'd thought, it was a larder. She was instantly reminded of her grandmother. Granny Archer had been a notorious hoarder. From the looks of things, so was Iris Braithwaite.

On the highest shelf Charlotte could see a tin of Bird's Custard Powder, and she knew that if she were to look inside, the ancient-looking tin would be half empty just like Granny Archer's, and its contents rock hard. Her eyes roaming the shelves, Charlotte counted ten rusting tins of evaporated milk, eight polythene-wrapped bags of sugar, four packs of Bisto, numerous jars of fish paste, rows of tinned pears and peach slices, and half a dozen bottles of gravy browning. The kettle began to whistle. Charlotte went to turn off the gas and then returned to the larder to continue her hunt. Surely amongst this hoard of goodies there had to be at least one packet of tea?

On the lowest shelf, crammed with tins of Campbell's soup and pilchards in tomato sauce, Charlotte saw an old Cadbury's tin commemorating the Queen's Coronation. She remembered Granny Archer's identical tin – Hilary had it now and kept old buttons in it. Out of curiosity, she took it down from the shelf and carefully prised the lid off. She wasn't expecting tea bags, but she was surprised to find a selection of used birthday-cake candles, along with some small plastic cake decorations. Iris had never had any children. She noticed that all the cake decorations were a variation on the same theme – a dog holding up a paw, a dog curled up in a basket and a dog with a bone in its mouth. Moving these objects to one side of the tin, Charlotte caught sight of a faded, stained envelope at the bottom. Ashamed of her nosiness but unable to stop herself, she opened the envelope and pulled out a set of photographs. Each photograph showed Iris's dog sitting in front of a decorated cake with writing in shaky blue icing that read 'Happy Birthday Henry'. Charlotte counted the photographs. There were exactly eleven.

'Damn!' she said out loud, and screwing up her eyes in a futile attempt not to cry, she pushed the tin back on the shelf and closed the larder door behind her. As she wiped away her tears with the palms of her hands, Alex came into the kitchen.

'You all right?' he asked.

She told him about the tin and the photographs of Henry. 'It's silly, isn't it?' she said. 'But it's always the trivia in life that gets to you. I saw poor Henry quite dead last night and that didn't upset me, but put a collection of sentimental plastic bits and pieces in front of me and I'm a hopeless wreck. Why do you suppose that is?' She paused, but not long enough for Alex to answer her. She went on, her words hurried and full of restrained emotion, 'Do you know, when I was told Peter was dead . . . I didn't cry . . . Can you believe it? I didn't cry, not one tear.' She bit her lower lip, clenched her fists, held her breath, all to keep her body in check, to stop it trembling and betraying her completely, but no matter how hard she tried she could not hold back the tears.

'Charlotte,' Alex said, 'you must—'

'No,' she said without looking at him. 'Don't. Just leave me . . .'

'I have only vague memories of last night . . .'

They both spun round to see Iris Braithwaite, looking pale and gaunt, framed in the doorway. She was wearing a dressing-gown and somehow managed to appear strangely majestic.

' . . . but I remember enough,' she carried on, 'to have woken up with the distinct impression that for some unaccountable reason I behaved very badly. I would prefer it if you never mentioned or referred to the event again. And now . . .' she hesitated slightly, as her voice began to waver, 'I would appreciate, Mr Hamilton, you taking Mrs Lawrence home, who, for her own reasons, seems to be quite overwrought. I would very much like to be alone with my poor Henry now. Thank you for being so kind as to dig a hole for me. I watched you from my window. You made a good choice, beneath the magnolia tree . . . it was planted the same year Henry came to live . . .'

Unable to continue, she went back upstairs.

They left The White Cottage in silence. Aware now that his role had been so clearly defined, Alex knew he had no right to intrude upon Charlotte's unhappiness. But he couldn't help wondering how much longer she would be able to fight back the need to free herself from the prison of her own making. For that was what it was, and he knew all about self-imprisonment. Standing in Iris's kitchen he had seen the pain in Charlotte's tormented face, and had recognised it as the same pain he himself had once experienced. Guilt. As surely as Charlotte was a willing prisoner of her guilt over Peter's death, so he too had been held captive after Lucy's death.

'I feel so angry,' Charlotte said, suddenly coming to a stop.

He looked at her, but she was turned away from him, staring up the drive of In The Pink. 'It's all *his* fault. How *dare* he come here with all his flash charm and ruin Iris's life. He's got no right hurting people like that.' She turned on Alex, her face flushed with angry indignation. 'I've got a good mind to go and have it out with him. Coming?'

Halfway up the drive, they were met by Barry jogging towards them.

'Is your father up?' Charlotte demanded.

Barry looked startled. 'I'm sorry?' he said, pushing a nervous hand through his hair.

'I asked if that rotten stinking father of yours was up yet? Probably enjoying a good laugh, is he?'

'Dad isn't at home, he's . . .'

'Out ruining somebody else's life, no doubt,' Charlotte said hotly.

'Look, Charlotte,' Alex intervened, knowing that Charlotte was taking out her frustration on the nearest person to hand, 'this has got nothing to do with Barry. Leave it till later, when Derek's back from wherever he is.' He tried to lead Charlotte away, but she was firmly rooted to the ground.

'Actually Dad won't be home until he's been discharged from hospital.'

'Ah, somebody got to him before me, did they?'

'Hold on a moment, Charlotte,' Alex said, placing a hand on her arm. 'Why, what's happened?' he asked Barry.

Slowly, Barry's earnest face cracked into a cautious smile. 'Dad broke his leg down at the village hall last night. I thought you were there. Surely you saw what happened?'

Two blank faces stared back at Barry. 'We left early,' Alex volunteered.

'Apparently the power went off and Dad slipped and . . .'

'And broke his leg,' finished Charlotte. 'Well thank goodness there's still a spark of justice in the world.'

'I'm going to see him later, do you want me to pass on a message?'

'No need. I think I'll go and see him in person.'

When Charlotte got back to Ivy Cottage she was horrified and shocked – horrified at the state of the kitchen and shocked that she could have forgotten poor Mabel so completely.

After cleaning up, feeding Mabel and generally making a fuss of her, Charlotte decided to take the dog for a walk down by the mere. She set off down Acacia Lane and turned left on to the footpath between In The Pink and

The White Cottage. She peered through the neatly trimmed privet hedge to see if Mrs Braithwaite was about. There was no sign of her so Charlotte pressed on, down the hill, towards the mere.

It was a beautiful morning with clear blue skies. While Mabel scampered on ahead, snuffling around in amongst the fir trees, Charlotte followed slowly behind, enjoying the moment of freedom. Freedom. It seemed she had been searching for this commodity all her life. Was this the only way to experience it? To be utterly alone? For it seemed to Charlotte, standing there in the clearing, over-looking the still water and breathing in the sweet smell of pine, that whenever people were involved, restrictions were applied and demands made. In her experience even the nicest of people pushed others about for their own purposes.

Calling Mabel to heel and turning for home, Charlotte thought of poor Iris again. She wondered how she must be feeling right now. All at once the anger she had felt standing there on the driveway of In The Pink came flooding back. Derek!

Charlotte lied to the nurse, saying she was 'family', then walked through the ward towards Derek's bed at the far end. It was seven-thirty and the ward was packed with evening visitors.

'Charlotte!' he called out, seeing her. Huddled visitors and patients all looked up as she made her way past them. 'My mistress,' Derek said loudly, with a big grin on his face.

'Shut up, Derek,' she said, when at last she stood over him.

'What, no kiss, not even a peck on the cheek?'

She glared at him. 'Not after what you've done.' Her

voice was raised and unmistakably angry and everyone else in the ward was making a poor job of pretending not to be listening.

'After what I've done? What on earth are you talking about? Here I am, recovering from major surgery, and you accuse me . . .'

'I said shut up, Derek. I don't know how that family of yours puts up with you.'

'Must be my magnetic . . .'

'I said shut . . .'

'All right, all right, you've used that line,' Derek said, frowning. 'And anyway, you sure you're not muddling me up with somebody else? I'm Derek Rogers, he of the compound fracture fame.' He pointed to the end of the bed. 'They've put a pin in my tibia-whatsit or something or other. I've been very brave. Surely I deserve just a little sympathy from you? One kiss would do it.'

'You're despicable. What you did last night was pathetic.'

'Charlotte, a guy can't help breaking his leg . . .'

'Not that. What you did to poor Mrs Braithwaite, that was such . . .'

'A laugh, I thought,' Derek said smiling. 'Got her a touch frisky, didn't it, relaxed the old bird a bit?'

'You've ruined her!' Charlotte shouted. 'And you don't give a damn, do you?'

'Oh come on, Charlotte,' Derek retorted with equal volume, 'don't exaggerate. You talk as though I'd raped her.'

An audible gasp rippled round the rest of the ward.

'Well, you might just as well have done. She's lost all her dignity and reputation in one go. She'll be the laughing stock of the village.'

'Rubbish! She was that already and why the hell are

you so defensive on her behalf? I would have thought after what she'd done to you, you would have been pleased with what I did, grateful even.'

'You . . . you don't understand, do you?' It was hopeless. Charlotte turned her back on Derek and rushed out of the ward, goggled-eyed faces following her as she went.

'Too bloody right I don't!' Derek threw after her, and then, as all faces turned back to look at him, he shouted angrily, 'Oh, sod off, the lot of you!'

What a day! Derek thought to himself, reaching for his jug of water – a day that had begun with Nurse Baker, of whom he had had high hopes, who had turned out to be a mustachioed, red-haired Cliff Baker and was probably as bent as a Uri Geller fork. He took a gulp of his water and looked up to see Cindy and Barry coming towards him.

'What did Charlotte want?' Cindy asked sharply, as she stood at the end of his bed. 'We passed her on the stairs. She looked upset.'

'If you must know, she's just been giving me a right mouthful and I don't mean we were snogging. Ask this nosy lot here,' he said, gesturing with his hand towards the rest of the ward, who were all, once again, not so discreetly tuning in.

Barry looked down at his father. 'Alex said you got Mrs Braithwaite drunk last night. Is that true?'

'Isn't anyone at all interested in how my operation went? I reckon I'm bloody lucky to be alive.'

'Well, is it true?'

'Of course I didn't,' Derek said, turning away from his son and looking out of the window. In the car park below, he could see Charlotte getting into her car. He watched her slam the door shut and then slump over the steering wheel, her hands covering her face.

'Dad?'

Derek turned and faced Barry. 'Okay,' he said irritably, 'so what if I did?'

'You stupid bloody fool,' Cindy said with undisguised contempt.

'I thought it would be a laugh.'

'Alex says Mrs Braithwaite's dog died last night,' Barry said.

'Oh Alex says this and Alex says that,' shouted Derek. 'I'm sick of that man.' Heads again turned their way.

Cindy suddenly smiled. Jealousy! How wonderful that at last her husband should have come to know that most self-destructive of emotions. 'Well, we're all sick of you,' she said, and walked away, her head held high as all eyes followed her down the ward.

Derek looked at his son. 'Are you leaving as well?'

Barry nudged his glasses. 'Not if you don't want me to.'

They stared at each other. Then Barry walked slowly round the bed and sat in the chair between the window and his father.

'Been a bit of a plonker, haven't I, Bas?'

'You could say that, Dad.'

Chapter Twenty-Six

My dear Carlotta, I am so very sorry, but I shall not be able to come and visit you this month. I have to be in Rome for a funeral. I think it will be quite a party! Forgive me for disappointing you. Love, Christina.

'No!' said Charlotte out loud, looking down at the letter in her hand which had just arrived by that morning's second post. 'No, I won't forgive you. I want you here with me.'

Charlotte had found Hulme Welford strangely quiet for the past five weeks. Flaming June had been and gone and for once had lived up to its name, being hot and dry, but July so far had been a wash-out, forcing people to stay indoors, abandoning their gardens to the daily downpour of torrential rain, which left delphiniums battered and cheap barbecues to fill up with water and rust.

Charlotte had put her time to good use, though, spending most days up a ladder with a paintbrush in her hand. She had even taught herself to stencil and had festooned the kitchen walls with wisteria and the bathroom with ivy, echoing exactly the exterior of the house. She was really quite pleased with her efforts at decorating. But she didn't feel pleased now. She had been looking forward to Christina coming to stay, had even decorated a bedroom specially for her. There was so much she wanted to talk to Christina about. What with all the rain and being cooped up inside the house, she felt as though she hadn't talked properly with anyone for weeks.

Everyone, it seemed, was busy. There was Dad with his gooseberries – trying to protect them from all the rain – and Mum with her shop and the passing holiday trade; even Alex, who previously had seemed always to be around, had been absent recently. Charlotte had missed their chats in the garden. Occasionally she would hear music coming through the wall, but Alex was a good tenant and the music was always to her liking, and never intrusive. She sometimes heard him going out early in the morning and not returning until late. Some nights, he didn't come home at all. She wondered what he did then. Was he with Heather? Perhaps not, not after Jonathan.

The last she had seen of Jonathan had been when she had got back from the hospital after giving Derek a piece of her mind and found him waiting for her on the doorstep. 'I need my things,' he had said, with not a hint as to where or what he had been doing since the previous evening. And then he had gone, accelerating smoothly down Acacia Lane in his hired Mercedes.

She had seen hardly anything of Hilary either. Her sister had been busy organising just about every end-of-term social activity for children and parents alike, at the same time getting ready for their annual camping holiday. Only two days ago Hilary had sat in the conservatory with Charlotte, the rain coming down like stair rods on the glass roof above their heads, and had said, very smugly Charlotte thought, 'Well, at least we'll be able to rely on the weather in Haute Provence.' They had set off yesterday morning, the Volvo weighed down with patched canvas, Marmite, Ribena, mosquito repellant, water-purifying tablets, factor twenty sun cream, as well as several bagfuls of pre-holiday tension. They were supposed to leave at the crack of dawn according to David's itinerary, but at nine o'clock he was still sitting in the car, revving the engine and waiting for Becky, who that morning had started complaining of an upset tummy, to get off the toilet.

She heard Mabel scratching at the conservatory door and went to let her in. The little dog was drenched. Charlotte picked up a towel and rubbed her down. The doorbell rang.

'Hello Tiffany,' Charlotte said, opening the door.

'You okay for a visitor?'

'Yes, of course, come in. I was just about to indulge in some comfort eating. Fancy joining me?'

They sat in the kitchen, Charlotte loading crumpets under the grill and Tiffany absentmindedly carving patterns in the butter. With her head bent over the table, Charlotte could see that Tiffany's own natural colour was showing through the defiant puce of the rest of her hair. She was no longer wearing the elaborate beehive, but a plait, which hung down her back like a stick of rock. Not for the first time Charlotte wondered how on earth Tiffany had got away with it at school. Didn't teenagers get expelled for such things?

'The house seems so empty without Barry,' Tiffany said, looking up at Charlotte. 'It's dead boring not having him around. I know he's quiet and all that, but at least, when he's there, I can . . .'

'Annoy him?'

Tiffany laughed. 'Isn't that what brothers are for?'

'Sisters too,' Charlotte said with a smile.

'You know, I don't think Dad can work Barry out. He's paid for us both to have a dead expensive education, expecting at least one of us to end up as a smart something or other, you know, an accountant or a barrister, something boring like that. Dad thinks you've got to spend money to make money.' She laughed scornfully and plunged the knife deep into the butter. 'And Barry's gone off to do charity work in an orphanage in Rumania for the summer. Ironic or what?'

'Have you heard from him yet?' Charlotte asked, setting a plate of hot crumpets down on the table.

'Yes, we got a letter yesterday. He's been sprayed for fleas and lice and is helping to install twelve new toilets.'

'Well, at least he's doing something positive,' Charlotte said, sitting down and passing Tiffany a knife and a plate.

'Meaning I'm not, I suppose.'

Charlotte shook her head. 'No,' she said emphatically. 'Meaning *I'm* not.'

'Do something, then.'

'Like what?'

'Hang on,' Tiffany said, balancing a thick slab of butter on a crumpet, 'isn't that supposed to be my line? I'm the awkward teenager, you're supposed to be the one with all the answers.' She took a huge bite of the buttery crumpet, and with her mouth full, said, 'Why don't you just get a job?'

Charlotte looked up from her plate. 'I know that's the answer. The trouble is I haven't got a clue what I really want to do.'

'There must be hundreds of things you could have a go at. I'll prove it to you. Got a newspaper?'

Charlotte went through to the sitting-room and came back with a copy of the *Chronicle*.

'Right,' said Tiffany, taking it from her and laying the relevant pages out on the table. ' "Receptionist required, must be smart in appearance".' She looked at Charlotte in her jeans, paint-splattered sweatshirt and hair scraped back in a rubber band. 'Well, we'd have to get Mum and

Dad to tidy you up a bit.' She continued with the advertisement. ' "Must have excellent communication skills and knowledge of Monarch system".' She lifted her head. 'What's a Monarch system?'

Charlotte shrugged. 'A computer for Royals? Helps them to foul up perhaps.'

'Okay then,' Tiffany grinned, returning to the paper. 'How about "Efficient organiser and administrator, must be confident and discreet and able to act under pressure".'

Charlotte gave a short derisive laugh. 'I think I've got enough pressure in my life just at the moment.'

Undaunted, Tiffany carried on. 'Well, that rules out secretarial and administrative. How about domestic? Some poshy over in Prestbury wants a housekeeper. You've only got to be conscientious and like children.'

'Grilled or fried?' laughed Charlotte.

'You're not taking this seriously at all, are you?' Tiffany said, throwing the paper on the floor.

'Let's forget about me. How's your dad's leg?'

'Covered in kisses,' Tiffany said in disgust. 'Every woman who comes into the place wants to sign her name on his plaster. By the way, did you know he tried to apologise to Mrs Braithwaite?'

'No, I didn't,' answered Charlotte, wondering what crass things Derek might have said.

'She wouldn't even speak to him, just slammed the door in his face. He said she looked awful, well, worse than she normally does.'

Charlotte frowned. She had been worried about Mrs Braithwaite for some time now. Ever since that dreadful night at the village hall and Henry's death it was as though Mrs Braithwaite had disappeared from the village. Nobody seemed to have spoken with her; nobody knew whether she was hiding her grief or her embarrassment, or even both. 'When was that exactly, when did your father see her?'

Tiffany thought for a moment. 'Ages ago, I think, before all this rain started anyway. Why?'

'I don't know, I just feel uneasy about Mrs Braithwaite. Even Hilary, before she left for France yesterday, said she hadn't seen her about, and Hilary usually sees most things going on in Hulme Welford.'

'Surely someone must have seen her down at the shops.'

'Apparently not.'

'What's she eating, then?'

Charlotte thought of all the jars of paste and tins of pilchards in Iris Braithwaite's larder and feared the worst.

In his study at the Vicarage, Malcolm Jackson pulled the telephone towards him and dialled a number from his parish address book. He waited and waited. At last he heard Neville Archer's voice.

'Hello Neville, it's Malcolm. You all right? You sound out of breath.'

'I'm fine. I was in the garden.'

'What, in this weather?'

'Especially in this weather. I was making sure I'd got enough rhubarb leaves covering the gooseberries. It's only a couple of weeks to go until the big day.'

A smile flickered over Malcolm's face. 'Oh yes, of course, the gooseberry show. I'd forgotten about that. How are they doing?'

'Best not say, not over the telephone, careless words, etc.'

They both laughed. Gooseberry growers were notorious for their rivalry and secrecy, and sabotage was not unheard of.

'So what can I do for you, Malcolm?'

'Actually, Neville, do you think you could leave the gooseberries for a short while and bob round? There's something I'd like you to do for me.'

Neville approached The White Cottage in the drizzling rain, taking each step with increasing trepidation. 'She might listen to you, Neville,' Malcolm had said. 'For so long in her life you've been a figure of standing in the village. You were her doctor for goodness knows how long, she's more likely to listen to you than anyone else. She's got to realise that we all care about her, that she can't hide in her house for ever, for whatever reason. She's got to come out.'

On the doorstep, Neville didn't feel a figure of any standing whatsoever. He lifted the brass knocker and brought it down sharply. He counted to twenty and knocked again, and then again. He bent down, pushed open the letter box and peered inside. 'Mrs Braithwaite,' he called out nervously. 'Are you there, Mrs Braithwaite?'

Why nervously? What was he afraid of? Afraid that they, that he, had left it too late, that Iris was lying on the floor . . . dead?

Why did he imagine Iris lying dead *on the floor*. Why be so dramatic? Why not just imagine her in her favourite comfy armchair? Not every old person living alone had to die on the floor. Stop being so useless, Neville Archer! he told himself. Get on and do something! Smash a window, do something heroic for once in your life. But be careful, let the gas out before you go in. Gas? Who mentioned gas? He breathed in deeply, then exhaled slowly. One more time and then I'll call the police, he told himself. 'Mrs Braithwaite,' he shouted through the letter box again, 'it's me, Dr Archer.'

'I can see that perfectly well, Dr Archer.'

Neville spun round at the sound of Iris Braithwaite's voice.

'Though why you should be shouting through my letter box for all the neighbours to hear, I really cannot think.'

'Mrs Braithwaite!' he said, revelling in the fact that Iris was looking wonderfully alive and not gasping her last in front of the gas cooker.

'Perhaps you would be so good as to help me with my case. It's heavy and I've just walked with it from the bus stop.'

'You've been away, then?' Neville said, watching Iris unlock the front door.

'My word, Dr Archer, retirement has done nothing to weaken your diagnostic powers, has it? Well of course I have, you don't think I've been shopping with a suitcase, do you?'

'It's just that we were all so . . .' Neville hesitated.

'Come on, Dr Archer, in with that case, if you please, and what were you all?'

'Pleased to see you back,' Neville said smiling.

In the hall Iris freed herself from her raincoat and stared at Neville. 'Well, that's very civil of you.' Then removing her plastic rain-hood and patting her hair into place, she said, 'Now don't let me keep you. I'm sure you must have plenty to do.'

'Yes,' he answered, edging towards the door. 'Been anywhere nice?' he ventured, realising that Iris was exhibiting a tan that could not possibly have been acquired anywhere in the North of England during the past few weeks.

'Yes, as a matter of fact, somewhere very nice. Goodbye.'

Chapter Twenty-Seven

When, three weeks later, the removal of his plaster cast coincided with two days of continuous sunshine, Derek decided to hold an impromptu barbecue. It was early Sunday morning and he sent Tiffany off to invite the neighbours. He told her to ask Louise and Neville. 'And you'd better ask Old Ma Braithwaite,' he added, 'and that vicar bloke.'

'The vicar?' Tiffany said, astonished. 'Why him?'

'I want to see what kind of man is going to baptise my son. I want to know whether he's into choirboys or not.'

Both the vicar and Iris Braithwaite sent their apologies, or rather Malcolm Jackson did. Iris informed Tiffany she would rather sup with the Devil. Undaunted, at one o'clock, resplendent in knee-length shorts, espadrilles, sunglasses, and with his hands stuffed inside the mouths of a pair of crocodile oven gloves, Derek greeted the rest of his guests, as well as their plates of microwave-defrosted meat and freezer-chilled bottles of wine. He was an incongruous sight with one evenly tanned leg and an elastic support stocking covering the lower part of his other leg which was white and scrawny. He was leaning on a walking stick, but mostly he used this to direct operations.

'Meat over there,' he said, pointing with the stick to the hostess trolley they had all seen at the fork supper, 'and booze over here, where I can reach it easily. A guy can only hobble so far. Tiffany, go and tell your mother to bring out that sangria I made earlier.'

Alex felt Charlotte wince at his side. They had arrived at the same time, though not together. He hadn't seen her to talk to in ages. Their landlady–tenant relationship had consisted of fleeting glimpses of each other, and that was all. Earlier in the summer their lives had been unexpectedly thrust together, but after that morning in Iris's kitchen they had gone their separate ways; and if he was truthful with himself, despite missing her company, life had been a lot more straightforward since then.

Standing slightly apart from the rest of the group, which numbered Louise and Neville and Hilary and David, along with their children, Alex turned to Charlotte. 'Good thing Mrs Braithwaite isn't here,' he said.

She responded with only a slight smile, though enough, he noticed, to set off those two dimples either side of her mouth. He couldn't read her eyes, for they were hidden behind dark glasses.

'Anyone found out where she went on holiday?' he asked.

'No,' she answered. 'Apparently she's been quite secretive about it, hasn't told a soul where she went. Dad reckons it's the first holiday she's had since she brought Henry home as a puppy.'

Alex looked directly at Charlotte, and – conscious that he was shifting a gear or two – said, 'To be honest, I'm surprised to see you here. Aren't you still angry with Derek?'

Charlotte returned Alex's unwavering gaze for a moment, then looked away towards Derek, who was prodding indiscriminately at the fake hot coals of his gas-fired barbecue. At the same time he was chatting to her mother and leaning on his stick. 'It's hard to stay mad with such a fool,' she said.

'And are you still mad with me?' he ventured.

'No,' she said.

He noticed there was no hesitation in her reply. 'Friends, then?'

She nodded. 'Friends.'

'Fancy a stroll?'

'Yes, if it means getting out of having to drink Derek's lethal sangria.'

They wandered down to the bottom of the garden, away from the smoke and the sound of Becky and Philip starting to argue, and Hilary and David telling Neville, yet again, about their eighteen hours of hell on the French roads coming back from Haute Provence.

'How have you been?' Alex asked, as they sat on a white-painted wrought-iron garden seat, overlooking a small pond with a spouting cherub and an ugly-looking ornamental toad.

'Quiet, but busy,' she answered. 'In fact I've struck up quite a relationship with Mr Dulux. How about you, you don't seem to have been around as much?'

'I've been busy with several . . .'

'You're not going back to your eighty-hour weeks, are you?'

'Would you be disappointed in me if I was?'

'Yes,' she said, 'I would. I had high hopes for you, Alex. I thought you were a real nineties man.'

Was it his imagination or was she more at ease, not just with him, but with herself? 'Oh don't worry about me, I'm way ahead in the emancipation of men stakes. I already organise my work schedule around *Neighbours* and *Home and Away*.'

'Now you have disappointed me. I had you down as an

Anne and Nick fan.' She pushed her sunglasses up over her head and closed her eyes. 'After all that rain this is wonderful. I feel as if I'm on holiday.'

'Do you think you'll go away this summer?'

'I shouldn't think so,' she said. 'I know it sounds like I'm being a bit of a wimp but I don't much fancy a holiday alone. And before you say anything, I'm too old for Club Eighteen and too young for a bowling holiday in Bourne-mouth with a bevy of grey-haired grannies. I'd rather stay at home.'

An idea occurred to Alex. 'Charlotte?' he said. 'Do you trust me?'

'What an extraordinary question,' she said, reminded of the morning she had discovered Alex cleaning her kitchen floor when he had given her that hangover cure. 'Trust me,' he had said then. 'Why, what have you done?'

'It's not so much what I've done, as what I'm about to suggest.'

Charlotte opened her eyes. She fixed her attention on a blackbird some six feet away, basking in the sunshine, its feathers so plumped up it looked like a sooty powder puff. 'Go on,' she said.

'I'm going to stay with some friends next week, over in Yorkshire. I've known them since we were at university together.'

'That's nice. I hope you have a lovely time.'

'Why don't you come with me? It might be fun for you to get away for a few days.' Was he pushing it? Was he already putting their re-established friendship in jeopardy?

She kept her eyes on the blackbird. Recently her life had begun to show signs of becoming trouble-free, with each day gently easing itself into the next. She had even started to feel better, the dreams had stopped and she couldn't remember the last time she had cried. Would going away with Alex complicate things again? But surely they were both over all that nonsense now. 'I don't know what to say,' she said at last.

'I am only offering you a few days in Yorkshire.'

'I know that. If I thought it was anything else I wouldn't be considering the idea.'

'Say yes, then, and before Long John Silver gets bored with his alfresco Keith Floyd impersonation and comes yo-ho-ho-ing down here to rout us out.'

She laughed.

'Hey you two,' shouted Derek, right on cue, 'quit your canoodling in my bushes. I've got a lovely steak for you, Charlotte. Alex, I'm sorry but your burger's burnt.'

'Subtle, isn't he?' Alex said, as they began walking back to the house. They hadn't got as far as the patio when Tiffany called from the kitchen French window.

'Dad, there's a man on the phone for you.'

'Well bring it out here. What's the point in having a mobile phone if it's stuck in the kitchen the whole time? You don't expect me to be Linford Christie with this leg, do you?'

Coming out into the garden and rolling her black-lined eyes, Tiffany slapped the phone down into her father's hand. He poked her with his stick.

'Hello,' he said, 'Derek Rogers here . . . yes, that's right . . . what, what kind of . . . what do you mean you don't know . . . what kind of agency are you . . . you send my son . . . too right I'm worried, pal!'

Derek pushed the aerial in and tossed the phone on to the pink-frilled hammock behind him.

'What is it, Dad?' asked Tiffany, seeing the look on her father's face.

'You'd better go and tell your mother. Bas is being

flown home from Rumania . . . he's ill, caught some . . . they don't know what. He'll be at Manchester, about six.'

'He'll be fine,' Hilary said brightly, looking inanely about her. 'It'll just be some kind of tummy bug, you know what these foreign places are like. Last year in the Dordogne we . . .'

'They've arranged for an ambulance to be there at the airport,' Derek said flatly.

Nobody said anything else.

They were met at the airport by a small nervous man in baggy trousers and a creased shirt. 'Mr and Mrs Rogers? I'm from Aid Now and I'd . . .'

'I don't give a shit about you,' Derek shouted, pointing an accusing finger at the man, 'so shut up until you're spoken to.'

An airport official escorted the tense group to a private lounge. 'We'll let you know the minute the plane lands,' he said. 'I'm afraid you won't be able to see your son straight away. We have a medical team on standby . . . we need to know whether he's infectious.'

When the man left them, Cindy began to cry and Tiffany put her arm round her mother's shoulders. She was shocked to feel how thin and insubstantial her mother really was – her mother, who had always seemed to be rock solid, fighting Tiffany every step of each day.

Derek breathed in deeply, and stood and glowered over the man in baggy trousers.

They saw the plane land and then watched in helpless disbelief through the triple-glazed window as a stretcher was carried down the steps of the aircraft and was pushed into the awaiting ambulance.

*

At the hospital Cindy looked through yet another glass window at her son. 'I can't believe this,' she said, 'I can't believe he's going to die.'

'He's not,' Tiffany almost growled. 'He's bloody well not going to die.'

Derek turned away from the sight of his son, twitching spasmodically, suffering God knows what. It was too much for him. 'I'm going to look for that doctor. It's been long enough for them to know something by now.'

Before he even got to the door it was opened by the young doctor they had spoken to earlier, a man who looked as though he would be more at home on a rugby pitch than in an intensive care ward. He came into the room, filling the small space. 'We've performed the lumbar puncture,' he said briskly, 'and it's as we thought: your son has meningitis. I think you should prepare yourselves for a long haul.' He turned away from them and looked through the glass at Barry and two nurses who were hovering over him. 'I have to tell you, the delirium may well wear off quite soon, but there's a strong possibility that he could lose consciousness.'

'Will he . . . ?'

The young doctor looked kindly at Cindy. 'We know exactly how to treat your son, Mrs Rogers, it's more a question of timing. If we can treat the illness in the early stages, there's a good chance of a full recovery, but . . .'

'What you mean,' Derek said, cutting in, 'is that we might be too late in Bas's case.'

'Dad,' shouted Tiffany, 'stop it!'

'I'm sure you'd like to see your son now,' the doctor said simply. 'First though, I'll show you where you can wash and put on some gowns.'

They stood at the foot of the bed, staring down at Barry's restless body. Tiffany was the first to move

235

forward. 'Oh Barry,' she cried, bending over his flushed, sweating face. 'Barry, what have you done?'

Slowly, as though using all his strength, Barry opened his eyes. Tiffany could see he was trying to focus on her. 'Tiffany?' he said faintly.

'Yes,' she said, 'it's . . .' Then, moving away from the bed, she began to cry quietly.

Cindy came forward, her hand covering her trembling lips. Behind her, Derek leaned over towards his son, and swallowing hard, he said, 'So Bas, it's your turn to be a bit of a plonker, is it?'

Barry's eyes closed.

They took it in turns to stay awake by Barry's side throughout the night, even though a nurse was constantly monitoring his progress. Each watched helplessly as Barry's restless, fevered body thrashed from side to side. A drip was in place, its plastic bag of liquid vanishing steadfastly into Barry's arm.

At about four in the morning, as Derek felt himself falling into a much needed sleep, he was brought up with the strongest of feelings that something was wrong. His son wasn't moving. 'Bas!' he cried, convinced that Barry was no longer breathing. There was no sign of the nurse, so he stumbled out of the room, forgetting his stick and trying to ignore the pain shooting through his leg. 'Help! Somebody come quickly,' he shouted down the empty corridor. At once Tiffany and Cindy were at his side, along with the nurse. 'He's not moving . . . I think he's . . .'

The nurse pushed past him and went to Barry. 'He's unconscious,' she said, hurrying out of the room. 'I'll fetch Dr Bawton.'

Alone again, Cindy sat by her son. She reached out her

hand and eased back his damp hair. It was such a simple gesture, but that lock of hair was such an integral part of her son's make-up. She felt Tiffany and Derek moving behind her. 'I want him baptised,' she said quietly. 'He's to be baptised, just as he wanted.'

Exhaustion, fear and bewilderment made Derek unusually quiet. He greeted Malcolm Jackson in the waiting-room with nothing more than a nod, taking him through to Cindy and Tiffany and Bas. What was there to say anyway? He listened to the vicar talking about Barry's courage and about pulling through and then about them joining him in a moment of prayer.

'I usually like to kneel,' Malcolm Jackson said, 'but if you'd feel more comfortable standing, that's fine.'

Derek watched the others to see what they would do. They knelt, and so he got awkwardly down on one knee. He couldn't concentrate on anything that was being said. He could only think how scared and isolated he felt, kneeling alone on his side of Bas's bed. More than anything he wanted to run away from this room, to be outside in the sunshine, in their garden, where only yesterday they had been drinking sangria and burning cheap steak. Oh God, he wasn't strong enough to cope with this.

At last it was over and they were getting to their feet. Derek limped over to the window and looked out over the car park. In the background he could hear more kind words being said. Then he lost it. Something deep inside him exploded and, bringing his fist down on the window-sill, he shouted, 'What's the bloody sense in all this?'

Chapter Twenty-Eight

'This doesn't feel at all right,' Charlotte said, as the Elton John cassette came to an end. Alex looked across at her briefly, wanting to keep his eyes on the motorway ahead. They were on the M62, just passing Hollingworth Lake, and for most of the journey neither of them had spoken much. He wondered whether Charlotte was beginning to regret coming.

He didn't know which had most surprised him; his impulsiveness while sat in Derek and Cindy's garden, or Charlotte's agreement to come away with him, and without any real persuasion on his part. All he could be sure of was that the anticipation he had experienced over the past few days at the prospect of spending some time with Charlotte had made him face up to how he really felt towards her. When they had first met at Hilary's, he had been intrigued by her. Intrigued because she had seemed determined from the word go not to like him. She had been on the attack as soon as Hilary had introduced them, and had been in that position ever since . . . until now possibly. When she had told him Derek had kissed her he had realised then that what he felt for her was more than just passing curiosity. Imagining Derek kissing Charlotte had not set him off down the path of jealousy as he might have supposed, but had made him want to protect her from any further advances from Derek . . . or any other kind of roué for that matter. From that moment on he had wanted Charlotte for himself, and the whole of her, not just the fragments she was prepared to share. During their brief time apart he had almost convinced himself that his feelings for her had changed. But they hadn't. He still wanted Charlotte, and now that he had somehow gained her trust, he didn't want to risk losing it.

'I said this doesn't feel right,' Charlotte repeated, looking pointedly at Alex.

'I'm sorry,' he said. 'I was miles away.' He pulled out into the fast lane and overtook a shirt-sleeved man in a Cavalier, his jacket hanging limply behind him on the specially designed hook. 'So what exactly doesn't feel right?'

'Oh, I don't know . . .'

'Come on, you can do better than that.'

'It feels . . .' She looked out of the window, realising that at some stage during the journey, the landscape had changed – ribbons of dry-stone wall had replaced the familiar hawthorn hedges of her native Cheshire. 'I feel bad about Barry. It's as though we don't care by coming away.'

'I know what you mean, but Barry could be in a coma for ages. Somehow life has . . .'

'Oh please no, not that old number,' Charlotte said. 'You're beginning to sound like Hilary.'

Her defiance made him want to smile; it was one of her traits he had missed these past few weeks. 'I called in at the hospital last night,' he said. 'Cindy was on her own. She looked worn out.'

'I know. Tiffany burst into tears when I went and poor Derek couldn't even talk to me.'

They drove on in silence, until Alex indicated to come off the motorway. 'Nearly there,' he said.

Charlotte tried to block out her anxiety for Barry.

Instead she began to wonder what Alex's friends would be like. He had barely said a word about Sally and Stephen, other than to say that he was sure she would like them and that they had a five-year-old son called Mark. She stole a quick glance at Alex, thinking how little she really knew about him. It wasn't so much that he was a secretive man, it was more that he seemed to prefer encouraging others to talk about themselves. Initially this had disturbed her – he had probed a little too deeply for her liking. Then he had frightened her, or rather her own response to Alex had made her scared of him. She hadn't expected to feel such a physical attraction to another man so soon after Peter's death. It had taken her completely unawares and she had found herself out of her depth, floundering through her inability to cope with her confused emotions. It had been her misreading of the situation that had led to all the problems, she could see that; she had simply read too much into Alex's relationship with her and had over-reacted. Thank goodness she had come to her senses and she could now enjoy Alex's friendship on a more down-to-earth level. He was good company and made her laugh, and since their truce he had stopped probing. Which was why she had decided to accept his invitation. A few days away from Hulme Welford might even help her to start thinking more clearly about what she was going to do with her life. She had spent long enough licking her wounds; it was time to think of the future.

'You're quiet. You okay?'

'These friends of yours,' she said, 'what are they like? Green wellies and Labradors?'

Alex laughed. He slowed the car down, eased it round a sharp corner and then turned through a gate that led into a small cobbled courtyard. Turning the engine off, he said, 'Do I look like the sort of man who has friends out of a Jilly Cooper novel?'

Charlotte gazed up at the house in front of them. It was lovely, possibly more than a century old. Its original light stone was now, in parts, blackened with age and dotted with small, staring, mullioned windows. Around the front door was an assortment of stone-coloured tubs, but not one was filled with the usual summer array of geraniums and lobelia. Instead, the pots were home to burgeoning tomato plants.

She got out of the car and instantly the front door opened and out came a petite blonde girl in jeans and an oversized T-shirt. Her hair was tied up on top of her head in a loose knot, and wisps of it framed a pretty face that was almost angelic in appearance. Charlotte thought she looked about nineteen and that she couldn't possibly have been at university the same time as Alex.

The girl rushed to Alex's side of the car and kissed him delightedly. Their pleasure at seeing one another was obvious, especially when Alex picked her up and swung her round.

'Stop it, Alex,' she called out, 'and let me say hello to Charlotte.'

Alex did as he was told and introduced them.

'Come on in. Don't bother about your luggage, Alex can see to that later. Can't you?' Sally said, looking over her shoulder as she steered Charlotte inside. 'I've just pulled some scones out of the oven, would you like one? I've even got some cream.'

She took them through to a large welcoming kitchen – welcoming because of the smell of baking and the fact that it was so colourful and looked as though it had evolved through use rather than careful planning. There was a large dresser painted royal blue, which dominated the room. It was packed with books rather than artfully placed pieces of china. In the centre of the stone-flagged floor was a table which held a further assortment of books and the floury remains of a baking session. The walls were covered in wrinkled pieces of artwork. Charlotte presumed the artist himself was the small blond-haired boy at the far end of the kitchen sitting with his back to her. Like Becky and Philip, he was engrossed in watching the television in front of him, but unlike Becky and Philip, the sound of the television was not at blaring pitch.

'I'll just go up and tell Stephen you've arrived,' Sally said, darting out of the room.

Charlotte watched Alex walk over to Mark. He said nothing until he was directly in front of the child. When the boy saw Alex he leapt excitedly to his feet. Alex gathered him up in his arms and brought him over to Charlotte. 'Mark, this is my friend Charlotte.' His voice was strangely slow.

'Hello,' she said, a little shyly and somewhat surprised at how gorgeous this particular child was. But there again, the only children she even vaguely knew were Philip, with his belligerent face, and Becky with her many pouting madam expressions.

An open smiling face looked at her with undisguised curiosity, but soon turned back to Alex. 'Uncle Lex,' Mark said, slowly and in a distorted voice, 'play monsters?'

Alex smiled and then put him down on the floor. 'Later, Mark,' he said slowly. 'Let me say hello to your father first.' Satisfied, Mark went back to the television and Alex joined Charlotte.

'Is he deaf?' she asked in a low voice.

'Yes. So there's no need to whisper. But isn't he great?'

'God, life's a bitch, isn't it?'

'I wouldn't say that.'

'Stephen!' The two men hugged each other with unrestrained affection, Charlotte noticed, and in a way so few men feel able to do. Alex introduced Charlotte.

Stephen smiled at her as he shook her hand. He was slightly taller than Alex and almost as blond as his pretty wife. It wasn't hard to see how between them they had created such a beautiful child.

'I hope my coming hasn't put you to any extra trouble,' Charlotte said, wanting to sound genuine but suspecting she sounded terribly trite.

'Not a bit of it,' Sally said, coming into the kitchen. 'Stephen, why don't you take Charlotte into the sitting-room and Alex can help me get some tea together.'

Leading the way but still within earshot of his wife, Stephen said, 'Round here we call Sally the Ayatollah. We pray to her at least six times a day.' A pair of rolled-up children's socks came flying through the door and hit him on the back of his neck.

He took Charlotte into a large square room with deep mullioned windows which overlooked the garden and a vast landscape of open moorland beyond. Late afternoon sunlight filtered through the windows giving a brilliant, almost theatrical light to the room. Like the kitchen, this room was no slave to fashion either, but held an eclectic assortment of homely-looking armchairs and tables, with a patchwork of paintings on the walls ranging from bucolic landscapes to a stunning watercolour portrait of Mark. There was a silver-framed photograph on a windowsill that caught Charlotte's eye. It was of Stephen and Sally on their wedding day and Alex was there too, with his arm round . . . a girl who looked just like Sally.

Stephen gestured to a squashy armchair for Charlotte. He sat down opposite her. 'You've caught us on a good day,' he said. 'The sun has barely shown itself all week. With a bit of luck, you and Alex might even be able to go on some decent walks. He has warned you about his passion for walking, hasn't he?'

'No, he's kept quiet about that.'

'Hold on, Stephen,' Alex said, coming into the room with a large tea tray, 'you're not giving away all my secrets, are you?'

'I wouldn't dream of it,' Stephen said.

Later that evening, while Stephen and Alex were both upstairs putting Mark to bed and Charlotte was helping to prepare supper, Sally caught her off guard. 'Alex told us your husband died earlier this year . . . in a car crash, he said.'

Charlotte concentrated hard on scraping the potato in her hand. 'Yes,' she said, simply. She felt annoyed at this untimely reminder of Peter. The day had been going so well. 'So what else did he tell you about me?' The thought occurred to her that perhaps Alex had asked Sally to do his probing for him.

Sally stopped what she was doing. She put the vegetable knife down on the chopping board. 'I'm sorry,' she said, 'I shouldn't have said anything. Here, have some wine and you can tell me to mind my own business.'

Grateful for Sally's change of tack, Charlotte took the glass from her. She remembered the silver-framed photograph she had seen earlier and asked, 'Is that your sister in the wedding photo of you and Stephen, in the sitting-room?'

'Yes, my twin sister Lucy,' Sally replied, bending down to the oven and sliding a large casserole in. 'She died seven years ago.'

Her voice was matter of fact, in a way Charlotte felt

sure hers would never be when talking about Peter's death. 'It's my turn to be sorry now,' she said.

'Don't be. It doesn't hurt any more to talk about her. You're not intruding on my grief . . . like I just did with you. It was crass of me. I should have realised it would be too soon for you to talk about your husband with somebody you hardly know.'

Was that another attempt to get her to open up, Charlotte wondered? She chose to ignore it. 'Was it a sudden death?'

'No. Leukaemia. It took her sixteen months to die . . . it was a long and painful time for us all . . . especially for Alex.' She saw the look on Charlotte's face. 'You did know that he and Lucy were . . .'

'No,' Charlotte said, her heart suddenly heavy with sadness for Alex. Why had he never said anything? Was it possible he was still in love with the memory of Lucy?

'You know, Lucy and I could never fool Alex,' Sally said, adopting a more cheerful voice. 'We led all our boyfriends a merry old dance. We'd swap dates and they'd never know. We even fooled poor Stephen. But Alex was the only one who could separate us. I used to joke that it was his sixth sense. Once he threatened to put us both over his knee if he ever suspected we were trying it on with him.'

'And did you?'

Sally laughed. 'Lucy was all set to give it a go but I chickened out. Believe it or not, I was the more timid of the two of us.'

'You must miss her. How did you come to terms with losing someone you were so close to?'

'This might seem strange but I don't think in terms of having lost her completely. Maybe because we were twins I feel a bit of Lucy is still with me.'

'And Alex, how did he . . . ?'

'It was so much harder for Alex. When Lucy died it was as though she took away his future. He had spent so long determined he was going to live the rest of his life with her. I had Stephen. But Alex had no one. He was alone and has been ever since.'

Chapter Twenty-Nine

As they were finishing breakfast the next morning, the telephone rang. Stephen went to answer it in his study. He came back after a couple of minutes. 'Sorry,' he said, picking up the remains of his toast, 'but I'm going to have to leave you. One of the surgeons has gone down with tonsillitis, so bang goes a rare day off.' He turned to Sally. 'I'll give you a ring when I think I'll be able to get away.'

'You didn't tell me Stephen was a surgeon,' Charlotte said, when Sally and Mark had gone to the front door to wave goodbye to him.

'I didn't think we needed to pin identity labels on everyone,' Alex said, getting up from the table and starting to clear away the dishes.

Charlotte laughed. 'What a horrid, nasty man you are.'

At Sally's insistence, Alex and Charlotte were sent out on a walk. Mark's disappointed face peered from the doorway as they set off.

They turned left at the gate and set off along the open moorland road. At a fork in the road Alex chose the right one and led Charlotte uphill until they came to a footpath, which took them to a small craggy outcrop. A dozen or so frightened rabbits scampered away at the sound of encroaching footsteps, their lean bodies slithering into crevices hidden deep in the rocks. A bird flew overhead and Charlotte watched Alex raise his head, shading his eyes against the sun. 'A curlew,' he said, coming to a stop.

'I'll take your word for it,' she answered, her eyes remaining on Alex. Since her conversation with Sally last night she had been unable to stop herself thinking of Lucy and the devastating effect her death must have had on Alex. But the most persistent thought running through her mind was what it must have been like for Lucy to be loved in such a way. Plainly Alex had adored her.

From where they stood, they had a clear uninterrupted view of a landscape of endless moorland. The purple heather was at its best, with a summer fragrance that carried lightly on the wind. Charlotte sat down on one of the rocks, letting the moment last. The sprawling landscape held a quietness that right now she needed. There was a timeless quality about it that meant just here, just now, she was held in its reassuring vacuum. 'Thank you,' she said, looking up at Alex.

'What for?' He joined her on an adjacent rock.

'For this, for bringing me here.'

'It was a risk though, wasn't it?'

She smiled. 'I hadn't got you down as a gambling man.'

'Full of surprises, me.'

'Mm . . . you're right, you are.' Charlotte decided it was now or never. She wanted Alex to tell her about Lucy. She knew if she didn't hear the words from him she would never be able to rid herself of the memory of what Sally had told her last night – *He was alone and has been ever since*. 'Sally told me about her sister dying.'

There was no shocked response from him, as she might have thought. 'Did she tell you about Lucy and me?'

'A little. She mentioned . . .'

'Come on.' He stood up and took her hand, pulling her

towards him. 'Let's walk and I'll tell you about my dark and murky past.'

They left the crags behind them and followed the footpath out across the purple heather. 'The four of us were all at university together,' Alex told her. 'We were a mixed bag to say the least. There was me, a complete freak as far as computers were concerned, and Stephen studying medicine. We were in our third year and both lodging with Mrs Holroyd. Remember, I told you about her? Then along came Sally and Lucy, into the house next door. They were both studying psychology – they really were identical, in everything. There were times when Stephen couldn't even . . .'

'Yes, Sally told me how he had trouble telling them apart, but that you always could.'

'Don't ask me how, I just knew.'

'I'm sorry, I interrupted. Carry on.'

'It wasn't long before I knew that I wanted to marry Lucy. I asked her several times and each time she turned me down, but refused to give a reason. Then we graduated and both ended up in London, independently of each other, but friends, close friends. I was working with Henderson and Wyatt and in a better position to ask Lucy to marry me, so I asked her one more time. Over dinner in her flat she told me she would never marry anybody and she explained why. She had this recurring dream – she'd had it since she was a child – that she was going to die before the age of thirty. She didn't want anyone to be saddled with that kind of heartbreak . . . she was so certain she was going to die.'

'But that's awful. Surely you must have convinced her otherwise.'

He shook his head. 'I managed to persuade her to live with me, and then, two years later, she was diagnosed as having leukaemia. She carried on working for as long as she could but she spent more and more time in hospital, until the doctors said there was nothing else they could do. She pleaded with me to bring her up here to Yorkshire to be with Sally and Stephen. They'd settled here by then. They nursed her to the end. Sally gave up her lecturing job at Leeds and I tried to spend as much time as I could helping . . . and just being there with Lucy. We all became very close during that time. I suppose the text books would call it a bonding experience.'

When he didn't carry on, Charlotte reached out to him. She touched his arm with her hand. 'Oh Alex. How *did* you cope, when you loved her so much?'

'I . . .' He looked down at his arm and without thinking he picked up Charlotte's hand, turned it over and pressed her palm to his lips, closing his eyes momentarily. 'It was Sally who held me . . . held us all together.' He lowered Charlotte's hand, but kept it at his side. 'She's incredibly strong. Nothing ever fazes her, not even after Mark was born and she and Stephen realised he was deaf.'

'Yes, I could see when she talked to me last night that there was a lot more to her than her youthful good looks.' But Charlotte wasn't only thinking of Sally's strength of character and courage, but of the determined love Alex once had for another woman. To be loved like that . . .'

'Shall we go back to the crags now? There's something I'd like to show you.'

They stood where they had been an hour earlier. Small puffy white clouds had bubbled up and were hanging listlessly in the blue sky; the persistent cry of curlews overhead provided the only sound to penetrate the emptiness of the landscape.

'What did you want to show me?'

Alex guided her round to the back of a massive rock, weathered smooth by wind and time. 'Stand just there,' he said, 'about four feet away from the rock, and tell me what you can see.'

She laughed, feeling slightly silly, but did as he asked. 'Nothing in particular, just a large dark stone.' She turned to face him. 'Is that it?'

'Charlotte – I asked you this before – do you trust me?'

'For goodness' sake, Alex, what is all this?'

He took a step closer to her. 'That large dark stone, as you call it, represents Peter.'

She stepped away from him and pushed her hands down deep into the pockets of her jeans. She felt cross with Alex for reminding her of her failed marriage. And anyway, she had all that under control now. She had already begun to close that particular box in her life. 'I thought I was supposed to come here to get away from my problems.'

Why had he started this? What was he doing risking everything with her all over again? But Alex's instinct told him that something was stopping Charlotte from putting Peter to rest, and he suspected he knew what it was. 'I think it's time you started facing up to the main problem in your life,' he said.

'Oh yes,' she said, scathing sarcasm ringing in her voice. 'And what would that be, Mr Know-it-all?'

'I'm only guessing, but for some reason I think you're blaming yourself for what happened to Peter. Am I right?'

'That's rubbish,' she shouted defiantly. 'And what gives *you* the right to make assumptions like that?' She started to walk away from him. She was furious. Why couldn't he leave her be? They had been happy a few moments ago. Why did he have to keep spoiling things?

'Because,' Alex called out, catching up with her, 'when

Lucy finally died . . . I felt such relief that it was all over. Suddenly I was free of the daily burden of grief that I'd experienced for two years. But that feeling of freedom soon passed and guilt took a hold of me and I nearly screwed up completely. I think guilt is your problem and, believe me, I know about it.' He was almost shouting at her now. He hadn't meant to, but he wanted to convince Charlotte that she was not alone.

She faced him. 'So what happened to you?'

'I pushed myself harder and harder at work, got more and more run down. Then Stephen came to stay. He saw the mess I was in and insisted I came back here to rest. One day Sally brought me to this very place and stood me behind that rock. She asked me what I could see and my answer was more or less what you just said, except I emphasised the darkness . . . for me the whole world had been eclipsed by what I was doing to myself.'

Charlotte swallowed hard. 'What did Sally say next?'

Alex led Charlotte back to the rock. When she was standing where she had stood a few moments ago, he said, 'Step back six paces and tell me what you can see now.'

She wanted to shout, oh stop all this nonsense, it's so facile, but instead she said, 'I can see . . . how much do you want me to tell you?'

'Everything you see.'

'Blue sky, white clouds, a bird flying, dry-stone walls, grass, some sheep, small houses over there, a church.' Without looking at Alex, she said, 'Is that where Lucy is buried?'

'Yes, but don't change the subject. Do you want to know what Sally said next?'

'Okay.'

'She told me it was time to step back from my boulder of guilt and take a look at the world behind it.'

'That's very interesting,' she said, 'but I'm over Peter's death, and I certainly don't have a problem with guilt.' She gave the rock a vicious kick and once again started to walk away.

But Alex was ready for her. He placed a firm hand on her shoulder and pulled her round to face him. 'Charlotte,' he said gently, 'stop pretending. Try talking to someone about it. Surely you must have a friend you could talk to.'

'No,' she answered. 'We were on the move so much I didn't make many close friends. Anyway, they're too busy, too wrapped up in their own lives and marriages to listen to me . . . apart from that, they all think that Peter and I . . .'

'Peter and you what?'

She remained silent, turned her face away from him.

And then he knew, understood at last what Charlotte's real pain was about. How stupid he had been! He had wondered at the time about those words she had uttered in the garden at Ivy Cottage, about her life in Belgium – *It was empty and cold and I hated it*. But that wasn't about her life in Belgium at all, that was her life with Peter. He said, 'So they all think that you and Peter had the perfect marriage? That you of all people couldn't possibly have stopped loving your husband. Is that it, Charlotte? Charlotte, talk to me.'

'Yes!' She yelled back at him. 'Yes, yes! Only hours before Peter died I'd asked him for a divorce . . . there, you're the first person I've told. Are you satisfied now?' Her words were angry and filled with pain as though they had been extracted from her under torture. And then suddenly her anger subsided and she fell against Alex and allowed him to lead her back to the rocks. There they sat, her shaking body held tightly against his own, while she sobbed and sobbed.

'I killed him, didn't I?' Charlotte said, when at last she had calmed down and had managed to tell Alex what had happened that snowy February morning and what had led to it. 'I upset him and he was in no state to drive. I shouldn't have let him go . . . I should have . . .'

Still with his arms round her, Alex said, 'But it was Peter who chose to walk out of the apartment that morning, it was Peter who was behind the wheel of his car, not you '

She pulled away from him and shook her head. 'But Alex, if I hadn't said anything, Peter would still be alive today. I'm sure of it.'

'Would he, though? He would still have driven on that same road, he would have been just as determined to get to his meeting in Luxembourg . . . would have encountered that same patch of ice.'

'Yes, but that conversation did take place and it must have affected the way he drove.'

'Look, Charlotte, you have to come to terms with the fact that we can't control other people's reactions, it's just not possible. What happened to Peter happened because he chose to make that journey.'

He took her hand in his and squeezed it gently. She sighed and leaned against him again. They sat in silence for a while, until Alex placed a hand under her chin. 'Okay now?' he said in a low voice.

'Yes.' She lifted her head. Her eyes fixed on him were heavy with sadness and wonder. His heart twisted with compassion and he stroked the stray wisps of hair away from her face. Her eyes closed at his touch. He kissed first one eye, then the other, and then he kissed her on the lips, tentatively at first, but when she responded with an eagerness that matched his own, he cradled her head and tilted her back on to the flat surface of the rock. The touch and feel of her body clinging to him filled him with desire. Then in the distance he heard voices, children's voices. He tried to ignore the noise, hoping he was imagining it, but Charlotte's body was shaking. He looked down into her face, concerned. But she was laughing, her eyes wide open and reflecting the blue sky above. 'God, you're beautiful,' he said. 'Do you suppose we're always going to be interrupted?' He sat up and pulled her towards him as the voices came nearer.

She sprang to her feet, still laughing as a Scout troop weighed down with enormous backpacks passed by. 'We'll have to see, won't we?' she said.

They headed for home, hand in hand.

That evening, Charlotte and Sally were left alone while Stephen and Alex disappeared off to the pub for a pint of beer. It was a warm evening and they sat out in the garden with a bottle of Chianti and a large bag of peas to shell for supper. Charlotte began to tell Sally some of what happened on her walk with Alex that morning.

Looking up from the bowl of peas on her lap, Sally said, 'Why do you think you and Peter got married in the first place?'

'I think he only asked me to marry him because his parents didn't approve of me. They thought I was just a shop girl. The fact that it was my own shop was immaterial to them. I wasn't good enough for their son and Peter wanted to get his own back. In fact I don't think he would have married anyone who his parents actually did approve of.'

'So why did you accept?'

'Because . . . oh dear, this is going to sound pathetic, but I truly believed I could undo all the harm of Peter's upbringing.'

'Saint Charlotte the Saviour, eh?'

'That's not nice,' Charlotte said, but she smiled all the same.

'So, you married and then found you didn't have the necessary saintly qualities. But what made you want to take that final step to end your marriage?'

Charlotte snapped open a pea pod and popped out the peas. She put one in her mouth. 'It was when I knew that Peter was always going to put work first, that he didn't need a wife, simply someone permanently on hand to massage his ego. Then I knew I couldn't carry on as we were. Selfishly, I suppose, I wanted more . . . I wanted to be loved.'

'Nothing particularly selfish in that.'

'Okay then, you might be able to convince me that I shouldn't feel guilty about wanting to be loved, but how about the fact that I'm responsible for Peter's death?'

Sally put her bowl of peas down on the grass and picked up her wine glass. 'You're *not* responsible for Peter's death. It's possible that you want to believe you're to blame, and then not forgive yourself for it, because you want to keep punishing yourself. It can be an insidious self-defence mechanism against grief. Focusing on the injustice means that you can't forgive yourself, can't grieve properly. Does that make any sense, ring any bells?'

Charlotte leaned back in her chair. 'Oh yes,' she said. 'Yes, it certainly does.'

'More Chianti?'

'Mm . . . please.'

As Charlotte reached forward with her glass Sally said, 'Now, what are you going to do about Alex? You do realise, don't you, that you're the first woman he's allowed himself to fall in love with since Lucy?'

Chapter Thirty

They drove back to Hulme Welford after breakfast the following day. Mark was disappointed that Alex wasn't staying longer. 'Come again,' he shouted as Alex started up the engine. And while Stephen said goodbye to Alex, Sally came round to Charlotte's side of the car.

'Now remember,' she said, 'stop being so hard on yourself.'

Charlotte leaned out of the car and gave Sally a kiss on the cheek. 'Thanks for everything.'

Once they had left the Pennines behind them and they were skirting round north Manchester, Charlotte realised that she was going home reluctantly. She had hoped her time away from Hulme Welford would give her the opportunity to think more clearly about her future. It hadn't. Her disclosure to Alex had left her battered and bruised, but it had made her see that she had been kidding herself that she was getting over Peter. Sally was right: she hadn't allowed herself to grieve for Peter, she had been too frightened of the consequences.

And Alex. What was she to do about him? Again she could no longer ignore what had been staring her in the face all these weeks. But love? Perhaps Sally was wrong. Maybe Alex might never be able to love another woman. Could anyone ever replace Lucy? Could she . . . did she want to?

With so much of the past hanging over her, Charlotte

knew there was a lot she had to consider before she could even contemplate the future. She had to speak to Alex, and soon, but she didn't know where to start.

'You've got something to say, haven't you?'

She looked across at Alex. 'Sally mentioned you had a sixth sense.'

'That's great coming from her. I've never known anyone more perceptive.'

You're the first woman he's allowed himself to fall in love with . . . 'And is she always right?'

'Usually. But I'm an amateur compared to her. I only know when you've got something important to say because you frown slightly and you get three lines, just here.' He took his eyes off the motorway briefly and placed a finger on her forehead.

Her stomach lurched as he touched her. 'You're right though,' she said, watching his hand move back to the steering wheel, 'I do have something I want to say.'

'Go on, then.'

'No, not now. Later. I need to think first.'

'How about tonight, then? I'll cook us a meal, and you can talk.'

'I don't . . .'

'Look,' he said patiently, 'I want to call on Cindy and Derek and then perhaps go and see Barry in hospital. Do you want to come with me? We could talk afterwards.'

'You're very sure Barry's still alive, aren't you?'

He moved his hand from the wheel and rested it on her knee. 'If there's one thing my time with Lucy taught me, it was never to give up hope.'

'But she *died*, Alex,' Charlotte said, mystified.

'Yes, but *I* didn't . . . I thought my life would end when hers did, but it didn't.'

*

They tried calling at In The Pink later that afternoon and found the whole place shut. They drove on to the hospital where, at Barry's door, they were greeted by Tiffany. 'Come in. We were just talking about you two.'

'You were?' Alex smiled and walked over to the bed. 'Hello Barry, how's it going?'

'Surprisingly good, considering. Just tired, mainly.'

Charlotte couldn't believe what she was seeing. There was Barry, sitting up in bed wearing his familiar glasses, with a book lying open at his side. He looked pale and tired, and was still attached to a drip, but there was no sign of death about him, nor that there ever had been. She was so pleased! She went straight up to Barry and gave him a kiss, and then, sensing his embarrassment at her unexpected display of euphoria, she said, 'We've all been so worried about you.'

'Sorry to have been a nuisance,' he said, pushing his glasses up on his nose.

'Muffin 'ell, will you listen to him!' Tiffany shouted. 'Get him to tell you his exam results, they came this morning.'

'No, Tiffany, they don't want to know about that.'

''Course they do.' She turned to Alex and Charlotte. 'They're brill. Pure genius, this lad.'

Barry picked up the piece of paper by the side of his bed and passed it to Alex.

'A for physics,' Alex read out, 'A for chemistry, A for biology and, wait for it, A for economics. I'll say one thing for you, Barry, you're consistent. Well done!'

'Yes,' agreed Charlotte. 'Congratulations! I used to hate people like you at school. Your parents must be delighted, and I don't just mean with your exam results.'

'Dad's been a real head-case,' Tiffany said. 'He was here on his own when Barry came round on Tuesday.' She laughed. 'I'm not sure Dad's the first person I'd want to see after being in a coma!'

'Don't be so hard on him,' Barry said.

'What?' she cried. 'After the things he's said to you?'

'It's just his way.'

'So where are your parents?' Alex asked. 'We called in at your place, but there was no sign of anyone there.'

'The salon and everything's been shut since Barry's been here, but Mum and Dad are somewhere in the hospital. They went off to find the doctor to see about Barry coming home. We're hoping it'll be in a few days, or rather Dad is – he won't want to be paying for this private room for too long, will he? So anyway, you two been away or what?'

'Stop being so nosy, Tiffany,' Barry said.

Alex laughed. 'So that's what you were talking about when we arrived.' Worried that Barry was more tired than he was letting on, he added, 'We'd better be going, don't want to wear out the patient.'

'We reckon you've been away, *together*,' Tiffany persisted.

'Correction,' said Barry. 'That's what my sister thinks. Honestly, Tiffany, you get more like Dad every day.'

'Bloody well don't!'

Charlotte looked at Alex and realised that he was leaving it up to her to decide what to say. 'You're absolutely right, Tiffany. Alex took me to see some friends of his.'

Tiffany was triumphant. 'Told you,' she said, looking at her brother.

'You know,' Alex said, in the car on the way home, 'I don't think I can take the suspense any longer. Do you want to tell me now what it is that's on your mind?' Since their drive back from Yorkshire, he had been conscious of Charlotte's preoccupation with her own thoughts and he suspected that it had something to do with what she wanted to talk to him about. He sensed it wasn't good.

'Yes, perhaps you're right,' Charlotte answered distantly, 'now is probably as good as later. I just want to say how grateful I am for these past few days. You were right about many things, especially my liking Stephen and Sally.'

'So, why is it I detect an unspoken "but" in what you've just said?'

'Alex, both you and Sally made me see that I haven't really begun to get over Peter . . . Sally also said . . .' Charlotte paused, unsure just how to carry on. In her mind, she had worked out exactly what to say to him; it had sounded perfectly reasonable when she had gone over it earlier, but now she didn't feel so convinced. Sitting close to Alex in the car, watching his hands on the steering wheel, she was reminded of their time at the crags, when his hands had caressed her with such tenderness. The memory was so provocative she could almost feel the weight of his body against her own, could remember exactly the sensation of his mouth on hers. She shifted awkwardly in her seat.

'She told you I loved you, didn't she?' Alex said, bringing the car to a stop at a red traffic light. He turned and looked at her.

'Yes, she did.'

'So where does that leave us?'

'Oh Alex, I don't know. I feel so confused. I don't want to lie to you, it wouldn't be fair. I just don't think I'm capable of loving anyone, not after . . .'

'But you might feel differently in time.'

'Please, please don't push me.'

262

The traffic lights turned to amber, then green, and they completed the rest of the journey in silence.

Sat in his office, Alex was strangely calm. Surely he hadn't really hoped for more. He had been a fool to think that anyone who had gone through what Charlotte had would be inclined to take up with another man so soon. He had to give her space, so that she could get over Peter's death properly. She may not have loved him when he died, but she still had to go through some sort of grieving process for the man she had been married to for eight years; a process which, up until now, she had avoided.

Patience. That's what was called for. Let's face it, he had been patient with Lucy for all those years. He stared into the VDU screen in front of him, its blank whiteness waiting expectantly for him to fill it. He switched it off. Why, he wondered, did he fall for women who were determined to keep him at arm's length? Why couldn't he be satisfied with the Heathers of this world?

Chapter Thirty-One

When Barry was discharged from hospital, he was welcomed home by the residents of Acacia Lane. Even Iris Braithwaite surprised everyone by calling round. 'A pot of honey for your son, Mrs Rogers. I recommend two spoonfuls a days, soon have him back on his feet.' Then Charlotte herself received a surprise.

She had just got back from the supermarket and emptied the car, when she looked out of the kitchen window and saw Alex sitting in the garden talking to an extraordinarily glamorous woman. It was a while before Charlotte realised who it was, because initially the combination of this particular woman sitting in this particular rickety old garden chair beneath her fig tree threw her completely.

'Christina!' she shouted, rushing outside. 'What on earth are you doing here?'

'Carlotta, my darling,' Christina said, rising elegantly from the old chair, 'I have been waiting here for you, so long.' She wrapped her graceful arms around Charlotte and kissed her several times. Then, standing back, she gave Charlotte a long hard stare. 'You still look dreadful, but slightly better than when you lived in Brussels. Carlotta, why are you looking like that, as though you weren't expecting me?'

'That's because I wasn't expecting you.'

'Did you not receive my letter, telling you I was coming?'

Charlotte shook her head. 'Sorry, no letter.'

'Oh, that is too bad. Then there is nothing else for it. I shall leave you to recover from your shock and return tomorrow. Perhaps that would suit you better?' She offered Alex one of her most seductive smiles. 'I am sure Mr Hamilton here would provide me with a bed for the night.'

Alex smiled, until Charlotte threw him a keep-out-of-this look. 'Don't be so silly, Christina,' she said. 'I'm delighted you're here. It's just that there's nothing ready for you and the house is such a mess.'

Christina shrugged her shoulders dismissively. 'What else do I need? I have your company and your nice Mr Hamilton to amuse me.' She laid a perfectly manicured hand on his arm. 'Oh yes, I have everything I could possibly desire.' She seemed to add an extra emphasis to the word desire. Charlotte began to feel uneasy.

'And why, Carlotta, have you never written to me of your charming neighbour? If I had been you I would have written of little else.'

Trying hard not to laugh, Alex got to his feet. 'I think I'd better leave you to it. I have some work I need to get on with.'

Christina looked up at him. 'I am so sorry to have kept you. But Carlotta darling, could we not invite Mr Hamilton for dinner?'

'I'm sure,' Charlotte said firmly, giving Alex a warning glance, 'that Mr Hamilton has far too much work to do to spare us any of his valuable time.'

'I have?' asked Alex.

'You have,' Charlotte repeated. 'You've probably got enough to keep you busy for days.'

'Oh, stacks to do,' Alex said, making a move towards his part of the house. 'I shan't surface for weeks probably. Goodbye.'

'Well,' Christina said, in a voice designed to carry, 'what a most desirable man and those gorgeous blue eyes. Have you slept with him?'

'Christina!' cried Charlotte in a shocked voice, watching Alex as he disappeared inside. Had he heard?

'What, what have I said? He's young, he's handsome, he's amusing and he's living in your house with you. Why in heaven's name do you not sleep with him?'

That, thought Charlotte, is the million-dollar question.

Charlotte unpacked the shopping and stuffed the empty carrier bags into the bin, ignoring Hilary's imaginary voice in her head reminding her of the recycling banks in the village. What on earth was she going to give Christina for supper that night? She pulled open the fridge, knelt down and stared at all the food she had just bought. She waited for inspiration to come, but it was no good – she had only chosen convenience foods in the supermarket. They would have to go out to eat. She'd drive them over to Knutsford; plenty of upmarket restaurants there to impress Christina with.

Charlotte opened a can of dog food for Mabel and was putting the dish down on the floor by the back door when a cloud of expensive perfume came into the kitchen, followed by Christina. She was dressed in a close-fitting, red and white striped dress, which would have made anyone else look like a stick of candy, but on Christina looked stunning.

Mabel obviously thought so too. Giving her dish of food not a second glance, she pattered across the kitchen floor, looked up at Christina and rolled over on to her back, her paws hanging limply in the air.

'Oh, what a perfectly splendid little *bambino*,' Christina cried. She bent down to Mabel and rubbed her tummy. 'Carlotta, you have much to tell me, I think. Why don't you take me out to one of your famous pubs for supper?'

Charlotte laughed. 'I don't think the Spinner is quite ready for you, Christina.'

'But I am ready for the Spinner. Come on, Carlotta, where is your sense of fun? Let me get you out of those drab clothes and into something to set the Spinner on fire.'

It was impossible not to catch Christina's infectious humour and it made Charlotte realise that up until that point she had acted quite churlishly towards her friend. She wondered why. Was it because Christina had flirted so outrageously with Alex in the garden?

They opened the wardrobe doors in Charlotte's bedroom and got to work. 'Too dull,' Christina said, as Charlotte took out a smart pair of fawn-coloured trousers. 'Too morbid,' she sighed in response to a black pair. 'Come on, Carlotta, go for lightness, lightness of heart and spirit. Oh, I can see I came just in time to save you from dying of dullness. Ah here, wear this.'

Charlotte looked doubtfully at the strapless cream dress in Christina's hands. She hadn't worn it since last summer, when she had gone with Peter to Nice, he to give a presentation at the company conference and she to sit next to him at the dinner afterwards and bask gratefully in his reflected glory. After the meal the chairman had stood up and thanked all his hard-working colleagues for their unstinting loyalty to the company, telling them to keep up the good work. Not a word did he say to those wives present who had given up so much of themselves to travel with their husbands so that they could feel fulfilled; not a word of thanks to those wives who had given up their own careers and possibly their children to boarding school for the sake of continuity in their education. When the last of the liqueurs had been tossed back and the cigars stubbed out, Charlotte had tried to tempt Peter into a walk along the beach, but he had refused, preferring instead the company of his overhead slides for another presentation he had to give the following morning. And so, beneath the midnight sky, her shoes in her hands, Charlotte had walked along the water's edge alone.

'Okay,' she said. 'I'll wear it.'

She slipped into the dress and sat on a stool in the bathroom to let Christina see to the rest of her. First her friend wove her hair into a French plait. Then came her face. Looking with disgust at Charlotte's haphazard collection of make-up, Christina fetched her own. When she declared that she was finished, Charlotte looked apprehensively into the mirror. She was delighted. The shadows under her eyes had magically disappeared and somehow Christina had managed, with a few simple strokes of powder, mascara and lipstick, to give her a facelift. She looked good and she felt wonderful.

'And now,' Christina said, 'you must wear my perfume. We must not clash, we must not compete with each other.' She sprayed Charlotte liberally. 'There now, you are ready, and I think it would be nice for us to have a chaperon for the evening.'

'No,' Charlotte said vehemently. 'Alex is busy.'

Christina laughed. 'What a charming idea. But no, I was thinking of your little *bambino*. This is strictly a girls' night out.'

When they strolled arm in arm down Acacia Lane Charlotte was aware of a strange feeling bubbling up inside her. It wasn't until they got as far as the village hall that she recognised what the strange feeling was. She felt incredibly sexy. Tottering along on her high heels, wearing her girlfriend's lipstick and feeling as radiant as a star, she was nineteen again. With sadness, she knew she had never felt like that with Peter. How out of touch with her emotions she had become . . . until now. She caught her breath. Oh Alex. There it was. The truth, at last. Alex had unwittingly frightened her because he had made her come to know what she had been missing all these years and as hard as she had tried to resist him it had only made things worse, had made her want him all the more.

They made a predictably striking entrance at the Spinner, causing heads to turn and Ted the Toup to lose contact with the cigarette drooping out of his mouth; it plopped and fizzed into his beer. While Charlotte herself wasn't entirely comfortable with the position of centre stage, she knew Christina was perfectly at ease. For Christina there was no other position.

Hoping there would be fewer people outside, Charlotte led the way through the noisy public bar and out to the garden. They sat in the evening sun at a large wooden table with two benches either side, and the landlord came out personally to serve them. He took their order with a flourish of efficiency that would have even impressed Iris Braithwaite.

'Now Carlotta,' Christina said, when they were alone, 'how have you been? Your letters tell me nothing about you, only about your sister and your parents, oh, and a Mrs Britwit.'

'Mrs Braithwaite,' Charlotte corrected, with a smile.

'Now, tell me about yourself. Are you happy?'

'I'm happier.'

Christina shook her head. 'That is not good enough. Let me ask you this: would you rather be back in Brussels in that miserable apartment with that miserable husband of yours?'

'Christina, you can't ask things like that.'

'But I just have.'

'Well, no. No, I wouldn't want to be back there.'

'Good, so we have progress; now all you have to do is forgive yourself.'

Charlotte looked up sharply. This was exactly what Sally had told her. Was there a conspiracy? 'Why do you say that?'

'Because it's true. I was there with you in Brussels, I saw how unhappy you were. I knew why too. I knew that you felt guilty because you could not make yourself fit your husband's requirements. Few wives truly can. I knew too that you did not love Mr Carlotta . . . and that Mr Carlotta did not love you. So simple really. Nobody's fault, so nobody to blame, just forgive and—'

'But you can't forget,' Charlotte interrupted.

'No, I was not going to say forget, I was going to say *move on*. You should be a Catholic like me: you get forgiven every week and you move on.'

Charlotte laughed and then she frowned. 'Would you like to hear a confession?'

'Why not?'

'Remember the morning Peter died?'

'Yes, I remember it well, all that snow.'

'While we were having breakfast I asked Peter for a divorce.'

Christina looked across the table at her friend. She took Charlotte's hand. 'Oh my poor little Carlotta, so that is why you are still sad, I see now. But why did you not tell me?'

'Because . . .'

'Because you are so very English.'

'And you are not, if you don't mind me saying,' said the landlord of the Spinner as he put their tray of food down on the table.

'My dear man,' smiled Christina, 'how clever of you. What gave me away?'

The man beamed. 'Oh you know, little things.' He passed them their chicken and chips. 'The drinks are on the house,' he added, almost bowing as he made his exit.

'Tell me, Carlotta, here is a phrase I do not know – the drinks are on the house. What does it mean?'

Charlotte laughed. 'It means they're free, because the landlord of the Spinner has fallen in love with you, Christina.'

'That is good, we shall come here tomorrow, I think,' she said, spearing a huge chip with her fork. 'And why have you not fallen in love with Mr Hamilton?'

Sprinkling salt on to her meal and then some vinegar, Charlotte said. 'To be honest, Christina, I think I probably could fall in love with him.'

'That is very good.'

'No, it's not good. I don't want to fall in love with him, or anyone else for that matter. Not at the moment.'

'Oh Carlotta, you make your life so very difficult.' She speared another chip. 'Delicious,' she said, putting it to her lips and managing to make it look like an erotic act. 'Now I will tell you all about my friend Henri the Diplomat. He's so beautiful and with legs to die for.'

Glad the pressure was off her, Charlotte said, 'You must be missing him.'

'I had thought I might, but that was before I met your delightful Mr Hamilton.'

Charlotte laughed. But Christina looked serious. 'Why are you laughing? What is so funny?'

'Come on, Christina, Alex is too nice to be added to your list of . . .' She paused, list of what? What did one call Christina's men friends? Were they clients or lovers? She settled for the latter. ' Lovers.'

'I think a little souvenir of England to take home might be nice though.'

Charlotte looked shocked. 'But you can't . . .'

Christina smiled. 'Oh, but I think I will. After all, you do not seem to want him, do you?'

Chapter Thirty-Two

'Just thought I'd pop round,' said Hilary coming through the open conservatory door. 'Heard you'd got a friend staying.'

I bet you did, thought Charlotte, knowing that last night's visit to the Spinner would have the village spinning on its axis in a tizzy of excitement and curiosity for days to come. And all because Christina had insisted, in a loud voice, that the Spinner wasn't the real thing. 'How can it be so, there is no piano, there is no one singing?' Hearing this, the landlord had fetched his son's keyboard down from upstairs and called upon Mr Phelps, the church organist, to come out of the snug and put his hands to good use. With everyone gathered round him ready to sing, including Christina and Charlotte, Mr Phelps rose to the occasion and surprised them all by revealing his true musical bent, which was honky-tonk. He opened up with 'Down at the Old Bull and Bush' and then moved through a repertoire that included 'We'll Meet Again', 'I'm Getting Married in the Morning', and because he knew Christina came from somewhere across the Channel he played 'Viva España' again and again, until Ted the Toup demanded 'The Birdy Song'.

'I heard there was a bit of a party down at the Spinner last night.' Hilary already knew all the details of last night's goings-on. Ted had been only too willing to impart his news when she had gone to pick up her copy of Hello!

'I danced with a fancy foreign piece last night,' he had told her with relish. 'She's a friend of your sister's from abroad, you know, got a real body on her, too.'

'So where is she, this friend of yours?' Hilary pursued.

'She's not here,' Charlotte said, scrubbing hard at a particularly stubborn stain on the cooker hob she was cleaning.

'Oh, you mean she's gone home already?' Hilary was unable to keep the disappointment out of her voice. She had rushed straight from Ted the Toup's to Charlotte's in the hope of meeting this incredible creature, who had apparently enslaved both Ted and the landlord of the Spinner in one fell swoop.

'She's out with Alex,' Charlotte answered through clenched teeth. 'He's taken her to see the Italian Gardens at Tatton.'

Hilary was shocked. She had thought that things were more or less in the bag, ever since Tiffany had told her Charlotte and Alex had been away together. But if Ted's description of this woman was anything to go by, then Alex was in serious danger. 'Why on earth didn't you go with them?'

'Because I had a headache,' Charlotte snapped back, 'and I didn't feel like it.' Reluctant as she was to admit it, this was not the truth. Over breakfast Christina had suggested they go out for the day, suggesting also, 'We could take your lovely Mr Hamilton with us?'

'Look, Christina,' Charlotte had said on the edge of losing her temper, 'let's just get this clear. Alex Hamilton is not my lovely anything, okay?'

'Okay, okay, but let's invite him anyway . . . I think I would very much like him to be my lovely something for the day.'

Before Charlotte could stop her, Christina was next

door inviting Alex to accompany them on an outing. Even worse, Alex proposed a trip to Tatton to show Christina the Italian Gardens. At the last moment, in a desperate attempt to sabotage things, Charlotte feigned a headache – a headache that had all the potential of a full-blown migraine.

'My poor Carlotta,' Christina sympathised, 'you must rest, you must stay out of the sun. I will put you to bed and there you will stay. But we cannot possibly disappoint Mr Hamilton. I shall try my best to amuse him in your absence.' She settled Charlotte in bed, pulled the curtains across and ignored her protestations of suddenly feeling so much better. 'No, no, you are only trying to be brave,' Christina insisted, shutting the bedroom door softly behind her and then the front door with a resounding bang.

'What time did they go out?' Hilary asked. 'And when are they due back?'

'What is this, Hilary, the Hulme Welford Inquisition?'

'I only asked.' Hilary decided she had better change the subject. 'What are you wearing to Barry's confirmation tomorrow?'

Charlotte moved over to the sink and rinsed out the cloth she had been using to clean the cooker. 'I really don't know. I haven't thought that far ahead.'

No, thought Hilary, I'm not surprised, not with Alex being seduced in amongst the topiary, right now this minute. 'Shall I help you choose something?'

'No!' shouted Charlotte. 'No, and I just wish everyone would leave me alone.'

Hilary tactfully withdrew to The Gables. Her only hope was that if her sister was ruffled by the fact that Alex was out with Christina, then all was not completely lost.

*

It was nearly ten o'clock that evening when Charlotte heard Alex's car pulling up on the drive, followed by the sound of Christina's light tinkling laughter. But it was well past midnight before Christina came and rang the door bell.

Charlotte let her friend in and tried to show indifference to Christina's profuse apologies for being so late. 'Carlotta, forgive me, please. I have never known the time to fly so fast.'

'Goodness, is that the time already?' Charlotte responded. 'I had no idea it was so late. I've been reading.'

Christina dropped gracefully on to the sofa and looked about her, to where her friend must have been sitting. The armchair with its squashed cushion was surrounded by a trail of late-night snacking debris – an empty coffee cup, a plate with the remains of some crackers and an empty packet of crisps. No sign of a book.

'I was reading upstairs,' lied Charlotte, knowing the conclusion Christina must have reached. Then, looking her friend in the eye, she said, 'What have you been up to all day and all evening?'

Christina laughed, eased off her shoes and stretched out her long painted toes, managing to make them perform a neat Mexican wave. Charlotte wondered whether those artful little piggies had just been caressed by Alex's hands. But the thought of Alex's hands, which she had so coveted, caught her off guard and exposed the depth of her anger.

'So come on, Christina,' she demanded, 'what have you done to Alex?'

Again that light tinkling laugh. 'Carlotta, please, do you have to be so blunt?'

'Ah! That's rich coming from you. What was it you said yesterday in the garden and quite loud enough for Alex to hear – "Have you slept with him?" Well, if that wasn't being blunt, I don't know what is.'

Christina stretched back lazily on the sofa. The smile was still in place, but her eyes were not looking so kindly. 'Tell me, Carlotta,' she said, 'what exactly is it you want to know? Whether I have been making love to your adorable Mr Hamilton, the lovely Alex, with his so, *so* blue eyes? By the way, have you ever noticed his hands, he has the most creative hands?' She noticed Charlotte's face blanch. 'Well, Carlotta, is that it, is that what you want to know?'

'Yes,' cried Charlotte, pacing the room, 'yes it bloody well is!'

Christina sighed and got up from the sofa. Carrying her shoes, she made for the door. 'I think I shall go to bed now, I am so very tired . . . but Carlotta, I think you already know the answer to your question, don't you? Good night.'

Chapter Thirty-Three

Tiffany came into the kitchen brushing her long pink hair with a heavily matted brush that had never been near the salon sterilising unit. She took one look at Barry and whistled. 'You look a bit of all right. Shame you're my brother!'

'For God's sake!' rebuked Derek, coming in behind her. 'Do you have to be so vulgar? This is Bas's bloody confirmation, not an episode of *Blind Date*.' He turned to his son. 'She's right though, Bas. That suit looks great on you. Makes you look quite a chip off the old block.'

Tiffany cringed. 'Let's hope not.'

Barry ran his hand through his hair, nudged his glasses, then fiddled with the knot of his new tie. Picking up on his son's nervousness, Derek said, 'Where's your mum? It's about time to get this show on the road, isn't it?' He looked up at the kitchen clock and then at his wristwatch, remembering that this was how he had felt twenty-two years ago, standing in his parents' tiny kitchen, before driving off to the church in his father's light green Zephyr to marry Cindy. God, how he had wanted to get all the churchy business over and done with, so that he could get on to the reception afterwards and pour a beer down his throat. He began strumming his fingers on the work-top.

'For goodness' sake, Dad, calm down,' Tiffany said,

tossing her hairbrush on to the table. She bent down to tie up a purple ribbon she had threaded through the lace-holes of one of her boots. The other boot wore an orange ribbon and both laces matched perfectly the tie-dye baby-doll smock she wore over aubergine-coloured Lycra leggings. Straightening up, she added, 'Mum was outside ordering the caterers about in the marquee the last time I saw her.'

'Well go and give her a shout, will you? Tell her it's time to hit Westminster Abbey.' He watched his daughter go clomping off, then called after her, 'And tell her nicely. I don't want you rattling her today. Nervous, Bas?' he said, when Tiffany had gone.

Barry smiled. 'A bit.'

'Jesus, so am I! Sorry, shouldn't have said that, should I?'

'What?'

'You know, the Jesus bit.'

Barry laughed. 'Relax, Dad, it's me who's getting confirmed, not you.'

Derek looked hard at his son and felt real pride. Bas hadn't put the weight back on that he'd lost and his face still showed signs of fatigue, but despite this, Derek found himself having to admit that Bas was better looking than he himself had ever been. A damned sight smarter as well. Ever since that dreadful phone call, the day of the barbecue, he had felt differently towards Bas. Strange, too, that since that day he hadn't made any further attempts on Charlotte; he had left the gate to that par-ticular field wide open for Alex. God, he hoped he wasn't going through some kind of midlife crisis.

He glanced across the kitchen at Bas again, seeing him no longer as some young kid who embarrassed him, but as a man . . . as a friend even. He cleared his throat.

'Look, Bas,' he started to say, 'things haven't always been . . .' He paused, frightened of making a complete fool of himself.

'What, Dad, what's up?'

Derek paced over to the French windows and looked out at the garden where there seemed to be dozens of people milling about, some with chairs, some with covered trays and some with bottles of wine. He ran his tongue over his lips, wanting more than anything a drink.

'What's wrong, Dad?'

He turned round to face his son. 'I just wanted to say . . . well, the thing is . . . I don't want to let you down today.'

'You won't.'

'But I have already. I mean, all these years I've been a . . . I've been a right bastard to you, haven't I?'

'Dad . . .'

'You see, Bas, I've never really understood you . . . Jesus, Bas, I've always been scared of you.'

'Scared!' Barry repeated, taken aback at this revelation. 'How do you mean?'

'It's no good, I need a drink,' Derek said, striding across the kitchen and pulling open the fridge. He offered a can of lager to Barry.

'No thanks.'

Derek hesitated, his hand poised over the ring pull, his dry throat gasping to be satiated, but his brain calling for restraint. 'Perhaps you're right,' he said, 'perhaps I shouldn't either. Don't want the old biddies at St John's keeling over from the fumes of probably the best lager in the world, do we?'

Barry watched his father move away from the fridge. 'Why are you frightened of me, Dad?'

Derek swallowed hard and pushed his hands down into

his trouser pockets. 'Because you're so bloody clever! You've always managed to make me feel such a prat.'

Barry looked shocked. 'I never meant to.'

Derek shook his head. 'I know, Bas, and let's face it, I don't need anyone's help to make me look an idiot. I do a pretty good job of it on my own.'

'Dad, I . . .'

'Yeah, well, keep it to yourself,' Derek said, his face breaking into a sudden smile as he heard the sound of his wife's voice coming towards the kitchen. 'Don't want everyone knowing I've been baring my soul to you, do we?'

Cindy stood still for a moment and stared at Barry. 'You look wonderful,' she said with a faint tremor to her voice.

Barry didn't know what to say; first a confession from his father and now, after all these years, for the first time in his life, he had pleased his mother.

Derek followed behind his family as they walked up the aisle towards their reserved pew. He tried not to look about him, tried hard to fix his eyes on the chequered floor ahead, but he found it impossible. He hadn't expected the church to be so full. He knew that Bas had invited a few friends, but he hadn't said half the school was coming. And wasn't that Mr Knox, the headmaster, sitting next to Louise Archer?

'Okay, Dad?' Barry whispered, as they sat down.

'Yes,' Derek rasped back, 'I'm fine.' No I'm not, he thought, panic-stricken and looking anxiously about the church. He caught sight of Iris Braithwaite beneath a stern black hat and felt the comforting urge to crack a joke. He turned to nudge Bas and found he wasn't there. Oh God, he said under his breath, seeing his son on his knees beside him. Was that really necessary? He waited for what seemed for ever before Bas surfaced. 'That better?' he asked.

At the end of the service, Charlotte tried to bundle Christina out of the church as quickly as she could. She had no intention of letting her friend stir up as much interest at St John's as she had in the Spinner.

'Oh Carlotta, such a handsome young man, that Barry is,' Christina said, as they passed through the lych-gate. 'No wonder you wanted to come back to Hulme Welford. How is it that there are so many gorgeous men in such a tiny village?'

'Good grief, Christina!' Charlotte said bad-temperedly. 'Isn't one conquest in the village enough for you?' She had barely opened her mouth to Christina all morning; breakfast had been distinctly chilly, just two cereal bowls and a jug of cold milk between them.

'Carlotta, you are very cross with me, aren't you?'

'Cross, me? Why on earth should I be cross with you?' Christina laughed. 'Oh, there's Alex.'

Charlotte turned and saw Alex coming up behind them as they were about to cross the road. Her mood wasn't improved by the wide smile on his face. 'Saw you sitting at the back of the church,' he said, drawing level.

'We were lucky to get a seat,' Charlotte said tersely. 'Madam here was so exhausted from your exploits in the Italian Gardens yesterday that she overslept.'

Christina rolled her eyes at Alex. 'I think our poor Carlotta still has her headache, she is in such a bad mood.'

'Oh rubbish!' Charlotte said, stepping off the pavement and causing a Lycra-clad cyclist to swerve out into the middle of the road. He threw his fist at her along with a few choice expressions.

'Neville, have you gone completely mad?' Louise raised her voice above the sound of Abba's 'Dancing Queen'. 'There's more than a thousand calories on your plate.'

'Yes dear, I know,' Neville answered, licking his lips in eager anticipation of sinking his teeth into the chicken drumstick on his plate, along with the large dollop of avocado dip, a couple of miniature sausage rolls and a slice of salmon and cream cheese roulade, 'and that's nothing compared to the calories I shall be consuming when it's pud time,' he added with a glint in his eye. 'Tiffany told me there's trifle, crème brûlée and strawberries and cream.'

Louise raised her eyebrows. 'I don't know what's got into you. Ever since you won that prize yesterday you've been quite unbearable. It was only second prize. Anyone would think you'd won the wretched cup.'

Neville beamed, took a large bite out of his chicken drumstick and chewed with lip-smacking delight. 'Time to circulate, I think. I should get yourself some lunch. Derek and Cindy have done Barry proud.' Leaving his wife floundering – for the first time in their marriage – Neville saw Charlotte and her famous friend sunning themselves on a bright pink swinging seat. He pulled in his stomach and strolled over.

'Hello, Dad,' Charlotte said, helping herself to a sausage roll from his plate. 'Mum know you've got all that?'

'Indeed she does.'

Something in her father's voice made Charlotte look at him more closely. 'You're looking very pleased with yourself. What have you been up to?'

He smiled broadly and cleared his throat as though preparing to make an important announcement. 'I won second prize yesterday at the gooseberry show: thirty-five pennyweights and sixteen grains with my Edith Cavell.'

Charlotte's mouth fell open. She was mortified. 'Dad, I was going to be there.' She looked sideways at her friend. 'But I forgot all about it, what with Christina turning up so unexpectedly.'

With perfect timing, Christina held out her hand to Neville. 'My dear man, I am so sorry to have kept Carlotta from you, do forgive me.'

Neville chuckled like a schoolboy. 'Think nothing of it.'

Christina patted the space between herself and Charlotte. 'Now sit here with us and tell me about this wonderful prize you have won. But first, what is a gooseberry show and who is Edith Cavell?'

Charlotte got up from her seat. 'Go on, Dad,' she said, 'don't hold back. This is your big opportunity. Tell Christina all about it while I go and get us some wine.'

She wandered over to the yellow and white striped marquee and saw Barry coming towards her, carrying a tray of glasses. 'Hello,' he said. Behind him a small, attractive girl appeared. She had a mop of curly red hair, which gave her an Orphan Annie appearance. She too was carrying a tray of drinks. 'I'll go on ahead and give these to the others,' she said, offering Barry a dazzling smile.

'Okay. I'll be there in a moment.'

'Nice girl,' Charlotte said, watching Orphan Annie make her way to the bottom of the garden where all the younger members of the party were congregated.

Barry nudged his glasses. 'She is, isn't she? Going to Leeds as well.'

'Really,' she said with a smile. 'Medicine?'

'No. Theology.'

'You do surprise me.' She turned to look up at the house as the sound of 'Sultans of Swing' came to a finish and 'Like a Bat out of Hell' started up.

'Dad loves this,' Barry said.

'And so does Malcolm Jackson, by the looks of things,' Charlotte replied, watching what was taking place on the patio.

Cindy's carefully placed tubs of pink geraniums had been moved out of the way and Malcolm – now in mufti – together with Derek, was giving Meatloaf a fair run for his money. They were each holding a stick of celery and singing into the leafy end as though it were a microphone, the volume of their voices matching that of the hi-fi system.

Charlotte and Barry looked at one another and began to laugh. Then Barry handed her the tray of drinks and, grabbing a baguette from a passing waitress, he went up to join his father and the vicar. But when Barry approached the patio Derek seemed to falter, losing his place. He watched his son take up the baguette and start to sing. He put his arm round Barry and they sang together.

Most of the guests started clapping and cheering, and Barry's schoolfriends, hearing the noise, came up from the bottom of the garden to see what was happening. They soon joined in with the cheering, and a few went on to the patio to give their voices an airing and to pluck a few imaginary guitars.

Coming out of the marquee with her hands full of dirty plates, Cindy took in the scene. Charlotte watched her anxiously. Cindy's eyes filled with tears and she began to cry. Charlotte ditched Barry's tray of drinks on a nearby table, took the pile of crockery from Cindy and hugged her.

'Oh God,' Cindy cried, 'why has it taken eighteen years for this moment? Why are families so horrible to each other?' She sniffed loudly and then pulled away from Charlotte. 'I'm sorry,' she said, patting her perfect hair into place, 'this is absurd.'

Charlotte stiffened. Peter had said exactly the same the morning he had died, the morning he had revealed to Charlotte that he was emotionally fragile after all, just like any other human being. Poor Cindy. Why couldn't she just throw away that self-protective mask she wore and let people see her for what she really was? But of course it wasn't that easy, was it? Wasn't that what she herself had been doing all the time she had been back in Hulme Welford, hiding behind her precious mask of widowhood?

They watched the show on the patio come to an end and joined in with the applause.

'Muffin 'ell!' shouted Tiffany, coming towards them with Becky on her back. 'Were they embarrassing or what?'

'I thought they were good,' Cindy said, reaching for the pile of plates Charlotte had taken from her. 'I'll go and put these in the dishwasher.' She walked towards the house.

'What's up with Mum?' Tiffany shifted Becky to a more comfortable position on her back.

'I think she's happy.'

'Happy? Mum? Never. Come on, Becky, let's go and find you something to eat.'

Remembering she was supposed to have been fetching some drinks, Charlotte followed Tiffany into the marquee and was knocked back by the mélange of canvas-induced heat, the scent of crushed grass and the not-so-sweet smell of fifty-seven varieties of overstretched deodorant. On one side of the marquee tables covered in yellow cloths held an assortment of buffet food and on the other side stood white-dressed tables laden with shining glasses and bottles of wine, mineral water and beer. Charlotte helped herself to three glasses of wine and, wanting to get out of the oppressive heat as fast as possible, she turned to go but crashed into another guest. She jerked at the splash of cold wine against her chest. She looked up to see Alex.

'I'm sorry, Charlotte,' he said.

She glared at him, and for a moment, neither seemed to know what to say next.

'Mrs Lawrence,' boomed Iris Braithwaite, who knew exactly what to say. 'Just look at the state of you. What kind of a confirmation party is this? First Reverend Jackson makes a fool of himself out there in the garden and now you, in here, revealing . . . revealing all!'

Charlotte followed Iris's pointed stare and saw to her horror that the top of her white shift dress was practically transparent. She wasn't wearing a bra and the material was clinging mercilessly to her breasts. She plucked frantically at the thin fabric, trying to pull it away from her nipples. Looking up, she saw that Alex was smiling.

'How dare you!' she shouted angrily. She crashed the now half-empty glasses on the table behind her and turned and slapped Alex hard on the cheek.

'Mrs Lawrence!' roared Iris. But she got no further as she watched in horror Alex seize Charlotte and kiss her full on the lips.

'Mr Hamilton!' Iris almost pleaded, looking about her for back-up. But none was in the offing and the only voice to be heard was, 'Ooh look, Mummy, Auntie Charlotte's bonking that man who lives next door to her.'

*

'How dare you!' Charlotte repeated as Alex dragged her out of the marquee and towards the bottom of the garden. 'How bloody dare you do this to me . . . and in front of everyone.'

'Oh, come on,' he said, rounding on her, 'that's not what this is all about.'

'And what's that supposed to mean?'

'You know perfectly well what I'm talking about. You're as angry as hell with me, aren't you?'

'Yes . . . I mean no. What am I supposed to be angry with you about, apart from drenching me and making me look a fool?'

'You're angry because you think I slept with Christina. Isn't that right?'

She gave a loud derisive laugh. 'What you get up to in the privacy of your own rented house has got nothing to do with me.'

'Admit it, you're jealous.'

'I am *not*!' she exclaimed contemptuously, raising her hand once more to slap him.

'Charlotte,' he said, catching hold of her wrist, 'do as you're told for once and listen to me, *please*.'

She snatched her arm away from him. 'Okay then, I'm listening.'

He placed his hand under her elbow and marched her to the seat they had shared once before, overlooking the small pond. The cherub was still spouting and the ornamental toad looked just as ugly.

'I'm sorry for what just happened, Charlotte. I shouldn't have done that. But haven't you any idea how incredible you looked, standing there . . .'

'Don't be ridiculous.' She crossed her arms in front of her.

'What in heaven's name do I have to do to make you understand what you mean to me? Tell me and I'll do it.'

She said nothing, her mouth tightly shut.

'Charlotte, I think you ought to know that I've simply no intention of letting you go. You should know me well enough by now to realise I don't give up easily. And as to last night . . .' He lifted his hand to stop her outburst. 'Please, just hear me out. I've asked you several times before if you trusted me, right?'

'Yes,' she said, heavy irony in her voice, 'you have.'

'Have I blown it now?'

'Well, what do you think? Christina's my friend.'

'Would it have been okay with Heather, then?'

'No! I mean yes . . . oh Alex. For God's sake stop it, please.'

'Charlotte,' he said, 'nothing happened last night. It was an idea I should never have agreed to.'

'Whose idea?'

'Christina's.'

'I might have known. And what was this *idea* supposed to achieve?'

'To make you jealous,' he said, shamefaced. 'I'm sorry. It was a rotten thing to do to you. I never wanted to hurt you. And now I have and I hate myself for it. You'd think at my age I'd be past playing juvenile games like that, wouldn't you?'

Charlotte thought for a moment, taking Alex's words in. Jealous. Of course she had been jealous. Christina's plan had worked perfectly. She had lain awake all last night picturing Christina and Alex in bed; the images of them together had tortured her hour after hour in the dark until finally dawn had filtered through the curtains, allowing her a couple of hours of precious sleep. 'Well, it worked, didn't it?' she said, looking straight ahead of her. 'I *was* jealous.'

Alex sighed. 'I've made a right bloody mess of things, haven't I?' He took her hand and raised it to his lips. 'Do you think you could forgive me?'

'You know, I told Christina the other night that I probably could fall in love with you . . .'

'Charlotte . . .'

'No, let me finish. It's just that I'm terrified of discovering that it's me . . . that I'm not capable of making a relationship work . . . I'm petrified of taking the risk, of hurting you.'

'Try me. I'm pretty tough.'

'There's something else I'm scared of: Lucy.'

'Lucy? My God, you don't think I'm still in love with . . .'

'It's possible, isn't it?'

He put his hands on her shoulders. She tried to turn away from him, but he held her firmly and forced her to meet his gaze. 'We all have a past,' he said slowly, 'and Lucy is mine. When she died I truly thought there'd never be anyone else in my life. But now there is. You. I just wish you could understand what that means to me.' He clasped her face in his hands and kissed her. 'Charlotte, I love *you*.'

She felt her throat tighten with emotion. She tried to swallow, but found she couldn't. 'Alex, I could never . . . I couldn't cope with being second best again.'

'Peter was a fool,' Alex said sharply. 'He didn't deserve you. And anyway, can't you see that I love you because you're not second best? Charlotte, you're special. You're bloody wonderful!' He kissed her again. 'If I had my way I'd spend the rest of my days making you feel unimaginably special.'

'Oh you sweet-talker,' she said, managing a smile.

'Don't look at me like that, Charlotte. I don't know which is more devastating, your smile or the sight of you in that wet dress.'

Charlotte cleared her throat and changed the subject. She said, 'If you weren't making mad passionate love with Christina till gone midnight, what were you doing?'

'Talking. She's a great listener, a vital ingredient in her line of work.'

'She told you what she does for a living?' Charlotte was shocked.

'Yes.'

'Were you surprised?'

'I don't know really.'

Charlotte laughed, kicked off her shoes and stretched out her toes in the warm sun. She closed her eyes. Suddenly she felt unbelievably happy.

'You have lovely feet.' He picked one up and man-oeuvred it into his lap. He began to stroke her ankle.

'Alex,' she said warningly.

'A shame your dress has nearly dried out.'

Charlotte looked at him. 'You don't give up, do you?'

'No,' he said, 'I don't. And I won't.'

Chapter Thirty-Four

The airport was full of eager travellers brandishing passports and pushing overloaded trolleys of luggage or wheeling tombstone-sized cases on small squeaky wheels. Standing in the departure hall waiting for Christina's plane to be called, Charlotte felt reluctant to part with her friend. There was so much to be said, especially since yesterday, when Alex had told her the truth about the night before. She had hoped they might have had a chance to talk after Barry's party, but it hadn't broken up until nearly two in the morning, with Derek and Malcolm Jackson forming a cabaret act. Poor Iris was the only guest to leave early. She went home to The White Cottage next door and pointedly banged all her windows shut.

'Now Carlotta, my dearest friend,' Christina said, bringing Charlotte's thoughts back to the crowded airport, 'promise me one thing, that you will try to be honest with yourself.'

'Are any of us?' Charlotte said, shaking her head.

Christina smiled. 'You know, it takes courage, real courage to know another person, but it is a supreme act of heroism to know oneself and one's own darkness – remember that, Carlotta. Remember also that you are now brave enough to stop being evasive with yourself or anybody else. You must believe that.'

Charlotte reached out to her friend and hugged her. 'I

wish you weren't leaving today. Can't you stay a few more days?'

'No, Carlotta, my plane will be called in a few moments, and anyway, I want to get back to my wonderful Henri. He will be waiting for me and I have a feeling that I do not want to keep him waiting for too long. He is quite a catch, you know, I think I may marry him.'

'Somehow I can't imagine you married.'

Christina feigned a look of shock. 'You want me to remain the old maid, as you call it?'

'You could never be that, Christina. But what does Henri think of your . . . your work, your profession?'

'He thinks it is a very good one. Why?' asked Christina, a mischievous smile on her lips.

'Oh,' Charlotte said. 'He won't want you to give it up, then, if you marry him?'

'I don't think so. Do you think I should?'

Charlotte wasn't sure what to say. This was an area of their friendship that had been discreetly tucked under the carpet, or perhaps under the bedclothes.

'Carlotta, you haven't answered my question.'

She felt she was being pushed into a corner. 'It's just that, well, you know, I wouldn't have thought that what you do – entertaining men, I mean – and being a diplomat's wife would be terribly compatible.'

Christina's beautiful eyes opened wide and she laughed. 'Oh my darling Carlotta, at last you have been honest with me.'

Charlotte looked confused.

'All this time,' continued Christina, 'you really did think I was a prostitute, or as Mr Carlotta called me, a high-class tart.'

'You mean . . . ?' But what about all those men who kept calling on you?'

'Of course I had men visiting me. I'm a sex therapist.'

'A what?'

'Surely I don't have to explain . . .'

'No. No, I didn't mean that.' Charlotte was stunned. How could she have got it so wrong? 'I just meant . . . Oh, Christina, I made such an awful assumption. A sex therapist. You!'

'Yes, me,' Christina said. 'You know, there are a lot of sexual problems in Brussels, so many men who have the big work drive at the expense of the sex drive.'

'But there was no sign on your door, no office, no surgery, or whatever it is you need.' Part of Charlotte still needed convincing.

'One has to be discreet, my clients have to be treated with sensitivity. A large sign saying "This way for all those who can't get it up" would not do.'

'But even inside your apartment, it looked quite normal, not like . . .'

'Ah, you did not see the whole of my apartment, but then so often, we only scan the surface of life, only perceive what we are prepared to let ourselves see . . . for instance, you view Alex as another Peter.'

Charlotte frowned.

'There, I'm right, aren't I? You think Alex will hurt you in the same way Peter hurt you. But he really loves you, Carlotta, and for all the right reasons. Now they have called my plane, I must go, Henri awaits.'

They hugged each other again. Christina kissed Charlotte flamboyantly. 'Forgive me for trying to make you jealous, Carlotta,' she said. 'Forgive Alex too.' Then she walked towards the passport control booth and turned round for a final wave.

Ivy Cottage felt uncomfortably quiet when Charlotte got

back from the airport. She wandered about the kitchen, absentmindedly picking things up, then putting them down. She made herself a drink, but left it untouched. She went into the conservatory and flicked through a magazine. Bored and restless, she tossed it on the table and went outside. She sat beneath the fig tree and looked up at the house. She saw Alex staring down at her from what she guessed was his bedroom window. She held his gaze. Her throat went dry and she felt her heart beat faster.

She walked purposefully across the lawn and pushed open the back door. She had never been inside Alex's part of Ivy Cottage before. She found him at the foot of the stairs, his hand on the banister. He looked as though he was waiting for her, as if he had known she would come. She went to him, and without speaking she kissed him. He covered her face with kisses and then her neck, whispering her name, over and over. Breathless with what she knew was relief, she moved away from him, to the first step of the stairs. He followed her up.

In the gathering twilight Hilary tugged at the weeds in amongst the fading nemesia in the front garden. The summer would soon be over, she reflected; new school uniforms to buy and label, and autumn term PTA functions to start thinking about.

From across the road she heard the sound of barking followed by laughter. She peeped over the low wall she was hidden behind. She saw Mabel first, then Charlotte and Alex, arm in arm. When they reached the end of the drive she saw Alex whisper something in Charlotte's ear and heard her sister laugh again. Hilary crouched a little lower behind the wall as in fascinated delight she watched Charlotte kiss Alex. Not just a peck, but a full-blown belter of a kiss, their hands and arms all over the place. Heavens! gawped Hilary, goggle-eyed. And to think it was all down to her.

Iris Braithwaite stood poised over her tomato plants, a green plastic watering can in her hand. In the dwindling light she peered through the privet hedge, hearing the sound of voices coming towards her along the footpath.

'If you ask me,' she said in a loud voice, 'it's time you got yourselves married. At least that way we'd all be spared scenes of depravity such as we witnessed yesterday afternoon.'

'I beg your pardon, Mrs Braithwaite,' said Charlotte, facing Iris through the hedge.

'It's what I should have done after Sidney died. I've regretted it ever since.' Her voice sounded out of character; wistfully pensive. 'Of course now I've left it too late. Who would want an old thing like me?'

'I'm so sorry, Iris,' Charlotte said, risking the uncustomary familiarity of using Mrs Braithwaite's christian name, albeit through the safety of the hedge. 'I had no idea. You've always given the impression . . .'

'That's as may be, but don't ever quote me as having said it. I shall deny it of course. Goodnight, Mrs Lawrence, you too, Mr Hamilton.'

With the smooth, darkening water of the mere behind them Charlotte rested her head against Alex's chest, his arms around her shoulders.

'I'm exhausted,' she said.

'Me too.'

She gave him a playful punch. 'I wasn't talking about this afternoon.'

'Oh,' he said.

'It's been an exhausting summer.'

'That's because you spent most of it fighting me.'

'Only because . . .'

He kissed her. 'I think I've found the only way to keep you quiet.'

'No. There is another way.'

He caught the look in her eye and laughed. 'You do realise, don't you, that I won't let you end up like Iris Braithwaite, blue rinse and sensible lace-up shoes?'

'Well, that's a relief.'

'Charlotte?'

'Be quiet, Alex, and take me home, please.'

'Your place or mine?'

'Alex!'

Chapter One

It happened so quickly.

She had been hurrying from the market side of the Rialto Bridge, trying to avoid the crush of tourists in the packed middle section of shops, when a single face appeared in the crowd as if picked out by a bright spotlight entirely for her benefit. She turned on her heel to get a better look. And that was when she missed her footing and ended up sprawled on the wet ground, the contents of her handbag scattered.

Any other time Lydia might have been appalled at this loss of dignity, yet all she cared about, whilst a voluble group of Americans helped her to get back on her feet, was the man who had caused her to slip. She scanned the crowded steps for his retreating figure in the fine, drizzling rain. But he was long gone.

If he'd been there at all, Lydia thought as she relaxed into the chair and felt the downy softness of the cushions enfold her. The doctor had left ten minutes ago, promising the delivery of a pair of crutches in the morning. Her ankle was now expertly strapped and resting on a footstool. *Dottor* Pierili's parting words had been to tell her to keep the weight off her foot for as long as possible. He'd wanted her to go to the hospital for an X-ray, just to be on the safe side, but she'd waved his advice aside, politely yet firmly. Bandages, rest and painkillers would suffice.

'I still don't know how you managed to get home,' Chiara said, coming into the living room with a tray of tea things. She put the tray on a pedestal table between a pair of tall balconied windows that looked down onto the Rio di San

Vio. The weak, melancholy December light had all but faded and the spacious room glowed with a soft-hued luminosity. Strategically placed lamps created a beguilingly serene atmosphere, making it Lydia's favourite room in the apartment. She was a self-confessed lover of beautiful things; it was what brought her to Venice in the first place. Living here she was surrounded by beauty on a scale she had never encountered anywhere else. Venice's glorious but crumbling architecture together with its proud history combined to produce a profoundly sad and haunting sense of identity that appealed enormously to Lydia. It was the apparent isolation of the place that touched her; it was somewhere she felt she could be separate from the rest of the world.

She would always remember her first glimpse of Venice. It was early evening and as the *vaporetto* entered the basin, the city was suddenly there before her, floating like a priceless work of art in the distance, the low sun catching on the gilded domes and *campanili*. It was love at first sight. From then on she was a willing victim to Venice's trembling beauty and the spell it cast on her. Even with the myriad challenges that the city was forced to cope with – the growing threat of *acqua alta*, the ever-increasing crowds that were choking the narrow *calli*, and the graffiti (almost worst of all to Lydia) that was spreading endemically through Venice – it was still a place of dreams for her. Even the relentless chorus of 'Volare' and 'O Sole Mio!' coming from the gondoliers as they cruised the waterways with their cargo of nodding and smiling Japanese tourists could do nothing to diminish her love for her adopted home.

'You're either the bravest woman I know or the stupidest,' Chiara said as she handed Lydia a cup of tea.

Lydia smiled, noting that Chiara had gone to the trouble of digging out her favourite bone china cup and saucer. 'Undoubtedly the latter,' she replied. 'That's certainly what your father would have said.'

'You probably did more damage walking on it than when you slipped.'

'He would have agreed with you on that point too. And said that for a forty-six-year-old woman I should have known better.'

Chiara crossed the room for her own cup then came and curled up in the high-backed chair next to Lydia. It was where Marcello always used to sit, his hand outstretched to Lydia as he quietly read the *Gazzettino*.

'I want you to know that this arrangement will only go on for a day or two,' Lydia said, keen to establish that she would soon be back at work, business as usual.

Chiara, all twenty-four years of her, gave Lydia a quelling stare, her eyes dark and shining in the muted light. 'Oh, no you don't. We can manage perfectly well without you.'

'That's what I'm worried about. I don't want you getting too used to my absence.'

'Now there's an idea. A boardroom coup.'

The shrill ring of the telephone in the hall had Chiara getting to her feet. Within seconds it was obvious the call wasn't for Lydia. Selfishly she hoped it wasn't one of Chiara's friends inviting her out for the evening; she could do with the company.

This neediness had nothing to do with her sprained ankle, and all to do with not wanting to be alone. If she was alone, she might dwell on that face in the crowd. And that was definitely something she didn't want to do. An evening with Chiara would be the perfect distraction.

It was a matter of pride to Lydia that she and Chiara didn't have the usual mother and daughter relationship. For a start Lydia wasn't actually Chiara's mother: she was her stepmother. It was a clumsy label Lydia had dispensed with at the earliest opportunity. Chiara had always called her by her Christian name, anyway.

Lydia had never told anyone this, but it had been Chiara who she had fallen for first – her love for Marcello, Chiara's father, had come later. They had met fifteen years ago, when Chiara was nine and Lydia had been employed to teach the little girl English. She received a phone call in response to one of her advertisements offering her services, and three days later a distinguished-looking Signor Marcello Tomasi and his only daughter arrived at her apartment in Santa Croce. She was a painfully shy, introverted child and it didn't take long to realize why: her mother, as her quietly spoken father explained, had died last winter. Nobody could have empathized more with the young girl. Lydia knew exactly how it felt to have your world turned upside down and inside out. Every ounce of her being made her want to take away Chiara's sadness, to make her face light up with a smile.

The lessons always started at four o'clock on a Saturday afternoon and took place in Lydia's tiny kitchen. She thought it would be a less intimidating environment for this fragile child than to sit at the formal desk in the sitting room. There would always be a pot of freshly made hot chocolate on the table, along with a box of delicious almond biscuits from her local *pasticceria*. Lydia's other students were never offered more than tea or coffee, or fruit juice if she happened to have any in the fridge. Gradually her young pupil began to grow in confidence, which meant she looked less likely to burst into tears if she got anything wrong.

Without fail Marcello Tomasi would return for his daughter as the bell from San Giacomo dell'Orio struck five. He would hand over the agreed amount of money, check that they were still on for the following Saturday and then wish Lydia a pleasant evening. However, one day, just as Lydia was opening the door for them to leave, Chiara did something that changed everything. She beckoned her father to bend down to her, cupped her hand around her mouth and whispered into his ear. Straightening up, he cleared his throat, rubbed his hand over his clean-shaven chin and said, 'Chiara would like to invite you to her birthday party next week.'

The thought of a roomful of over-excited, noisy Italian children held no appeal for Lydia. As if reading her mind, Marcello Tomasi said, 'It will be just a small party. I think Chiara would very much like you to be there. And so would I,' he added.

The party was bigger than Lydia had been led to believe, but it was very much a family affair with the only children present being a handful of Chiara's cousins, most of whom were younger than her and blessedly well behaved. After six months of teaching this man's only daughter and forming a strong, protective relationship with her, but exchanging no more than a few words with him, it was strange to be in his home; it felt oddly intimate. She was suddenly seized with the urge to snoop and pry, to find out more about this immaculately dressed, taciturn man. She knew that he worked on the mainland in Marghera, the nearby industrial zone that was generally considered to be the Beast to Venice's Beauty. She also knew, from Chiara, that he was *very*, *very* important and had *lots* of people working for him. Judging from the house – a two-storey, stylishly restored property a stone's throw from Ca'Doro – he had excellent taste and lived in a degree of comfort. But this scant amount of detail wasn't enough for Lydia; she wanted to know what he did for pleasure. Did he read? If so, what books did he read? What music did he listen to? What did he eat for his supper? More to the point, who cooked his supper? Did he cook it himself, or did he have help? Chiara had never mentioned anyone.

Even if she had had the nerve to carry out any actual unseemly rifling through Marcello's personal effects for answers to her questions, there was no opportunity to do so. Chiara took her excitedly by the hand and introduced her in overly rehearsed English to her many relatives, one by one. 'This is Miss Lydia, my very nice English teacher . . . This is Miss Lydia, my very nice English teacher.' The responses were all in Italian, which was fine by Lydia; she had been speaking Italian since she was eighteen. She might only have been in Venice for two years but she could manage a passable version of *la parlata*, the local dialect, which seemed to her to be entirely made up on a whim solely to vex outsiders.

Everyone at the party was very welcoming and took it in turns to press plates of tempting food onto her as well as top up her glass of Prosecco. But she took pains not to outstay her welcome; this was a family affair, she reminded herself. Shortly after the children had been called upon to sing for the adults, accompanied on the piano by Fabio, Marcello's brother – apparently a family tradition – she tried to make her exit as discreetly as possible, but Chiara was having none of it and announced to everyone that her *very nice English teacher* was leaving. Endless goodbyes then ensued until at last she was rescued by Marcello who, having instructed Chiara to offer her sweet-toothed great-grandmother another helping of *dolce*, steered Lydia away.

'I hope that wasn't too awful for you,' he said when they were standing outside in the courtyard garden, the cool night air making her realize how warm she'd been inside and how much Prosecco she'd drunk. She could feel the heat radiating from her cheeks.

'I had a lovely time,' she said truthfully, thinking how much she really had enjoyed herself.

'It wasn't too overwhelming?'

'Not at all. It was good to see Chiara so happy. She's a delightful child; you must be extremely proud of her.'

'She is and I am. I don't know if you're aware of it, but she's grown very close to you.'

'The feeling is mutual. She's charming company.'

'Are you busy tomorrow evening?'

'I don't think so. Why?'

'Will you have dinner with me?'

And that, six months after losing her heart to his daughter, was the start of her relationship with Marcello. A man who, ten years older than her, in no way fitted her idea of a typical Italian. He wasn't one of those rumbustious Italian men who constantly argue about politics and corruption in high places and claim they could change everything overnight if only given the chance. Nor did he have the infuriating habit of shouting '*Ascoltami!*' ('Listen to me!') every other sentence. And not once did he grab her arm to make sure he had her full attention during a conversation. Instead there was a quiet and intelligent

6

reserve about him. He was courteous to a fault and very astute. He realized and accepted that there was a part of her he would never know or understand. 'Your life is like a photograph album with occasional blank spaces where some of the pictures have been removed,' he said on the day he asked her to be his wife.

'Does it matter to you?' she replied.

'No,' he answered. 'I think it's those mysterious gaps I love most about you.'

Perhaps if he had pressed her, she might have shared more of herself with him.

The sound of Chiara's happy laughter, as she continued talking to whoever it was on the phone, broke through Lydia's thoughts and, not for the first time, she wondered how the painfully shy child she had met fifteen years ago had grown into this confident, carefree young woman, a young woman who had had to cope with the loss of both her parents before she'd turned twenty-one. Lydia liked to think that she'd played a part in Chiara's recovery from the death of her mother – Marcello always believed she had – but all she'd done was give the child what she had never experienced when she was that age: love and stability.

Having children had never been something Lydia had particularly craved. However, having Chiara in her life had felt exactly the right thing to do.

That night she slept badly, her sleep disturbed by a host of fragmented dreams. In one dream the siren sounded, signalling *acqua alta*. Venice was sinking. The water was lapping at her feet as she tried desperately to make it home to Chiara. But she was lost; every *calle* she ran into was a dead end. The siren continued to ring out. The ancient wooden supports creaked and groaned and finally they gave way and the buildings crumbled and slid slowly but surely into the lagoon.

She woke with a start and lay in the dark remembering a Bible story from her childhood, about the man who built his house upon the sand. Pastor Digby had his long, bony finger raised accusingly to her; he was asking if she understood what the story was teaching her.

Once she'd allowed one memory to enter her thinking, others began flooding in too. Her next mistake was to attach too much meaning to the dream. Was her life disintegrating? Had she built her life on foundations that were about to give way?

She pulled the duvet up over her head, blaming that wretched face in the crowd. Who was he? A ghost?

All Orion/Phoenix titles are available at your local bookshop or from the following address:

Mail Order Department
Littlehampton Book Services
FREEPOST BR535
Worthing, West Sussex, BN13 3BR
telephone 01903 828503, *facsimile* 01903 828802
e-mail MailOrders@lbsltd.co.uk
(Please ensure that you include full postal address details)

Payment can be made either by credit/debit card (Visa, Mastercard, Access and Switch accepted) or by sending a £ Sterling cheque or postal order made payable to *Littlehampton Book Services*.
DO NOT SEND CASH OR CURRENCY

Please add the following to cover postage and packing

UK and BFPO:
£1.50 for the first book, and 50p for each additional book to a maximum of £3.50

Overseas and Eire:
£2.50 for the first book plus £1.00 for the second book and 50p for each additional book ordered

---

BLOCK CAPITALS PLEASE

name of cardholder ....

address of cardholder ....

....

....

postcode ....

delivery address
(if different from cardholder)

....

....

....

postcode ....

☐ I enclose my remittance for £....................................

☐ please debit my Mastercard/Visa/Access/Switch (delete as appropriate)

card number ☐☐☐☐☐☐☐☐☐☐☐☐☐☐☐☐☐☐

expiry date ☐☐☐☐   Switch issue no. ☐☐

signature ....

prices and availability are subject to change without notice